RANSOM CANYON

Praise for Jodi Thomas

"Jodi Thomas is a masterful storyteller. She grabs your attention on the first page, captures your heart, and then makes you sad when it's time to bid her wonderful characters farewell. You can count on Jodi Thomas to give you a satisfying and memorable read."
—Catherine Anderson, *New York Times* bestselling author

"Thomas sketches a slow, sweet surrender."
—*Publishers Weekly*

"Compelling and beautifully written, it is exactly the kind of heart-wrenching, emotional story one has come to expect from Jodi Thomas."
—Debbie Macomber, #1 *New York Times* bestselling author

"Tender, realistic, and insightful."
—*Library Journal*

"Extremely powerful and gripping writing."
—*Roundtable Reviews*

"This book is like once again visiting old friends while making new ones and will leave readers eager for the next visit. A pure joy to read."
—*RT Book Reviews*

"This is terrific reading from page one to the end. Jodi Thomas is a passionate writer who puts real feelings into her characters."
—*Fresh Fiction*

JODI THOMAS

RANSOM CANYON

HQN™

HQN™

ISBN-13: 978-0-373-78939-9

Ransom Canyon

This edition published by arrangement with Harlequin Books S.A.

For questions and comments about the quality of this book, please contact us at CustomerService@Harlequin.com.

www.Harlequin.com

Printed in U.S.A.

Recycling programs for this product may not exist in your area.

I dedicate this book to my dear friend DeWanna Pace.
We met in a writing class and spent the next twenty-five years
helping each other follow our dreams.
I miss her, but know she's Heaven's blessing now.

CHAPTER ONE

Staten

Staten Kirkland lowered the brim of his felt Resistol as he turned into the wind. The hat was about to live up to its name. Hell was blowing down from the north, and he would have to ride hard to make it back to headquarters before the full fury of the storm broke. His new mount, a roan he'd bought last week, was green and spooked by the winter lightning. Staten had no time to put on the gloves in his back pocket. He had to ride.

When the mare bucked in protest, he twisted the reins around his hand and felt the cut of leather across his palm as he fought for control of both his horse and the memories threatening as low as the dark clouds above his head.

Icy rain had poured that night five years ago, only he hadn't been on his ranch; he'd been trapped in the hallway of the county hospital fifty miles away. His son had lain at one end, fighting for his life, and reporters had huddled just beyond the entrance at the other end, hollering for news.

All they'd cared about was that the kid's grandfather was a United States senator. No one had cared that Staten, the boy's father and only parent, held them back. All they'd wanted was a headline. All Staten had wanted was for his son to live.

But, he didn't get what he wanted.

Randall, only child of Staten Kirkland, only grandchild of Senator Samuel Kirkland, had died that night. The reporters had gotten their headline, complete with pictures of Staten storming through the double doors, swinging at every man who tried to stop him. He'd left two reporters and a clueless intern on the floor, but he hadn't slowed.

He'd run into the storm that night not caring about the rain. Not caring about his own life. Two years before he'd buried his wife, and now he would put his son in the ground beside her because of a car crash. He'd had to run from the ache so deep in his heart it would never heal.

Now, five years later, another storm was blowing through, but the ache inside him hadn't lessened. He rode toward head-quarters on the half-wild horse. Rain mixed with tears he never let anyone see. He'd wanted to die that night. He had no one. His wife's illness had left both father and son bitter, lost. If she'd lived, maybe Randall would have been different. Calmer. Maybe if he'd had her love, the boy wouldn't have been so wild. He wouldn't have thought himself so invincible.

Only, taking a winding road at over a hundred miles per hour *had* killed him. The car his grandfather had given him for his sixteenth birthday a month earlier had missed the curve heading into Ransom Canyon and rolled over and over. The newspapers had quoted one first responder as saying, *"Thank God he'd been alone. No one in that sports car would have survived."*

Staten wished he'd been with his boy. He'd felt dead inside the day he buried Randall next to his wife, and he felt dead now as memories pounded.

He rode close to the canyon rim as the storm raged, almost wishing the jagged earth would claim him, too. But, he was fifth generation born to this land. There would be no more Kirklands after him, and he wouldn't go without a fight.

As he raced, he remembered the horror of seeing his son pulled out of the wreck, too beat up and bloody for even a father to recognize. Kirkland blood had poured over the red dirt of the canyon that night.

He rode feeling the pounding of his horse's hooves match the beat of his heart.

When Staten crossed under the Double K gate and let the horse gallop to the barn, he took a deep breath, knowing what he had to do.

Looking up, he saw Jake there at the barn door waiting for him. The rodeo had crippled the old man, but Jake Longbow was still the best hand on the ranch.

"Dry him off!" Staten yelled above the storm as he handed over the mare to Jake's care. "I have to go."

The old cowboy, his face like twisted rawhide, nodded once as if he knew what Staten would say. A thousand times over the years, Jake had moved into action before Staten issued the order. "I got this, Mr. Kirkland. You do what you got to do."

Darting across the back corral, Staten climbed into the huge Dodge 3500 with its Cummins diesel engine and four-wheel drive. The truck might guzzle gas and ride rough, but if he slid off the road tonight, it wouldn't roll.

Half an hour later he finally slowed as he turned into a farm twenty miles north of Crossroads, Texas. A sign, in need of painting and with a few bullet holes in it, read simply "Lavender Lane." Even in the rain the air here smelled of lavender. He'd made it to Quinn's place. One house, one farm, sat alone with nothing near enough to call a neighbor.

Quinn O'Grady's home always reminded him of a little girl's fancy dollhouse: brightly painted shutters and gingerbread trim everywhere. Folks sometimes commented on how the house was as fancy as the woman who owned it was plain, but Staten had never thought of her that way. She was shy, had kept to herself even in grade school, but she was her own woman. She'd built a living out of the worthless land her parents had left her.

He might have gone his whole life saying no more than hello to her, but Quinn O'Grady had been his wife's best friend. Even after he'd married Amalah, she'd still have her "girls' days" with Quinn.

They'd can peaches in the fall and take courses at the church on quilting and pottery. They'd take off to Dallas for an art show or to Canton for the world's biggest garage sale. He couldn't count the times his wife had climbed into Quinn's old green pickup and simply called out that they were going shopping as if that were all he needed to know. Half the time they didn't come back with anything but ice-cream-sundae smiles.

Quinn hadn't talked to him much in those early years, but she'd been a good friend to his wife, and that mattered. Near the end, she'd sat with Amalah in the hospital so he could go home to shower and change clothes. That last month, it seemed she was always near. The two women had been best friends all their lives, and they would be to the end.

Staten didn't smile as he cut the engine in front of Quinn O'Grady's house. He never smiled. Not anymore. For years he'd worked hard thinking he'd be passing on the Double K to his son. Now, if Staten died, the ranch would probably be sold at auction to help support his father's run for the senate or, who knows, the old guy might run for governor next time. Even though Samuel Kirkland was in his sixties, his fourth wife was keeping him young, he claimed. He'd never had much interest in the ranch and hadn't spent a night on Kirkland soil since Staten had taken over the place.

Quinn caught Staten's attention as she opened her door and stared out at him. She had a big towel in one hand as she leaned against the door frame and waited for him to climb out of the truck and come inside. She was tall, almost six feet, and ordinary in her simple clothes. He couldn't imagine Quinn in heels or her hair fixed any way except the long braid she always wore down the center of her back. She'd worn jeans since she started school; only, there had been two braids trailing down her back then.

Funny, Staten thought as he climbed out and tried to outrun the rain, *a woman who wants nothing to do with frills or lace lives in a dollhouse.*

After he reached the porch and shook like a big dog, she handed him the towel. "When I saw the storm moving in, I figured you'd be coming. Tug off those muddy boots while I dip up some soup for supper. I made taco soup when I saw the clouds rolling in from the north."

No one ordered any Kirkland around. No one. Only here, in her house, he did what she asked. He might never have another drop of love in him, but he'd still respect Quinn.

His spurs jingled as his boots hit the porch. In his stocking feet he stood only a few inches taller than her, but with his broad shoulders he guessed he probably doubled her in weight. "Any chance the clouds made you think of coconut pie?"

She laughed softly. "It's in the oven. Be out in a minute."

They watched the stormy afternoon turn into evening, with lightning putting on a show outside her kitchen window. He liked how he felt comfortable being silent around her. They sometimes talked about Amalah and the funny things that had happened when they were growing up. He felt as if he and Quinn were the leftovers, for the best of them had both died with Amalah.

Only, tonight his thoughts were on his son, and Staten didn't really want to talk at all. As the sun set, the temperature dropped, and the icy rain turned to a dusting of soft mushy snow while they ate in silence.

When he reached for his dishes and started to stand, she stopped him with a touch on his damp sleeve. "I'll do that," she said. "Finish your coffee."

He sat quiet and still for a few minutes, thinking how this place of hers seemed to slow his heart and make it easier to breathe. He finally left the table and silently moved to stand behind her as she worked at the sink. With rough hands scabbed over in places where the reins had cut, he began to untie her braid.

"I did this once when we were in third grade. I remember you didn't say a word, but Amalah called me an idiot after school."

Quinn nodded but didn't speak. Shared memories settled comfortably between them.

He liked the way Quinn's sunshine hair felt, even now. It was thick and hung down straight except for the slight waves left by the braid.

She turned and frowned up at him as she took his hand. Without asking questions she pulled his injured palm under running water and then patted it dry. When she rubbed lotion over his hand, it felt more like a caress than doctoring.

He was so close behind her their bodies brushed as she worked. Leaning down, he tickled her neck with a light kiss. "Play for me tonight," he whispered.

Turning toward the old piano across the open living area, she shook her head. "I can't."

He didn't question or try to change her mind. He never did. Sometimes, she'd play for him, other times something deep inside her wouldn't let her.

Without a word, she tugged him to the only bedroom, turning off lights as they moved through the house.

For a while he stood at the doorway, watching her remove her plain work clothes: worn jeans, a faded plaid shirt that probably belonged to her father years ago and a T-shirt that hugged her slender frame. As piece by piece fell, pale white skin glowed in the low light of her nightstand.

When he didn't move, she turned toward him. Her breasts

were small, her body lean, her tummy flat from never bearing a child. All she wore was a pair of red panties.

"Finish undressing me," she whispered, then waited.

He walked toward her, knowing that he wouldn't have moved if she hadn't invited him. Maybe it was just a game they played, or maybe they'd silently agreed on unwritten rules when they'd begun. He couldn't remember.

Pulling her against him, he just held her for a long time. Somehow on that worst night of his life five years ago, he'd knocked at her door. He'd been muddy, grieving and lost to himself.

She hadn't said a word. She'd just taken his hand. He'd let her pull off his muddy clothes and clean him up while he tried to think of a way to stop breathing and die. She'd tucked him into her bed and then climbed in with him, holding him until he finally fell asleep. He hadn't said a word, either, guessing that she'd heard the news reports of the crash. Knowing by the sorrow in her light blue eyes that she shared his grief.

A thousand feelings had careened through his mind that night, all dark, but she'd held on to him. He remembered thinking that if she had tried to comfort him with words, even a few, he would have shattered into a million pieces.

Just before dawn, he remembered waking and turning to her. She'd welcomed him, not as a lover, but as a friend silently letting him know it was all right to touch her. All right to hold on.

In the five years since, they'd had long talks, sometimes when he sought her out. They'd had stormy nights when they didn't talk at all. He always made love to her with a gentle touch, never hurried, always with more caring and less passion than he would have liked. Somehow, it felt right that way.

She wasn't interested in going out on a date or meeting him anywhere. She never called or emailed. If she passed him in the little town that sat between them called Crossroads, she'd wave, but they never spoke more than a few words in public. She had no interest in changing her last name for his, even if he'd asked.

Yet, he knew her body. He knew what she liked him to do and how she wanted to be held. He knew how she slept, rolled up beside him as if she were cold.

Only, he didn't know her favorite color or why she'd never married or even why sometimes she couldn't go near her piano. In many ways they didn't know each other at all.

She was his rainy-day woman. When the memories got to him, she was his refuge. When loneliness ached through his body, she was his cure. She saved him simply by being there, by waiting, by loving a man who had no love to give back.

As the storm raged and calmed, she pulled him into her bed. They made love in the silence of the evening, and then he held her against him and slept.

CHAPTER TWO

When her old hall clock chimed eleven times, Staten Kirkland left Quinn O'Grady's bed. While she slept, he dressed in the shadows, watching her with only the light of the full moon. She'd given him what he needed tonight, and, as always, he felt as if he'd given her nothing.

Walking out to her porch, he studied the newly washed earth, thinking of how empty his life was except for these few hours he shared with Quinn. He'd never love her or anyone, but he wished he could do something for her. Thanks to hard work and inherited land, he was a rich man. She was making a go of her farm, but barely. He could help her if she'd let him. But he knew she'd never let him.

As he pulled on his boots, he thought of a dozen things he could do around the place. Like fixing that old tractor out in the mud or modernizing her irrigation system. The tractor had been sitting out by the road for months. If she'd accept his help, it wouldn't take him an hour to pull the old John Deere out and get the engine running again.

Only, she wouldn't accept anything from him. He knew better than to ask.

He wasn't even sure they were friends some days. Maybe they were more. Maybe less. He looked down at his palm, remembering how she'd rubbed cream on it and worried that all they had in common was loss and the need, now and then, to touch another human being.

The screen door creaked. He turned as Quinn, wrapped in an old quilt, moved out into the night.

"I didn't mean to wake you," he said as she tiptoed across the snow-dusted porch. "I need to get back. Got eighty new yearlings coming in early." He never apologized for leaving, and he wasn't now. He was simply stating facts. With the cattle rustling going on and his plan to enlarge his herd, he might have to hire more men. As always, he felt as though he needed to be on his land and on alert.

She nodded and moved to stand in front of him.

Staten waited. They never touched after they made love. He usually left without a word, but tonight she obviously had something she wanted to say.

Another thing he probably did wrong, he thought. He never complimented her, never kissed her on the mouth, never said any words after he touched her. If she didn't make little sounds of pleasure now and then, he wouldn't have been sure he satisfied her.

Now, standing so close to her, he felt more a stranger than a lover. He knew the smell of her skin, but he had no idea what she was thinking most of the time. She knew quilting and how to make soap from her lavender. She played the piano like an angel and didn't even own a TV. He knew ranching and watched from his recliner every game the Dallas Cowboys played.

If they ever spent over an hour talking they'd probably figure out they had nothing in common. He'd played every sport in high school, and she'd played in both the orchestra and the band. He'd collected most of his college hours online, and she'd gone all the way to New York to school. But, they'd loved the same person. Amalah had been Quinn's best friend and his one love. Only, they rarely talked about how they felt. Not anymore. Not ever really. It was too painful, he guessed, for both of them.

Tonight the air was so still, moisture hung like invisible lace. She looked to be closer to her twenties than her forties. Quinn had her own quiet kind of beauty. She always had, and he guessed she still would even when she was old.

To his surprise, she leaned in and kissed his mouth.

He watched her. "You want more?" he finally asked, figuring it was probably the dumbest thing to say to a naked woman standing two inches away from him. He had no idea what *more* would be. They always had sex once, if they had it at all, when he knocked on her door. Sometimes neither made the first move, and they just cuddled on the couch and held each other. Quinn wasn't a passionate woman. What they did was just satisfying a need that they both had now and then.

She kissed him again without saying a word. When her cheek brushed against his stubbled chin, it was wet and tasted newborn like the rain.

Slowly, Staten moved his hands under her blanket and circled her warm body, then he pulled her closer and kissed her fully like he hadn't kissed a woman since his wife died.

Her lips were soft and inviting. When he opened her mouth and invaded, it felt far more intimate than anything they had ever done, but he didn't stop. She wanted this from him, and he had no intention of denying her. No one would ever know that she was the thread that kept him together some days.

When he finally broke the kiss, Quinn was out of breath. She pressed her forehead against his jaw and he waited.

"From now on," she whispered so low he felt her words more than heard them, "when you come to see me, I need you to kiss me goodbye before you go. If I'm asleep, wake me. You don't have to say a word, but you have to kiss me."

She'd never asked him for anything. He had no intention

of saying no. His hand spread across the small of her back and pulled her hard against him. "I won't forget if that's what you want." He could feel her heart pounding and knew her asking had not come easy.

She nodded. "It's what I want."

He brushed his lips over hers, loving the way she sighed as if wanting more before she pulled away.

"Good night," she said as though rationing pleasure. Stepping inside, she closed the screen door between them.

Raking his hair back, he put on his hat as he watched her fade into the shadows. The need to return was already building in him. "I'll be back Friday night if it's all right. It'll be late, I've got to visit with my grandmother and do her list of chores before I'll be free. If you like, I could bring barbecue for supper?" He felt as if he was rambling, but something needed to be said, and he had no idea what.

"And vegetables," she suggested.

He nodded. She wanted a meal, not just the meat. "I'll have them toss in sweet potato fries and okra."

She held the blanket tight as if he might see her body. She didn't meet his eyes when he added, "I enjoyed kissing you, Quinn. I look forward to doing so again."

With her head down, she nodded as she vanished into the darkness without a word.

He walked off the porch, deciding if he lived to be a hundred he'd never understand Quinn. As far as he knew, she'd never had a boyfriend when they were in school. And his wife had never told him about Quinn dating anyone special when she went to New York to that fancy music school. Now, in her forties, she'd never had a date, much less a lover that he knew of. But she hadn't been a virgin when they'd made love the first time.

Asking her about her love life seemed far too personal a question.

Climbing in his truck he forced his thoughts toward problems at the ranch. He needed to hire men; they'd lost three cattle to rustlers this month. As he planned the coming day, Staten did what he always did: he pushed Quinn to a corner of his mind, where she'd wait until he saw her again.

As he passed through the little town of Crossroads, all the businesses were closed up tight except for a gas station that stayed open twenty-four hours to handle the few travelers needing to refuel or brave enough to sample their food.

Half a block away from the station was his grandmother's bungalow, dark amid the cluster of senior citizens' homes. One huge light in the middle of all the little homes shone a low glow onto the porch of each house. The tiny white cottages reminded him of a circle of wagons camped just off the main road. She'd lived fifty years on Kirkland land, but when Staten's granddad, her husband, had died, she'd wanted to move to town. She'd been a teacher in her early years and said she needed to be with her friends in the retirement community, not alone in the big house on the ranch.

He swore without anger, remembering all her instructions the day she moved to town. She wanted her only grandson to drop by every week to switch out batteries, screw in lightbulbs, and reprogram the TV that she'd spent the week messing up. He didn't mind dropping by. Besides his father, who considered his home—when he wasn't in Washington—to be Dallas, Granny was the only family Staten had.

A quarter mile past the one main street of Crossroads, his truck lights flashed across four teenagers walking along the road between the Catholic church and the gas station.

Three boys and a girl. Fifteen or sixteen, Staten guessed.

For a moment the memory of Randall came to mind. He'd been about their age when he'd crashed, and he'd worn the same type of blue-and-white letter jacket that two of the boys wore tonight.

Staten slowed as he passed them. "You kids need a ride?" The lights were still on at the church, and a few cars were in the parking lot. Saturday night, Staten remembered. Members of 4-H would probably be working in the basement on projects.

One kid waved. A tall, Hispanic boy named Lucas whom he thought was the oldest son of the head wrangler on the Collins ranch. Reyes was his last name, and Staten remembered the boy being one of a dozen young kids who were often hired part-time at the ranch.

Staten had heard the kid was almost as good a wrangler as his father. The magic of working with horses must have been passed down from father to son, along with the height. Young Reyes might be lean but, thanks to working, he would be in better shape than either of the football boys. When Lucas Reyes finished high school, he'd have no trouble hiring on at any of the big ranches, including the Double K.

"No, we're fine, Mr. Kirkland," the Reyes boy said politely. "We're just walking down to the station for a Coke. Reid Collins's brother is picking us up soon."

"No crime in that, mister," a redheaded kid in a letter jacket answered. His words came fast and clipped, reminding Staten of how his son had sounded.

Volume from a boy trying to prove he was a man, Staten thought.

He couldn't see the faces of the two boys with letter jackets, but the girl kept her head up. "We've been working on a project for the fair," she answered politely. "I'm Lauren Brigman, Mr. Kirkland."

Staten nodded. *Sheriff Brigman's daughter, I remember you.* She knew enough to be polite, but it was none of his business. "Good evening, Lauren," he said. "Nice to see you again. Good luck with the project."

When he pulled away, he shook his head. Normally, he wouldn't have bothered to stop. This might be small-town Texas, but they were not his problem. If he saw the Reyes boy again, he would apologize.

Staten swore. At this rate he'd turn into a nosy old man by forty-five. It didn't seem that long ago that he and Amalah used to walk up to the gas station after meetings at the church.

Hell, maybe Quinn asking to kiss him had rattled him more than he thought. He needed to get his head straight. She was just a friend. A woman he turned to when the storms came. Nothing more. That was the way they both wanted it.

Until he made it back to her porch next Friday night, he had a truckload of trouble at the ranch to worry about.

Twenty miles away Quinn O'Grady curled into her blanket on her front porch and watched the night sky, knowing that Staten was still driving home. He always came to her like a raging storm and left as calm as dawn.

Only tonight, she'd surprised him with her request. Tonight when he'd walked away at midnight, it felt different. Somehow after five years, their relationship felt newborn.

She grinned, loving that she had made the first move. She had demanded a kiss, and he hadn't hesitated. She knew he came to her house out of need and loneliness, but for her it had always been more. In her quiet way, she could not remember a time she hadn't loved him.

Yet from grade school on, Staten Kirkland had belonged to her best friend, and Quinn had promised herself she'd never try to step between them. Even now, seven years after Amalah's death, a part of Staten still belonged to his wife. Maybe not his heart, Quinn decided, but more his willingness to be open to caring. He was a man determined never to allow anyone close again. He didn't want love in his life; he only wanted to survive having loved and lost Amalah.

Amalah had wanted to be Mrs. Kirkland since the day she and Quinn had gone riding on the Double K ranch. She'd loved the big house, the luncheons and the committees. She knew how to smile for the press, how to dress, and how to manage the Kirkland men to get just what she wanted. Amalah had been a perfect wife for a rich rancher.

Quinn only wanted Staten, but never, not for one moment, would she have wished Amalah dead. Staten was a love Quinn kept locked away in her heart, knowing from the beginning that it would never see light.

When her best friend died, Quinn never went to Staten. She couldn't. It wouldn't have been fair. She never called or tried to *accidentally* run into him in town. Amalah might be gone, but Staten still didn't belong to her. She was not the kind of woman who could live in his world.

Two years passed after Amalah died. Staten would stop by now and then just to check on Quinn, but her shyness kept their conversations short.

Then, Randall died.

She'd heard about the car crash on the local radio station and cried for the boy she'd known all his life.

Tears for a boy's life cut short and for a father who she knew must be hurting, but who she couldn't go to. She wouldn't have known what to say. He'd be surrounded by people, and Quinn was afraid of most people.

When she'd heard a pounding on her door that night, she almost didn't answer. Then she'd seen Staten, broken and needing someone, and she couldn't turn him away.

That night she'd held him, thinking that just this one time, he needed her. Tomorrow he'd be strong and they'd go back to simply being polite to one another, but for one night she could help.

That next morning he'd left without a word. She had never expected him to return, but he did. This strong, hard man never asked anything of her, but he took what she offered. Reason told her it wouldn't last. He'd called the two of them the leftovers, as if they were the ones abandoned on a shelf. But, Staten wasn't a leftover. One day he would no longer suffer the storms. One day he would go back to living again, and when he did, he'd forget the way to her door.

As the five years passed, Quinn began to store up memories to keep her warm when he stopped coming. As simple as it seemed, she wanted to be kissed. Not out of passion or need, but gently.

Every time he walked away might be the last time. She wanted to remember that she'd been kissed goodbye that last time, even if neither of them knew it at the moment.

CHAPTER THREE

Lauren

A midnight moon blinked its way between storm clouds as Lauren Brigman cleaned the mud off her shoes. The guys had gone inside the gas station for Cokes. She didn't really want anything to drink, but it was either walk over with the others after working on their fair projects or stay back at the church and talk to Mrs. Patterson.

Somewhere Mrs. Patterson had gotten the idea that since Lauren didn't have a mother around, she should take every opportunity to have a "girl talk" with the sheriff's daughter.

Lauren wanted to tell the old woman that she had known all the facts of life by the age of seven, and she really did not need a buddy to share her teenage years with. Besides, her mother lived in Dallas. It wasn't like she died. She'd just left. Just because she couldn't stand the sight of Lauren's dad didn't mean she didn't call and talk to Lauren almost every week. Maybe Mom had just gotten tired of the sheriff's nightly lectures. Lauren had heard every one of Pop's talks so many times that she had them memorized in alphabetical order.

Her grades put her at the top of the sophomore class, and she saw herself bound for college in less than three years. Lauren had no intention of getting pregnant, or doing drugs, or any of the other fearful situations Mrs. Patterson and her father had hinted might befall her. Her pop didn't even want her dating until she was sixteen, and, judging from the boys she knew in high school, she'd just as soon go dateless until eighteen. Maybe college would have better pickings. Some of these guys were so dumb she was surprised they got their cowboy hats on straight every morning.

Reid Collins walked out from the gas station first with a can of Coke in each hand. "I bought you one even though you said you didn't want anything to drink," he announced as he neared. "Want to lean on me while you clean your shoes?"

Lauren rolled her eyes. Since he'd grown a few inches and started working out, Reid thought he was God's gift to girls.

"Why?" she asked as she tossed the stick. "I have a brick wall to lean on. And don't get any ideas we're on a date, Reid, just because I walked over here with you."

"I don't date sophomores," he snapped. "I'm on first string, you know. I could probably date any senior I want to. Besides, you're like a little sister, Lauren. We've known each other since you were in the first grade."

She thought of mentioning that playing first string on a football team that only had forty players total, including the coaches and water boy, wasn't any great accomplishment, but arguing with Reid would rot her brain. He'd been born rich, and he'd thought he knew everything since he cleared the birth canal. She feared his disease was terminal.

"If you're cold, I'll let you wear my football jacket." When she didn't comment, he bragged, "I had to reorder a bigger size after a month of working out."

She hated to, but if she didn't compliment him soon, he'd never stop begging. "You look great in the jacket, Reid. Half the seniors on the team aren't as big as you." There was nothing wrong with Reid from the neck down. In a few years he'd be a knockout with the Collins good looks and trademark rusty hair, not quite brown, not quite red. But he still wouldn't interest her.

"So, when I get my driver's license next month, do you want to take a ride?"

Lauren laughed. "You've been asking that since I was in the third grade and you got your first bike. The answer is still no. We're friends, Reid. We'll always be friends, I'm guessing."

He smiled a smile that looked like he'd been practicing. "I know, Lauren, but I keep wanting to give you a chance now and then. You know, some guys don't want to date the sheriff's daughter, and I hate to point it out, babe, but if you don't fill out some, it's going to be bad news in college." He had the nerve to point at her chest.

"I know." She managed to pull off a sad look. "Having my father is a cross I have to bear. Half the guys in town are afraid of him. Like he might arrest them for talking to me. Which he might." She had no intention of discussing her lack of curves with Reid.

"No, it's not fear of him, exactly," Reid corrected. "I think it's more the bullet holes they're afraid of. Every time a guy looks at you, your old man starts patting his service weapon. Nerve-racking habit, if you ask me. From the looks of it, I seem to be the only one he'll let stand beside you, and that's just because our dads are friends."

She grinned. Reid was spoiled and conceited and self-centered, but he was right. They'd probably always be friends. Her dad was the sheriff, and his was the mayor of Crossroads, even though he lived five miles from town on one of the first ranches established near Ransom Canyon.

With her luck, Reid would be the only guy in the state that her father would let her date. Grumpy old Pop had what she called Terminal Cop Disease. Her father thought everyone, except his few friends, was most likely a criminal, anyone under thirty should be stopped and searched, and anyone who'd ever smoked pot could not be trusted.

Tim O'Grady, Reid's eternal shadow, walked out of the station with a huge frozen drink. The clear cup showed off its red-and-yellow layers of cherry-and-pineapple-flavored sugar.

Where Reid was balanced in his build, Tim was lanky, disjointed. He seemed to be made of mismatched parts. His arms were too long. His feet seemed too big, and his wired smile barely fit in his mouth. When he took a deep draw on his drink, he staggered and held his forehead from the brain freeze.

Lauren laughed as he danced around like a puppet with his strings crossed. Timothy, as the teachers called him, was always good for a laugh. He had the depth of cheap paint but the imagination of a natural-born storyteller.

"Maybe I shouldn't have gotten an icy drink on such a cold night," he mumbled between gulps. "If I freeze from the inside out, put me up on Main Street as a statue."

Lauren giggled.

Lucas Reyes was the last of their small group to come outside. Lucas hadn't bought anything, but he evidently was avoiding standing outside with her. She'd known Lucas Reyes for a few years, maybe longer, but he never talked to her. Like Reid and Tim, he was a year ahead of her, but since he rarely talked, she usually only noticed him as a background person in her world.

Unlike them, Lucas didn't have a family name following him around opening doors for a hundred miles.

They all four lived east of Crossroads along the rambling canyon called Ransom Canyon. Lauren and her father lived in one of a cluster of houses near the lake, as did Tim's parents. Reid's family ranch was five miles farther out. She had no idea where Lucas's family lived. Maybe on the Collins ranch. His father worked on the Bar W, which had been in the Collins family for over a hundred years. The area around the headquarters looked like a small village.

Reid repeated the plan. "My brother said he'd drop Sharon off and be back for us. But if they get busy doing their thing it could be an hour. We might as well walk back and sit on the church steps."

"Great fun," Tim complained. "Everything's closed. It's freezing out here, and I swear this town is so dead somebody should bury it."

"We could start walking toward home," Lauren suggested as she pulled a tiny flashlight from her key chain. The canyon lake wasn't more than a mile. If they walked they wouldn't be so cold. She could probably be home before Reid's dumb brother could get his lips off Sharon. If rumors were true, Sharon had very kissable lips, among other body parts.

"Better than standing around here," Reid said as Tim kicked mud toward the building. "I'd rather be walking than sitting. Plus, if we go back to the church, Mrs. Patterson will probably come out to keep us company."

Without a vote, they started walking. Lauren didn't like the idea of stumbling into mud holes now covered up by a dusting of snow along the side of the road, but it sounded better than standing out front of the gas station. Besides, the moon offered enough light, making the tiny flashlight her father insisted she carry worthless.

Within a few yards, Reid and Tim had fallen behind and were lighting up a smoke. To her surprise, Lucas stayed beside her.

"You don't smoke?" she asked, not really expecting him to answer.

"No, can't afford the habit," he said, surprising her. "I've got plans, and they don't include lung cancer."

Maybe the dark night made it easier to talk, or maybe Lauren didn't want to feel so alone in the shadows. "I was starting to think you were a mute. We've had a few classes together, and you've never said a word. Even tonight you were the only one who didn't talk about your project."

Lucas shrugged. "Didn't see the point. I'm just entering for the prize money, not trying to save the world or build a better tomorrow."

She giggled.

He laughed, too, realizing he'd just made fun of the whole point of the projects. "Plus," he added, "there's just not much opportunity to get a word in around those two." He nodded his head at the two letter jackets falling farther behind as a cloud of smoke haloed above them.

She saw his point. The pair trailed them by maybe twenty feet or more, and both were talking about football. Neither seemed to require a listener.

"Why do you hang out with them?" she asked. Lucas didn't seem to fit. Studious and quiet, he hadn't gone out for sports or joined many clubs that she knew about. "Jocks usually hang out together."

"I wanted to work on my project tonight, and Reid offered me a ride. Listening to football talk beats walking in this weather."

Lauren tripped into a pothole. Lucas's hand shot out and caught her in the darkness. He steadied her, then let go.

"Thanks. You saved my life," she joked.

"Hardly, but if I had, you'd owe me a blood debt."

"Would I have to pay?"

"Of course. It would be a point of honor. You'd have to save me or be doomed to a coward's hell."

"Lucky you just kept me from tripping, or I'd be following you around for years waiting to repay the debt." She rubbed her arm where he'd touched her. He was stronger than she'd thought he would be. "You lift weights?"

The soft laughter came again. "Yeah, it's called work. Until I was sixteen, I spent the summers and every weekend working on Reid's father's ranch. Once I was old enough, I signed up at the Kirkland place to cowboy when they need extras. Every dime I make is going to college tuition in a year. That's why I don't have a car yet. When I get to college, I won't need it, and the money will go toward books."

"But you're just a junior. You've still got a year and a half of high school."

"I've got it worked out so I can graduate early. High school's a waste of time. I've got plans. I can make a hundred-fifty a day working, and my dad says he thinks I'll be able to cowboy every day I'm not in school this spring and all summer."

She tripped again, and his hand steadied her once more. Maybe it was her imagination, but she swore he held on a little longer than necessary.

"You're an interesting guy, Lucas Reyes."

"I will be," he said. "Once I'm in college, I can still come home and work breaks and weekends. I'm thinking I can take a few online classes during the summer, live at home, and save enough to pay for the next year. I'm going to Tech no matter what it takes."

"You planning on getting through college in three years, too?"

He shook his head. "Don't know if I can. But I'll have the degree, whatever it is, before I'm twenty-two."

No one her age had ever talked of the future like that. Like they were just passing through this time in their life, and something yet to come mattered far more. "When you are somebody, I think I'd like to be your friend."

"I hope we will be more than that, Lauren." His words were so low, she wasn't sure she heard them.

"Hey, you two deadbeats up there!" Reid yelled. "I got an idea."

Lauren didn't want the conversation with Lucas to end, but if she ignored Reid he'd just get louder. "What?"

Reid ran up between them and put an arm over both her and

Lucas's shoulders. "How about we break into the Gypsy House? I hear it's haunted by Gypsies who died a hundred years ago."

Tim caught up to them. As always, he agreed with Reid. "Look over there in the trees. The place is just waiting for us. Heard if you rattle a Gypsy's bones, the dead will speak to you." Tim's eyes glowed in the moonlight. "I had a cousin once who said he heard voices in that old place, and no one was there but him."

"This is not a good idea." Lauren tried to back away, but Reid held her shoulder tight.

"Come on, Lauren, for once in your life, do something that's not safe. No one's lived in the old place for years. How much trouble can we get into?"

Tim's imagination had gone wild. According to him all kinds of things could happen. They might find a body. Ghosts could run them out, or the spirit of a Gypsy might take over their minds. Who knew, zombies might sleep in the rubble of old houses.

Lauren rolled her eyes. She didn't want to think of the zombies getting Tim. A walking dead with braces was too much.

"It's just a rotting old house," Lucas said so low no one heard but Lauren. "There's probably rats or rotten floors. It's an accident waiting to happen. How about you come back in the daylight, Reid, if you really want to explore the place?"

"We're all going now," Reid announced, as he shoved Lauren off the road and into the trees that blocked the view of the old homestead from passing cars. "Think of the story we'll have to tell everyone Monday. We will have explored a haunted house and lived to tell the tale."

Reason told her to protest more strongly, but at fifteen, reason wasn't as intense as the possibility of an adventure. Just once, she'd have a story to tell. Just this once…her father wouldn't find out.

They rattled across the rotting porch steps fighting tumbleweeds that stood like flimsy guards around the place. The door was locked and boarded up. The smell of decay hung in the foggy air, and a tree branch scraped against one side of the house as if whispering for them to stay back.

The old place didn't look like much. It might have been the remains of an early settlement, built solid to face the winters with no style or charm. Odds were, Gypsies never even lived in it. It appeared to be a half dugout with a second floor built on years later. The first floor was planted down into the earth a few feet, so the second floor windows were just above their heads giving the place the look of a house that had been stepped on by a giant.

Everyone called it the Gypsy House because a group of hippies had squatted there in the '70s. They'd painted a peace sign on one wall, but it had faded and been rained on until it almost looked like a witching sign. No one remembered when the hippies had moved on, or who owned the house now, but somewhere in its past a family named Stanley must have lived there because old-timers called it the Stanley house.

"I heard devil worshippers lived here years ago." Tim began making scary movie soundtrack noises. "Body parts are probably scattered in the basement. They say once Satan moves in, only the blood of a virgin will wash the place clean."

Reid's laughter sounded nervous. "That leaves me out."

Tim jabbed his friend. "You wish. I say you'll be the first to scream when a dead hand, not connected to a body, touches you."

"Shut up, Tim," Reid's uneasy voice echoed in the night. "You're freaking me out. Besides, there is no basement. It's just a half dugout built into the ground, so we'll find no buried bodies."

Lauren screamed as Reid kicked a low window in, and all the guys laughed.

"You go first, Lucas," Reid ordered. "I'll stand guard."

To Lauren's surprise, Lucas slipped into the space. His feet hit the ground with a thud somewhere in the blackness.

"You next, Tim," Reid announced as if he were the commander.

"Nope. I'll go after you." All Tim's laughter had disappeared. Apparently he'd frightened himself.

"I'll go." Lauren suddenly wanted this entire adventure to be over with. With her luck, animals were wintering in the old place.

"I'll help you down." Reid lowered her into the window space.

As she moved through total darkness, her feet wouldn't quite touch the bottom. For a moment she just hung, afraid to tell Reid to drop her.

Then, she felt Lucas's hands at her waist. Slowly he took her weight.

"I'm in," she called back to Reid. He let her hands go, and she dropped against Lucas.

"You all right?" Lucas whispered near her hair.

"This was a dumb idea."

She felt him laugh more than she heard it. "That you talking or the Gypsy's advice? Of all the brains dropping in here tonight, yours would probably be the most interesting to take over, so watch out. A ghost might just climb in your head and let free all the secret thoughts you keep inside, Lauren."

He pulled her a foot into the blackness as a letter jacket dropped through the window. His hands circled her waist. She could feel him breathing as Reid finally landed, cussing the darkness. For a moment it seemed all right for Lucas to stay close; then in a blink, he was gone from her side.

Now the tiny flashlight offered Lauren some much-needed light. The house was empty except for an old wire bed frame and a few broken stools. With Reid in the lead, they moved up rickety stairs to the second floor, where shadowy light came from big dirty windows.

Tim hesitated when the floor's boards began to rock as if the entire second story were on some kind of seesaw. He backed down the steps a few feet, letting the others go first. "I don't know if this second story will hold us all." Fear rattled in his voice.

Reid laughed and teased Tim as he stomped across the second floor, making the entire room buck and pitch. "Come on up, Tim. This place is better than a fun house."

Stepping hesitantly on the upstairs floor, Lauren felt Lucas just behind her and knew he was watching over her.

Tim dropped down a few more steps, not wanting to even try.

Lucas backed against the wall between the windows, his hand still brushing Lauren's waist to keep her steady as Reid jumped to make the floor shake. The whole house seemed to moan in pain, like a hundred-year-old man standing up one arthritic joint at a time.

When Reid yelled for Tim to join them, Tim started back up the broken stairs, just before the second floor buckled and crumbled. Tim dropped out of sight as rotten lumber pinned him halfway between floors.

His scream of pain ended Reid's laugher.

In a blink, dust and boards flew as pieces of the roof rained down on them and the second floor vanished below them, board by rotting board.

Lucas reached for Lauren as she felt the floor beneath her feet crack and split. Her legs slid down, scraping against the sharp teeth of decaying wood.

The moment before she disappeared amid the tumbling lumber, Lucas's hand grabbed her arm just above her wrist and jerked hard. She rocked like some kind of human bell as boards continued to fall, hitting her in the face and knocking the air from her lungs.

But Lucas held on. He didn't let her disappear into the rubble. He'd braced his feet wide on the few inches of floor remaining near the wall and leaned back.

When the dust settled, she looked up. He'd wrapped his free arm around a beam that braced a window. His face was bloody. The sleeve had pulled from his shirt, and she saw a shard of wood like a stake sticking out of his arm, but he hadn't let her go. His grip was solid.

Tim was crying now, but in the darkness no one could see where he was. He was somewhere below. He had to be hurting, but he was alive. The others had been above when the second floor crumbled, but Tim had still been below.

Reid jumped into the window frame that now leaned out over the remains of the porch. The entire structure looked as if it were about to crash like a hundred deformed pickup sticks dumped from a can.

Reid didn't look hurt, but with the moon on his face, Lauren had no trouble seeing the terror. He was frozen, afraid to move for fear something else might tumble.

"Call for help." Lucas's voice sounded calm amid the echoes of destruction. "Reid! Reach in your pocket. Get your phone. Just hit Redial and tell whoever answers that we need help."

Reid nodded, but his hand was shaking so badly Lauren feared he'd drop the phone. He finally gripped it in one hand and jumped carefully from the window to the ground below. He yelped a moment after he hit the dirt and complained that he'd twisted his ankle. Then he was yelling into his cell for help. They were still close enough to town to see a few lights in the distance. It wouldn't be long before someone arrived.

Lucas looked down at Lauren. "Hang on," he whispered.

She crossed her free hand over where his grip still held her arm. "Don't worry. I'm not letting go."

Slowly, he pulled her up until she was close enough to transfer her free hand to around his neck. Her body swung against his and remained there. Nothing had ever felt so good as the solid wall of Lucas to hang on to.

"Can you walk?"

"I think so. Don't turn loose of me, Lucas. Please, don't turn loose."

She felt laughter in his chest. "Don't worry, I won't. I got you, *mi cielo.*"

They inched along the edge of the wall where pieces of what had once been the floor were holding. "Tim?" she called. She tried to shine her light down to see Tim, but there was too much debris below. His crying began to echo through the night, as did Reid talking to Mrs. Patterson on the phone.

"She must have been the last person he called," Lucas whispered near Lauren's ear. "So when he hit Redial, he got her."

Lauren brushed her cheek against his. "She's the last person I'd turn to for help."

"I agree," Lucas answered.

Their private conversation amid the chaos helped her relax a bit.

"Send everybody!" Reid kept yelling. "We need help, Mrs. Patterson." When he hung up he must have dialed his brother because all at once Reid was cussing, blaming the mess they were in on whoever answered.

"Hang on, Lauren," Lucas whispered against her hair. "I'll try to reach the window."

"I'm scared. Don't let me fall."

He bumped the top of her head with his chin. "So am I, but I promise I'm not letting you go."

Finally Lucas reached the window that Reid had dropped from, and he lowered Lauren slowly to the ground outside.

"I got her," Reid shouted just as car lights began to shine through the trees. Emergency vehicles turned off the main road and headed toward the Gypsy House—one volunteer ambulance, a small fire truck, along with one sheriff's cruiser and Mrs. Patterson's old gray Buick tailing the parade.

Lauren watched Reid move toward the men storming through brush.

"We're all right," he shouted. "I got Lauren out, but Lucas and Tim are still in the house. I was going in after them next." When he spotted the sheriff in the half dozen flashlights surrounding him, he added, "I tried to tell them this was a bad idea, sir, but thank God I went in to help Lauren, just in case she got into trouble."

The first men hurried past Reid, ignoring him, but finally Sheriff Brigman and an EMT stopped.

Men with bright flashlights moved into the house with ropes and a portable stretcher. She could hear Lucas yelling for them to be careful and guiding their steps. Tim was somewhere below, still crying.

Her father shone his light along her body. She could feel warm blood trickling down her face, and more blood dripped down from a gash on her thigh. "I'll take her from here, son," he said to Reid as if she were a puppy found in the road. "You all right to walk, Reid?"

"I can make it, sir." Reid limped, making a show of soldiering through great pain.

"We've got the boy," someone yelled from inside the house. "He's breathing, but we'll need the stretcher to get him out. Looks like his leg is broken in more than one place."

Her father never let go his hold of her as they watched Tim being lifted out of the house. One of the EMTs said that, besides the broken leg, the boy probably had broken ribs. The sound of Tim's crying was shrill now, like that of a wounded animal.

She listened as her father instructed the ambulance driver to take Reid and Tim. They needed care on the way to the hospital. He picked up Lauren and carried her to his car as if she were still his little girl. "I'll transport her to the emergency room. She's got wounds, but she's not losing much blood."

"Lucas is hurt, too," she said as the boy who'd saved her life was helped down from the second floor window. Lucas was the last to leave the haunted house. He'd made sure everyone got out first.

The sheriff nodded. "Make sure he's stable and put him in my car, too. I can get them both there faster than the ambulance can."

Two firemen followed his orders.

Lauren looked over her father's shoulder as Lucas moved clear of the shadow of the house. She'd had far more than the little adventure she'd wanted tonight. When her father set her in the back of his cruiser, she wondered at what point she'd gone wrong and swore for the rest of her life she'd never do something so dumb again.

One of the men from the volunteer fire department bandaged up Lucas's arm and wrapped something around her leg. The sheriff oversaw the loading of the other two injured, then returned. She could almost feel anger coming off him like steam, but he wouldn't step out of his role here. Here he was the sheriff. Later he'd be one outraged father.

Wrapped in blankets, she sat in the backseat of her father's cruiser with Lucas and watched everyone load up like a small army. Mrs. Patterson had tripped in the darkness, and two firemen were taking her home for treatment.

She looked over at Lucas sitting a foot away. He was leaning his head back, not seeming to notice that his forehead dripped blood. He'd saved her and helped bring out Tim. She realized he'd passed her to Reid so he could go back for Tim. No one was patting him on the back and saying things like "great job" as they were to Reid.

Lauren seemed to have been labeled "poor victim" and Lucas was invisible.

"You saved me tonight," she whispered. "Why didn't you tell my dad? He thinks this whole thing was your fault, thanks to Reid."

"The truth isn't worth crossing Reid. Let him play the hero. All I care about is that you're all right. If I spoke up, I might not have a job tomorrow. One word from Reid and the foreman will take me off the list of extras hires, or worse, tell my father to find another job."

"We're alive, thanks to you." She was touched that he worried about her. "The cut on my leg isn't deep. But I owe you a blood debt for real now."

"I know." His white teeth flashed. "I'll be waiting to collect it. You've got to save my life now."

Her father climbed into the car without saying a word to them. He spoke into his radio and raced toward the county hospital, half an hour away.

Lauren didn't feel like talking. She knew the sheriff was probably already mentally composing the lecture he planned to give her for the next ten years. Worry over her would be replaced by anger as soon as he knew she was all right. She'd be lucky if he let her out of the house again before she was twenty-one.

In the darkness, she found Lucas's hand. She didn't look at him, but for the rest of the ride, her fingers laced with his. They might never talk of this night again, but they both knew that a blood debt bound them together, and sometime in the future she'd pay him back.

CHAPTER FOUR

Yancy

The Greyhound bus pulled up beside the tiny building with Crossroads, Texas, United States Post Office painted on it in red, white and blue, and Yancy Grey almost laughed. The box of a structure looked like it had been rolled in on wheels and set atop a concrete square. He had seen food trucks at county fairs that were bigger.

This wasn't even a town, just a wide spot in the road where a few buildings clustered together. He saw the steeples of two churches, a dozen little stores that looked as though they were on their last legs framed in the main street, and maybe fifty homes scattered around, not counting trailers parked behind one of the gas stations.

A half mile north there stood what looked like a school, complete with a grass football field with stands on either side. To the east was a grain elevator with a few buildings near the base. Each one was painted a different shade of green. Yancy couldn't see behind the post office, but he couldn't imagine that direction being any more interesting than the rest of the town.

"This is the Crossroads stop, mister," a huge bus driver called back to Yancy from the driver's seat. "We're early, but I guess that don't matter. Post office is closed Sundays anyway."

Yancy stood and moved down the empty aisle as the bus door swished open. He'd watched one after another of the mostly sorry-looking passengers step off this bus at every small town through Oklahoma and half of Texas. He didn't bother to thank the driver for doing his job. Yancy had been riding for ten hours and simply wanted to plant his feet on solid ground.

"You got any luggage?" the driver asked. "It's been so long since Oklahoma City, I forgot."

"No," Yancy answered as he took his first breath of the dawn's damp air. "Just my pack."

"Good." The driver pulled out his cigarettes. "Normally I stop here for breakfast. That café across the street serves an endless stack of pancakes, but since there are no cars out front, I think I'll move on. I'll be in Lubbock next stop, and that's home."

Yancy didn't care what the driver did. In fact, he hoped the fat guy would forget where he left off his last passenger. All Yancy Grey wanted was silence, and this town just might be the place to find it.

For the past five years in prison he'd made a habit of not talking any more than necessary. It served no purpose. Friends, he didn't need, and enemies didn't bother chatting. He kept to himself. The inmates he'd met and got along with weren't friends. In fact, he'd just as soon never see any of them again. One of them, a dead-eyed murderer named Freddie, had promised to kill him every time he'd passed within hearing distance, and another who went by "Cowboy" would skin a dead man for the hide.

And the guards and teachers for the most part were little more than ghosts passing through the empty house of his life. He had learned one fact from every group-counseling session he'd attended, and that was if he was going to stay out of prison, he needed to plan his life. So he'd taken every course offered and planned how not to get caught when he next stepped out into the free world.

He dropped his almost empty backpack on the post office steps and watched the bus leave. Then, alone with nothing but the sounds of freedom around him, he closed his eyes and simply breathed for a while. He'd known he was low-down worthless since he was five, but now and then Yancy wanted to forget and just think of himself as a regular person like everyone else who walked the planet.

At twenty-five, he wasn't the green kid who'd gone to jail. He was a hardened man. He had no job or family. No future. Nowhere to go. But, thanks to positive-thinking classes, he had goals.

The first one was simple: get rich. After he got past that one all the others would fall in line: Big house. Pool. Fast car.

On the positive side, he had a lot going for him. Without a plan, he didn't have to worry about holes in his strategy. He wasn't running away from anything or anyone, and that was a first. He'd also learned a little about every trade the prison tried to teach.

Yancy had bought a bus ticket to a town he'd once heard his mother say was the most nothing place on earth. Crossroads, Texas. He figured that was where he'd start over, like he was newborn. He'd rebuild himself one brick at a time until no one who ever knew him would recognize Yancy Grey. Hell, he might even give himself a middle name. That'd be something he hadn't had in twenty-five years of being alive.

Sitting down on the steps, he leaned against the tin door of the twelve-foot square post office and looked around at a tiny nothing of a town that sparkled in the early light. He might not have much, but he had his goals, and with some thinking, he'd have a plan.

He wasn't sure, but he thought his mother met his dad here. She never talked about the man who'd fathered him except to say he'd been a hand on one of the big ranches around. She'd fallen in love with the hat and boots before she knew the man in between. Yancy liked to think that, once, she might have been happy in Crossroads, but knowing his mother, she wouldn't be happy anywhere unless she was raising hell.

Yancy warmed in the sun. The café would probably be open in an hour or two. His first plan was to eat his fill of pancakes, and then he'd think about what to do next. Maybe he'd ask around for a job. He used to be a fair mechanic, and he'd spent most of his free time in the prison shop. There were two gas stations in town. One might have an opening. Or maybe the café needed a dishwasher? He'd worked in the prison kitchen for a year. If he was lucky, there would be a community posting somewhere around for jobs, and he'd bluff his way into whatever was open.

If nothing came up, he'd hitch a ride to the next town. Maybe he'd steal enough lying around here to hock for pocket money. Six years ago he'd caught a ride with a family in Arkansas. By the time they let him out a hundred miles down the road, he'd collected fifty dollars from the granny who rode in the back with him. The old bat had been senile and probably wouldn't ever remember having the money in the first place. That fifty sure had felt good in his pocket.

Another time, when he was about sixteen, he'd hitched a ride with some college kids. They'd been a fun bunch, smoking pot as they sang songs. When he'd said goodbye, they'd driven away without a camera that was worth a couple hundred. Served them right for just wandering around the country spending their parents' money. No one ever gave him a dime, and he'd made it just fine. Except for one dumb partner and one smart cop in Norman, Oklahoma.

Yancy pushed the memories aside. He had to keep his wits about him. Maybe try to go straight this time. He was halfway through his twenties, and hard time would start to take a toll on him soon. He'd seen guys in prison who were forty and looked sixty.

Taking a deep breath, he let the air sit in his lungs for a minute. It felt pure and light. Like rain and dust and nothing else.

A few cars passed as the sun warmed, but none stopped at the café. Yancy guessed the place might not open until eight or even nine on Sunday. He'd wait. With twenty dollars in his pocket, he planned to celebrate. Maybe if they had pie out early, he'd have it for breakfast.

One man in a pickup stopped and stuffed a few letters in the outside drop. He tipped his hat in greeting, and Yancy did the same with his baseball cap. It had been so long since he'd been in the free world he wasn't sure how to act. He needed to be careful so no one would recognize him as an ex-con. Most folks probably wouldn't anyway, but cops seemed to have a knack for spotting someone who'd served time.

Yancy went over a few rules he'd made up when he was thinking about getting out of jail. Look people in the eyes but not too closely. Greet them however they greeted him. Stand up straight. At six-one he wasn't tall enough to be frightening or short enough to be bothered. He continued with his rules. Answer questions directly. Don't volunteer much information, but never appear to be hiding anything.

About eight o'clock he heard one of the church bells. The day was cold but sunny and already promising to be warm. The dusting of snow from last night was blowing in the street like a ghost snake wiggling in the frosty air. In an hour it would be gone.

He decided to set his first freedom goal. He'd buy a coat. After all, winter was already here. The first year in prison he'd been either hot or freezing. If he had a good wool coat, he could be warm all winter, and then if he ever got hot, he'd just take off his good coat. He sighed, almost feeling it already covering his shoulders. The old sweatshirt he'd found in the lost-and-found bin at one of the bus stops last night was too worn to last the winter.

Yancy smiled, knowing that if anyone passed by, they'd think he was an idiot, but he didn't care. He had to start somewhere. Daydreaming might not get him anywhere, but a goal—now, that was something he could sink his teeth into. He'd listened to all the tapes. He had to think positive and do it right this time, because he was never going back to prison.

Two old men came out of a couple of the small houses across the street. One had a saw and the other carried a folding chair. They must live in the cluster of little bungalows surrounded by a chain-link fence. The sign out front, looking as old as the two men, said Evening Shadows Retirement Community.

As he watched the men, he almost felt sorry for them. In Yancy's mind the place looked little better than prison. The homes were in bad shape. One roof sank in at a corner. One porch was missing a railing. The yard had been left on its own for so long it looked like nothing but prairie grass and weeds. A few of the homes had flowers in pots with leftover Christmas greenery, and all had tiny flags tacked up by the door as if they'd been put up as Fourth of July decorations, and no one had bothered to take them down.

Yancy stopped studying the place and decided to pass his time watching the old men. One at a time they each tried to stand on the folding chair to cut dead branches off the elms between the little houses. One kept dropping the saw. The other fell through the opening in the back of the chair and would have tumbled to the ground if his partner hadn't braced him.

Yancy laughed. The two were an accident about to happen, and he had a front row seat.

The second time he laughed, one of the old men turned toward Yancy and pointed his cane like a rifle. "You think you can do any better, mister, you get over here and try."

"All right, I will." He headed toward them. "If one of you

break a leg I'll probably get blamed." With nothing to do until the café opened, he might as well lend a hand. That's what normal people did, right? And Yancy wanted to be nothing but normal.

Sawing a branch that had been scraping against the house was no problem, even with both the old guys telling him how. Yancy had planned to stop there, but they pointed to another branch that needed cutting and then another. As he moved from house to house, more old people came out. Everyone had elms bothering their roof or windows or walls. Before long he felt as if he was leading a walker parade around the place. Every time he cut a branch down, one of the residents would grab it and haul it outside the chain-link fence to the lot beyond.

Listening to them chatter and compliment him was like music to his ears. None of the senior citizens ordered him around or threatened him. They all acted as if he was some kind of hero fighting off the dragon elms that had been torturing them when the wind blew or robbing them of sleep.

"We should pile them up and have us a bonfire," yelled the one old man with *Cap* written on his baseball hat.

"Great idea," his friend said, joining in. "I'll buy the hot dogs and we can have us a weenie roast."

"Won't that be a fire hazard?" Yancy asked as he used a stool to climb high enough to cut the last of the dead branches off a tree.

Cap-hat puffed up, making him about half an inch taller. "I was the captain of the volunteer fire department here for twenty years. I think if I say it's all right, nobody will argue."

To Yancy's shock they all agreed, and now the rush was on to collect firewood.

In general, Yancy hated people. He thought of some of them as evil, like Freddie and Cowboy who'd threatened to murder him for no reason, and others he feared were simply fools. The rest were stupid, destined to be played by the evil walking the earth. That pretty much summed up the population he'd been living with for five years, and those he'd grown up with were no better.

Only, these folks were different. They treated him as if he were a kid who needed praise and direction. Each had stories to tell, and each, in their way, appeared to have lived rich, full lives. None suspected the crimes he'd committed or regrets he had in life. To them he was a hero, not an ex-con.

Yancy swore he felt like Snow White stumbling into the elderly dwarves' camp. All of them were at least a head shorter than him, and most offered him a cup of coffee or something to eat. One little round woman dressed in pink from her shoes to her hair even brought him out a slice of pie. Mrs. Butterfield was her name, and she claimed her husband always ate pie for breakfast.

She also giggled and told Yancy that he reminded her of her first husband when he was young. "Black hair and strange eyes," she whispered. "Just like you, young man."

"Yancy," he said. "My name's Yancy Grey." He didn't want her thinking he was the ghost of husband number one returning.

All agreed that was a strong, good name, except Mrs. Butterfield who'd gone inside to look for a picture of her first husband.

An hour passed, and the café still wasn't open, but Yancy felt stuffed. By now the trees were trimmed and the eight geezers pulled their chairs around a crumbling swimming pool full of tumbleweeds and dead leaves. The pool deck was one of the few places that was out of the wind and offered sunshine.

Yancy used the tree-trimming chair to join them and was welcomed with smiles. Thank goodness Mrs. Butterfield had forgotten what she'd gone to look for and returned with another slice of pie for him.

The short senior citizen who'd fallen through the chair earlier introduced himself as he offered Yancy a wrinkled hand. "Leo is my name and farming was my game until I settled here.

I used to grow pumpkins so big we could have hollowed them out and used them for carriages."

A few rusty red hairs waved at the top of Leo's head as he laughed. "Let me fill you in on the protocol here. Every Sunday we get up early and sit out here, if the weather permits, until ten-thirty when two vans drive up. Until then we eat Mrs. Ollie's deliciously sinful banana bread and Mrs. Butterfield's pie if she remembers it's Sunday. Of course, we do this so the Catholics will have something to confess and the Baptists will have something to sing about. Those feeling the calling load the vans for church and the rest of us finish off the bread before our kin drop by to take us to their low-fat, no sugar, high-fiber Sunday dinners."

"Which van you climbing into, Mr. Leo?" Yancy smiled as he took another piece of the best banana bread he'd ever eaten.

"Neither," Leo snapped. "I was married twice. Once to a Baptist. Once to a Catholic. After spending twenty years in each church I gave up religion for superstition." Mr. Leo leaned forward. "Like, I've been noticing something about you, Yancy. You may be a good-looking fellow, but you got one gray-colored eye and one blue. Like Mrs. Butterfield said, that's strange. Some folks might think you to be the son of a witch, or maybe a witch yourself. I've heard tell a man with two colored eyes can see death coming for any one he stares at. Gypsy blood in you, I'm guessing, with that black hair. They say every Gypsy is born with a gift, and yours just might be death's sight. Am I right, Yancy?"

"That's me," Yancy lied. He had no idea where his people came from, but seeing death hanging around these folks wouldn't be too hard. He was surprised the Grim Reaper didn't make regular minivan stops by this place.

Miss Ollie passed by to offer him the last slice of bread. "Don't believe a word Leo says," she whispered. "He ain't never farmed in his life. He taught drama at the high school for forty years, and if he had two wives he must have kept them in a box, because no one in town ever saw them." She laughed. "We don't know if his brain is addled, or if he's just trying to make life more interesting. Either way, he's always fun to listen to."

It took Yancy a moment to wrap his mind around what he heard. He'd known many liars but not one who did so for fun, and nobody in the group seemed to care.

"Don't rat me out, Ollie," Leo grumbled, "or I'll tell him about when you came to town as a lazy streetwalker and settled here just so you'd only have to walk a few blocks to cover the whole town."

The very proper baker hit him with her empty banana-bread pan. Crumbs showered over him, but Leo didn't seem to notice. He just grinned and winked at her because he knew he'd flustered her. "She's Baptist," he whispered. "Never confesses to a thing she's done all her life. Taught home economics down the hall from me, and I can tell you there were some wild parties in that food lab."

She raised the pan as if planning to hit him again, but decided to laugh.

Yancy studied the circle of people. "How many of you taught school?"

To his surprise all but one raised his hand. A tall, frail man in a black suit, wearing hearing aids in both ears, finally lifted his hand to join the others. "I think I qualify, even though I was the principal. I'm Mr. Halls. Many a student made a joke about my name." His announcement was a bit loud. "A man's name sets his course at birth."

They all nodded as if he were the bravest among the brave. Battle-scarred veterans of decades of fighting their grand war against ignorance might have honed them, but age now left them crippled and alone. One to a house. No husbands or wives surviving, apparently. But they had each other. Somehow in the middle of nowhere, they'd found their place, like a flock of birds huddled together on a tiny lake.

When the two church vans arrived, most of the group climbed on. Only Leo, Cap and the principal remained in the circle with Yancy. When the principal went inside to get his cap, Yancy had to ask, "Isn't he going to church? He's all dressed up."

Cap shook his head. "He dresses like that every day. Old habits are hard to break. He's almost deaf, so whoever sits on his right tends to yell."

When Mr. Halls returned wearing his very proper hat, he didn't seem to notice they were still talking about him.

Yancy leaned back in his metal chair and relaxed. *This is it,* he thought, *my river of peace that prison preacher used to talk about.* They might not know it, but these old folks were offering him the bridge to cross from one life to another. He listened as they told him of Crossroads and their lives growing up, of growing old in the Panhandle of Texas, where canyons cut across the flat land and sunsets spread out over miles rich in history wild and deep.

Finally when one of the old men got around to asking what he was doing here in Crossroads, Yancy pointed to the post office and explained that he was looking for a job.

"I'm traveling light. Just a pack." As he said the words, he stared at the steps and noticed his pack wasn't where he'd left it.

"My pack!" he yelled as he stood and ran toward the post office.

By the time the three old men caught up to him, Yancy had been around the little building twice. The pack was nowhere to be found. No one was around. He'd been in sight of the post office all morning, and he hadn't seen a soul walk past. The only person he'd observed stop had been the guy in the pickup, and he'd been long gone before Yancy walked across the street.

"I've been robbed," he said, more surprised that a crime had been committed against him before he'd had time to commit one himself than he was worried about his few possessions.

"Everything I had was in that pack." He didn't mention that most of it was stuff the prison had given him. A toothbrush. All his socks and underwear. The bloody shirt he'd worn when he was arrested and a deck of cards he'd spent hours marking.

"This is serious," Cap said, passing like an elderly, short General Patton before his troops. "This is a crime right in the middle of town. This is outrageous."

Leo didn't seem near as upset. "What'd you have, sonny?"

Yancy didn't move. He couldn't tell them how little he had. They'd probably figure out he'd come from prison. All he'd walked out with were his goals. "I had a good winter coat made of wool," he lied. "And a great pair of boots. A shaving kit in a leather carrier and three hundred dollars."

All three old men patted him on the shoulder. They all agreed that that was a great deal to lose.

Cap spoke first. "Come on home with me, son. We'll call the sheriff, then you can join the few of us who are lucky enough not to have family dragging us to Sunday dinner. Mrs. Ollie always cooks for us."

Yancy was getting into his lie now. "I don't have the money to make it to Arizona. A friend of mine said if I could make it to Flagstaff I might have a job waiting."

They patted him again. "Don't you worry," Mr. Halls said. "We'll take up a collection if we don't find who did this. And do you know, my daughter gave me a winter coat that's too big for me. You can have it. I got half a dozen in the closet. She sends either that or two sweaters every Christmas."

"Is your coat wool?" Yancy asked. After all, it had to match his dream.

"It is," Mr. Halls said, "and if I remember right, it's got one of them heavy zip-out linings."

Yancy tried not to sound too excited. "I think it'll do, thanks."

"Don't thank me. It's the least I can do for a man who was robbed right under our noses."

"I can cover the shaving kit," Leo added. "I have four I've

never used. If you need gloves, I got half a dozen you can try on. Can't seem to convince my daughter-in-law that I don't like gloves. Why waste time on gloves when you got pockets, I always say, but I swear that woman never listens. Since my birthday is in November, she mails gloves every year. Lucky I wasn't born in July or I'd be getting a swimsuit."

Yancy choked down a laugh. This was better than stealing. These folks were giving him more than he could carry off. "One thing, Mr. Leo, I'd rather not call the sheriff. You see, it's my religion to forgive any wrong done me."

Leo swore. "Hell, I knew you was one of them van riders all along. Well, if you won't consider converting to my religion of superstition, I'll have to be tolerant of yours. But I got to tell you, son, that forgive-and-forget kind of thinking will lead you down a penniless path."

Yancy did his best to look thoughtful. "I'm set on my faith, Mr. Leo. For all I know, whoever stole my pack thought he needed it more than I did." Yancy didn't add that was usually his philosophy when he robbed someone.

Leo saw the light. "You're a good man, Yancy Grey, and we'd all be lucky to call you a friend. It'll be our pleasure to help you out with anything you need. We might even offer you some handyman work around this place to help you get back on your feet."

"Thanks," Yancy managed as he started a list of things that he'd forgotten were in his pack. A watch. A new wallet. "I'd be thankful for any work. I've been laid off for a while."

Everyone jumped as Mr. Halls shouted, "A man on a mission is a man who can't be bested."

Leo and Cap nodded, but Yancy had a feeling the old principal was walking the halls in his mind reading quotes he'd seen along the walls of the high school.

CHAPTER FIVE

Lauren

The county hospital had its own kind of sounds. Like echoes in Ransom Canyon and the lone clank of a windmill turning on the prairie or the rustle of paper in empty school hallways, hospital noise was unique.

The place rumbled like a train station. Phones rang, pagers beeped, and machines hummed and ticked like the final clock measuring someone's life away.

There was a rush about the people in white one moment and a stillness the next. Lauren had no idea what time it was. She'd seen a clock not long after she'd been wheeled in that said 2:00 a.m., but that had been hours ago.

In a hospital, only the smell of antiseptic seemed to remain the same. In her windowless space, she could have been waiting a few hours or a day.

Lauren sat alone in the third curtained-off emergency room cubicle, drifting off now and then, only to wake to the same nightmare.

She knew Tim was in the first bed. Everyone had rushed toward him when the emergency room doors opened, which told her he was in danger. Funny Tim O'Grady, whom she'd known all her life, might die! No one she'd ever been close to had ever died. Thinking about it wasn't funny at all, she realized.

A nurse had helped her onto the examination table when she'd first arrived and checked her leg. At least she thought she was a nurse. Without her glasses she couldn't read any of the name tags. For all she knew, she was the janitor. For a while she worried that Pop would be mad that she'd lost another pair of glasses, but decided that was so far down the lecture list it didn't matter.

The nurse was back.

"You're going to need a few stitches and a few shots," no-name in white said. "You're lucky. That first boy looks like he took a Humpty Dumpty fall."

"Can they put him back together again?" Lauren smiled at their nursery-rhyme code.

The nurse frowned as if she'd crossed some line in protocol. "I'm sure he'll be fine. He's getting the best care here."

Lauren nodded, but she didn't feel very lucky, and she wasn't at all sure Tim would be fine. If she were lucky, she wouldn't have gone into that haunted house. Following Reid Collins was the dumbest thing she'd ever done. He might have twice her muscles, but he only had about half her brain cells. If his dad wasn't rich, Reid would be lost. As it was, he'd probably run for Crossroads mayor in another twenty years. First he thought he was a football star because he had the jacket, and now he considered himself a hero.

No-name carefully pulled the curtain closed as she vanished. Lauren waited, fighting the need to slip under one of the fabric walls and escape. In her mind she kept backtracking all the way to the church, thinking of every wrong turn she must have taken to end up here. If she could get do-overs, she'd have stayed with Mrs. Patterson to talk about all the things the old lady thought were on Lauren's mind.

As time dragged by, her father dropped in twice to glare at her. She was in major trouble. During his first one-minute visit, he said he had to call Tim's and Reid's parents and get them out of bed. The second visit, an hour later, was to inform her that Tim was going into surgery. After that, Lauren just acted as if she was asleep when he made his hourly rounds.

He said the word surgery as if it was something terrible she'd done to Tim, but Lauren couldn't bear to think about it. Somewhere in this very building someone was cutting into Tim.

She wanted to ask about Lucas Reyes. Her father seemed to have forgotten about him. Or maybe he was still angry, thinking that somehow this was all Lucas's fault.

When the nurse finally came back, she was with a doctor who looked as though he wasn't old enough to be out of college. The nurse did all the talking, and the young doc just nodded and signed the chart. As Lauren had suspected, her injury wasn't worth much attention. A few stitches, just like the no-name nurse had said. Within minutes both the nurse and the doctor were finished. They had that why-are-you-wasting-our-time look about them. The emergency room had been busy for hours, and she'd been shoved to the back of the line several times.

About the time Lauren wondered whatever happened to bedside manner, the nurse poked her with an injection and announced, "Tetanus shot going in."

"Do I get a sucker?" Lauren asked, and to her surprise the nurse smiled.

Encouraged, Lauren continued, "How are the others?"

The nurse patted her hand. "They'll all be fine. Two will be released this morning, but the boy they took upstairs to surgery will have to stay a few days."

"You mean Tim's not going to die?"

The nurse shook her head. "Not from a broken leg. They're doing X-rays to make sure he didn't break a rib."

Lauren was so relieved that Tim wasn't headed for the afterlife she didn't feel the second needle. He might be dumb as a rock, but if his brain ever caught up to his imagination, who knows, he could make something of himself, other than being Reid's sidekick.

"What about Lucas?"

"Lucas Reyes?"

Lauren nodded.

"He's fine. Lost some blood, but we stitched him up. I think he's already been released. I saw him sitting in the lobby about half an hour ago."

"And Reid Collins?" Lauren was so mad at him she really didn't care. First, he'd gotten them into this mess, and then, when help showed up, he took all the credit for saving everyone.

"The Collins boy sprained his ankle. He was really complaining about the pain until the doc told him he'd have to use crutches for a few weeks. He seemed to cheer up after that." The nurse grinned. "He might have been cured if they'd offered him a wheelchair."

Lauren smiled, knowing that Reid would make the most of his injury. She thanked the nurse then closed her eyes, deciding that now that she knew all the guys were all right, she might as well sleep awhile. Her dad wouldn't be by to take her home until Reid and Lucas were released and Tim was settled into a real hospital room.

She almost drifted into a dream when she felt someone take her hand. The touch was gentle, comforting, and for a moment she smiled, thinking that her Pop was finally showing her how much he cared.

But when she opened her eyes, Lucas was standing beside the examining table.

"How you feeling?" he said quietly, so low no one on the other side of the curtain could have heard.

She rose to her elbows. "I'll survive."

"I gotta go. Half my family came to pick me up, and I think

the hospital is worried about the mob scene. I just wanted to say goodbye. Despite all that happened, I liked being with you tonight."

"Me, too," she said, wishing that she could think of something clever to add. But fighting down nervous giggling seemed to be the limit of her communication skills. Lucas was at least a year older than her, good-looking, and *he* was holding her hand.

"You ever been kissed?" He flashed a smile.

"No," she answered. He could have probably already figured that out. Glasses, sheriff's daughter, homely, brainy type. How many more strikes against her did she need? Oh, yeah, and flat chested.

Without a word, he leaned in and touched his lips to hers. As he pulled away he winked. "How about we keep this to ourselves?"

She nodded, deciding one kiss and her brain cells must be dying. Now she couldn't even talk.

"See you around." He backed away.

As he vanished through the curtain door, she whispered, "See you around."

CHAPTER SIX

Staten

Staten dropped by his grandmother's house, but she didn't have any chores for him. It seemed the cluster of retirees at Evening Shadows had hired a handyman to run the place. In truth, he'd never seen the community looking so good. The swimming pool had been cleaned out, the fence fixed and the porches painted, every house a different color.

"Yancy says," Granny shouted over the news blaring from her TV, "if each door is a different color, some of the folks won't get confused and keep going in the wrong house." She shook her head. "I've never been so embarrassed in my life than when I saw Leo naked."

Staten stood, his fists clenched. He didn't care how old the little man was, he wasn't putting up...

Granny continued, "It was my fault. I must have miscounted. I thought I turned into my house, but it was his. But I blame him, of course, for not locking his door."

Staten calmed. "Granny, you live in number three, he lives in four. How hard could it be to count to three?"

She shook her finger at him. "Now, don't get smart with me. After about eighty years, things like numbers started falling out of the back of my head. I can't even remember my phone number, much less anyone else's."

"Don't worry about it. Everyone you know is programmed into your phone. All you have to do is flip it open, punch a button and say their name."

She raised an eyebrow as if she suspected a trick. "So, what is going to happen if one day I'm somewhere lost and lose my phone? Even if I can borrow someone else's phone, I won't know a number to call, and the stranger I asked to help probably doesn't have Aunt Doodles's number in his phone anyway." She crossed her arms over her chest. "With my luck, the stranger will be one of them serial killers, just looking for his next victim, and there I'll be, up a creek without a phone."

Staten patted her shoulder. Every week she had a new worry. He should keep a list. Eventually she was bound to get around to repeating one. "First of all, you can't drive. So if you're lost, you're still in the county. Anyone you stop will probably know you and be happy to bring you back here. Second, if you do see a serial killer, he probably does know Aunt Doodles. She went to jail several times, remember."

Granny's finger started wagging again. "She did not. Not many anyway. And every single time was that dumb husband of hers' fault, not hers."

Staten leaned down and whispered, "How do you know? You can't count to three."

She slapped his cheek too hard to be a pat. "Stop it, Staten. You remind me of numbers I couldn't remember, and that reminds me of Mr. Leo and his wrinkled...body. Now, that's a sight I'd like to unsee."

All at once laughter erupted from her. Staten enjoyed the sound from the dear old woman who'd loved him every day of his life.

As always, her sweet chuckle was music to Staten's ears. When he was growing up, his parents were either traveling or fighting. By the time he was in middle school, his father had divorced his mother and found wife number two. Neither of them had seemed to want custody of him in the split. His mother had remarried and moved to England within six months, without leaving a forwarding address.

Staten had spent most of his time with his grandparents on the ranch. He'd loved working the land with his granddad and living in their little place where his granny's laughter always seemed to fill every nook and cranny. The visits from his father and wife number whatever had grown further apart. Senator Samuel Kirkland showed no interest in the ranch. No one was surprised when Granddad died and left it to Staten, his only grandson.

"Sorry you had to see Old Leo, Granny." He smiled at his grandmother. "Maybe the new handyman was right about the doors. It must have been a shock for you and Leo when you walked into his house."

Granny was busy cleaning up the coffee cups. "Not so much. I've seen him naked before." She turned and headed to the tiny kitchen.

Staten had no intention of asking more. He didn't want to know.

Since it was too early to go to Quinn's for supper, he dropped by the volunteer fire department's weekly meeting.

This time of year grass fires were rare, and guys were drinking coffee and talking about how the chamber of commerce was planning something big. The men got their information from their wives, who'd passed it around some. So, no telling how accurate it might be. The leaders in Crossroads were looking for ideas to help the town grow and that meant raising money.

"A fund-raiser to beat all fund-raisers," Hollis shouted. "We plan to raise enough money to improve both the fire station and the clinic. Ellie could use the space at the clinic, and when she graduates, most folks would like to see her stay in town and run it full-time."

"That waiting room is too small," one of the other farmers said. "She'll be stacking folks in chairs before long. With all the pregnancies lately, she'll want to add a birthing room. We can handle a doc coming in once a week, but we need a nurse there full-time."

G.W. Polk, who farmed next to Hollis, shook his head. "There's a good hospital in Lubbock. I was born in a car headed that way. To my way of thinking, kids should be born the same place they're conceived."

Hollis nodded. "My point exactly. You were born in a car and you haven't been the same since."

Staten was distracted by thoughts of Quinn and the way she kissed him, but he tried his best to listen. He rarely participated in the town's problems, but he always sent a check to help out with any fund-raiser. Every year the chamber of commerce thought up a grand plan to improve the town, but nothing ever really changed. Correction, he thought, the dozen reindeer they'd put up at Christmas on all the light posts along Main looked great.

After an hour, he excused himself and told the men that whatever they decided, he was behind the chamber one hundred percent. He took his time leaving. Reason told him he was being a fool worrying about what time he got to Quinn's house. She was the same shy woman he'd known all his life. Nothing unusual would happen tonight, and he'd be wasting worry to think otherwise.

For the past five years he had never given their unusual relationship much thought. Maybe because it seemed to have grown naturally with neither of them planning it. He never considered finding another woman, though he knew a few who'd welcome him in their bed if he showed up.

Only, they would come with strings. They'd want eventually

to become Mrs. Kirkland, and Staten wasn't sure he ever wanted that again. Being numb most days was far better than hurting.

Maybe he should just be satisfied with what he had with Quinn. It was good. It was enough. She probably felt the same, even if she had asked to be kissed.

He told himself when he got to her house he'd act exactly the same as he always did. Nothing different. Nothing changed. One little kiss didn't mean anything.

As he pulled up to her place, he noticed her working in the barn, elbow deep in the engine of her old tractor. Even after all his stops, he'd arrived early. He'd said supper. It wasn't even five o'clock.

Halfway to her barn he remembered the bag of barbecue in the truck. If she hadn't already waved, he would have turned around. But it was too late. Maybe she'd rather drive over to Bailee and eat hamburgers or maybe even try something at the café in town. They didn't have to always do everything the same. He could be flexible. The kiss was proof, wasn't it?

No, going into a café would seem too strange. They never ate out. They both thought it would seem too much like a couple thing.

"Need some help?" he asked when he reached her.

"No. I've about got it." She stepped down to face him. "Where's the barbecue?"

"In the truck. I brought beer, too. That all right with you?"

He rubbed away a smudge on her cheek with his finger. The touch was casual, but her eyes watched his every movement.

Stepping out of his reach, Quinn moved toward the house. "I'll clean up while you get the food." She was almost to the porch when she looked back and added, "I already set the table."

He watched her until she disappeared. She'd never seemed quite so nervous around him. Suddenly, he wished he could take back the kiss from last week. He wanted everything to stay the same. They had it good and good was enough.

The shower pipes rattled from down the hallway as he set out the food. The paper containers looked out of place amid her china. He hadn't given it much thought before, but she always set the table with her few pieces of hundred-year-old china and nice flatware. He tossed the plastic cutlery he'd picked up into the trash.

When she finally joined him in the kitchen, he was halfway through his first beer. He offered one to her, but she poured herself a glass of cold tea instead.

She was wearing a blue silk blouse that floated around her. He liked the look. Something different. Brushing his hand over the soft material, he breathed in her fresh smell. "It seems like I've been fighting all week to get back to you."

"I know how you feel." She leaned against him. "I missed you, too."

They sat down where they always ate and filled their plates. He wasn't sure what she'd like, so he'd bought a pound of every kind of grilled meat the café had. Then he'd tossed in fries and okra for the vegetable.

She asked about the meeting, and he told her the gossip that she probably cared nothing about. Neither ate much. Neither wanted to talk.

Finally, Staten stood. She hadn't offered to take him to her bedroom, and if he stayed longer, he'd say more than he should.

"I should call it a night." He reached for his hat. "We saddle up before dawn tomorrow."

"All right," she said in a flat tone that revealed nothing as she stood.

He took two steps to the door and remembered how he'd promised he would kiss her goodbye before he left.

With his hat in one hand and Quinn holding their plates between them, he leaned over and kissed her cheek.

When he straightened, he saw a tear roll down her face.

He doubted he'd get an answer if he asked her why she was crying, but it was obvious that he was doing something wrong.

Tossing his hat on the bar, he took the plates from her and set them aside. "I didn't do that right," he muttered, more like a swear than an apology.

She waited.

He brushed her shoulders lightly as he leaned in again and touched his lips to hers.

Quinn's mouth was so soft. Her bottom lip trembled slightly.

His fingers tightened over her shoulders, and he pulled her closer, kissing her lightly until her mouth opened. Then, without hesitation, he kissed her completely.

She didn't pull away. She simply accepted his advance. He lifted her arms and set them on his shoulders as he continued. If she wanted to be kissed, by hell he'd kiss her.

Slowly, her body melted against him.

He finally broke the kiss, but he didn't turn loose of her. "Any objections if I undress you?" His hand moved over her back and came to rest on her hip. "I've never said so, but I like doing that."

She leaned her head back as his fingers moved over her blouse. He watched her face as he slowly unbuttoned first her blouse, then her jeans. He liked the way she always left something on for him to finish, and tonight he was doing it all.

Standing before him she closed her eyes as he kissed his way down her body. Then, she took his hand and led him to her bedroom.

They made love slowly, tenderly, as they always did. Only after both were satisfied Staten held her tighter than ever before as though just discovering what a treasure he had in his arms.

When she drifted to sleep, he found himself kissing her. He couldn't get enough of the feel of her. He'd been starving all week and finally she was beside him, warm and soft. For a while she moved in her sleep, welcoming his touch, but when he deepened the kiss she woke with a jerk.

For a few minutes he held her tight, gently caressing her, whispering her name in the darkness.

When she calmed, he pulled her close. "I want you again if you've no objections, Quinn. I don't want to leave and wait a week to be with you again."

Her big eyes widened with uncertainty, but she nodded slightly, and he made love to her for the second time. But this time they both knew he wasn't just loving a woman out of need. He was loving Quinn.

CHAPTER SEVEN

Lucas

Lucas Reyes stood in the corner of the cafeteria and watched the mayhem. School was like the gathering of the clans in Scotland at Culloden. He'd read all about the great battle on the moors when the MacDonalds, the Jacobites and the French all met to fight the English in 1746. The English brought rifles and the men of the mighty clans of Scotland were wiped out that day. Highlander blood turned the earth red, and some said the thunder of the muskets still echoed off the hills.

Maybe the cafeteria wasn't quite that bad, but the cliques were clear. In his grandfather's day they would have been separated by race, but that no longer played a role. Neither did money. Now the division was more by interest. Each clan at Ransom Canyon High wore the markings of their tribe, though. The geeks, who always seemed to carry more books than anyone else. The jocks in their letter jackets. The cheerleaders with their designer purses and perfect spray-on tans even in January.

Several tiny towns and dozens of ranches fed into Ransom High, so there were more groups than he could name. Lately the goths were making an appearance, along with a dozen or so freshmen who looked like they were straight out of the Harry Potter movies. Big round black glasses and all that.

For a country school, this place was the best, Lucas thought. Folks around poured money into computer labs and libraries for their kids. Where city schools were cutting extra programs, Ransom Canyon High had the best in music and arts. Lucas knew when he headed to college he'd be prepared.

The idea of learning, without the cliques around, excited him.

"Hi, Lucas," Sarah Rodriguez said as she circled him.

"*Hola*, Sarah," he answered. He'd known Sarah most of his life and she'd always been sweet. He almost hated to see her grow up and join one of the groups. Maybe she'd be one of the few, like Lauren, who kept her own identity.

"My folks are having a belated New Year's party this weekend. You coming with your folks?"

"If I get off work in time. I'm riding for the Kirkland ranch all weekend. He'll have us working cattle until dark, but I'm not complaining. He pays great."

The bell rang, and she started off. "See you, if you make it in."

He waved back, thinking that with her three older brothers, she was comfortable talking to guys. Sarah was pretty, like her mother, with long midnight-black hair that hung down to her waist, but Lucas couldn't help but think he was starting to prefer sunny blond hair that fell down straight without a hint of a curl and bangs long enough to shade eyes framed in glasses.

Lucas glanced across the cafeteria as Lauren left a table where she'd been studying alone. Despite the noise, she read her history book while she ate her sack lunch. Her blond hair had curtained her off from the world. He thought of catching up with her but decided not to.

Somehow in all the talk about what had happened at the Gypsy House last Saturday night, Lucas had fallen out of the picture. Reid Collins had told everyone about how he saved Tim and Lauren, about how they were trapped at one point, about how Tim almost died. But Lucas's part in the whole thing must have gotten left on the cutting room floor.

He didn't care. If kids knew he'd been there, they'd only ask him questions, and at some point, his account of the night and Reid's would cross.

Better to let Reid tell the story. Tim wouldn't be back at school for another week or more, and by then the topic would be past tense. Lauren was so shy, he was sure she wouldn't talk about it. If Tim had any brains left, he would say he couldn't remember how it all happened, so with luck the whole thing would be yesterday's news very soon.

Lucas walked toward class, smiling. He'd remember the blood debt Lauren owed him. Maybe someday he'd tease her about it. And, he remembered kissing her. She was the first girl he'd really liked that he had kissed. He might be leaving after summer for college, but he'd remember Lauren long after he forgot everyone else at this school.

He rushed alone down the emptying hallway, feeling proud that he'd managed to stay out of any cliques. He saw no point to them. High school was only a passageway to what he wanted in life, nothing more.

To his surprise, Lauren caught up to him and fell into step beside him. For several seconds they just walked, but he slowed his pace a bit to match hers.

"I want to talk to you," she finally said without looking at him. "The story of what happened Saturday night has changed so much I don't even think I was there. Now Reid Collins claims Tim was hanging on by a thread, and we could all hear the ghosts whispering. I would have probably broken both legs in the fall from the window if he hadn't caught me. And—"

"I know," Lucas interrupted her. "According to Reid, I wasn't even there. Which is fine with me."

She stopped and turned to him. "But you were there. You

saved my life. Reid can lie all he wants to, but I'll never forget. I owe you a blood debt."

"Let Reid's legend live, *querida*. You and I will remember and that is enough."

"Like the kiss at the hospital. Between you and me, right?"

"Right." He smiled, remembering.

"It was the best kiss I ever had." She laughed.

"It was the only one you've ever had," he teased. "When I find you in a few years, I'll ask you again how I compare and see where I stand then."

She blushed and ran ahead of him into her class.

Lucas stood watching her disappear, knowing they were both late but not caring. She'd forget about him, but he'd remember Lauren. She'd be the only girl he'd ever call darling in any language. Funny thing was, Lauren would probably never know just how special she was.

"Reyes?" Mr. Paris, his math teacher, snapped. "Are you planning on joining us this afternoon?"

"Of course," Lucas answered. "I'm sorry I'm late."

He wasn't sorry at all, but Mr. Paris didn't need to know that. Being late because he was talking to a girl didn't compute in the old guy's world.

CHAPTER EIGHT

Yancy

Yancy Grey had worked ten days straight at the Evening Shadows Retirement Community and loved every minute. The first
few evenings he'd cleaned out an old office that stood apart from
the rest of the bungalows. The front of the building was lined
with dirty windows with a long counter separating the lobby
area from the back storage and living quarters. A tiny, windowless bedroom and bath ran across part of the back. The living
quarters were barely wide enough to fit a full bed, but it was
bigger than his cell had been.

Originally, in the '50s, this place had been a motel, boasting
that every cabin had a kitchen, bath and sun porch. Eventually,
the sun porches had been enclosed to make living rooms, and
the bungalows had been rented by the month. Oil field workers
and seasonal farmhands had taken over the place, but the owner
had never bothered repairing any of the buildings. Finally, he'd
let them sell to pay his back taxes.

Cap had told him the school board bought them in the '90s,
planning to offer discount housing to new teachers for the first

two years in the county school system. That had only lasted a short time before retiring teachers asked to buy them.

Yancy hadn't figured out why only teachers wanted to live in the place, but he didn't really care. All he knew was he had a great find. All eight of the residents, except maybe Miss Bees who lived in the first unit, seemed to like him. Old lady Bees didn't like anyone. She sometimes came out to sit with the group, but, if she talked, she only complained. She went to church on Sunday and played bingo over in Westland on Wednesday nights, but she didn't talk to Yancy.

Mr. Halls told him that she thought every stranger was probably a criminal. Yancy figured she might have a few more marbles than the others. He'd be smart to stay out of her way. He had Cap ask her what color she wanted her door and wasn't surprised she chose white. Only interesting thing about Miss Bees seemed to be her nickname, Bunny.

Yancy, with the advice of everyone except Miss Bees, had painted his one-room-and-bath behind the office. He'd used leftover paint from the porches, so every wall was a different color, but he didn't care. He'd spent too many years without color. He'd bought a used mattress and frame from the secondhand store a block away and a desk he could also use as his one table. The owner agreed to let him pay the furniture out at twenty-five dollars a week.

He'd turned what had been the front office into a sunny sitting room. That way, on cold days the old folks could sit in the long row of sunshine and watch their former students go by. The men would drink coffee while the women knitted or worked puzzles. Then, just for fun they'd argue politics. Cap, Leo and Mrs. Kirkland kept up with what was going on, but Mr. Halls only heard half of any news, and Mrs. Butterfield kept forgetting who was president.

About three in the afternoon they'd all wander back to their little cottages for naps.

Yancy started lists on the office wall. The first was things that needed fixing fast, like Miss Bee's roof and Mr. Halls's porch. The second list was for repairs that he could get to when he had time, like Mrs. Ollie's sink that had been dripping for six months and Mrs. Kirkland's broken window in the back. She'd covered it up with colored paper so her grandson wouldn't notice.

"If he sees it, Staten will only ask questions, and I'm not in the mood to tell him the truth," she'd said one morning.

As soon as she'd left, all the men stayed behind, trying to guess what she'd been doing to break a window higher than her head. Leo had explained that during World War II, he'd seen a female member of the French underground who could kick higher than six feet and knock a man out cold. Mr. Halls had pointed out that, since Leo was seventy-four, he would have been fourteen when the war ended.

Yancy went back to his lists, angry that he'd bought into Leo's story completely before Mr. Halls did the math.

The last list he kept on the wall was a wish list. Everyone had something to add to that list.

Miss Abernathy wanted bookshelves in the living room. Miss Ollie needed a railing for her hand-painted plates running high around her dining area. She explained to him that they were very valuable, but Yancy figured they'd be the last thing he'd steal if he robbed her place.

Leo wanted his TV hooked up high almost to the ceiling so he could watch sports in bed all night. He grinned and said that if he lost the remote control he could always get Mrs. Kirkland to come in and kick it off and on.

Yancy had worried at first that he wouldn't know how to do any of the repairs well enough to please them, but, to his surprise, Cap Fuller was a wealth of information. His hand wasn't steady, but his mind was sharp. By the end of the first week, Yancy had learned enough about plumbing, woodworking, painting and bricklaying to feel like he could hire himself out as a repairman.

Lying in his little room behind what everyone called the office, Yancy thought about all he had accomplished so far: Working in the sun without anyone yelling at him. Learning. Laughing. Talking to folks he'd never thought he would ever talk to about everything. For the first time in his life he was living a regular life.

Of course, the main topic of conversation was always their health, but he didn't mind. All he had to say was "how you feeling today" and they'd be off talking for half an hour. But, they knew so much more than him, things he'd never even heard about. The minute he acted interested, they showed up with a book or an article he should read. They worried if he was warm at night or if he ate proper meals.

No one had ever worried about him, and now he was into overload.

As each day passed he thought less and less about robbing them and more about how for the first time in his life he felt as if he had something to contribute.

The whole group had even gotten together and decided to up the dues of their home owner's association a hundred dollars each and pay him eight hundred a month, plus a free place to stay.

Cap had slapped Yancy on the back and said that should beat any offer he'd get in Flagstaff, so he might as well stay here. "A for-sure job here has got to be better than a maybe job there."

Yancy hadn't argued.

In truth, Yancy felt rich. If he could winter here, he could save enough money to buy a car and drive wherever he wanted. Even if he ate at the café three times a week and bought something new to wear once a month, he'd still have plenty of money to save.

On the nights one of them didn't bring him food, he'd heat up a can of soup over a hot plate in his room and swear, right out of the can, it was better than anything he'd had to eat in prison. The kitchen workers used to say they served miracle meals because it was a miracle if you kept it down.

On the eleventh day of work, Yancy was curled up in one of the office chairs reading a book Cap had given him on brick-laying when the glass door banged open.

He felt the cold air rush ahead of a young woman as if to get out of her way as she stormed into the room wearing a navy cape and a frown.

Yancy stood up, wondering if she was lost, or maybe she thought this place was a motel. With the roof fixed and a few of the bungalows painted, it *was* starting to look better.

But when he finally faced her nose to nose, he knew she wasn't lost. He saw anger firing in her gaze, and it all seemed to be aimed directly at him.

"You are not," she started as she slammed a case on the counter and raised her hand like a pointed weapon, "going to take advantage of these dear people."

"All right," he answered carefully, thinking it might not be too healthy to object. She still held a huge purse in one hand and was close enough to reach the case. Either was big enough to pack a gun. Plus, at almost his height and thirty pounds heavier, she'd have the advantage in a fight. The leather bag could prove a weapon if she knew how to use it, and this no-makeup, flat-shoed warrior looked as though she probably could.

Her tight mouth relaxed, but she didn't smile. "I care about these people, and I want you to know that I come by twice a month to check on them. So don't even think about trying anything."

Out of curiosity more than any need to continue the conver-sation, he asked, "Exactly what is it you think I'm going to do?"

"I don't know. I'm not a criminal."

"Neither am I," he lied, shoving all his thoughts of robbing the old folks blind under the carpet in his mind. "They just offered me a job, lady, so I took it."

"Why is that?"

She set her purse down next to the case and crossed her arms over what he noticed was an ample chest beneath her navy blue cape.

He studied her short hair and unpainted fingernails. "You any kin to Miss Bees?"

"No. Answer the question. Why did they offer you a job?"

"I guess because I needed one, and they needed work done around the place. Seems all their kids say they'll drop by and help with fixing stuff, but Mrs. Kirkland's grandson is the only one who even makes an effort."

She cocked her head. "Jerry at the hardware store said you've charged several hundred dollars to this place."

"I have." He didn't like her tone. "Who are you, lady?"

He swore he saw fire flash in her green eyes for a second. "I'm Miss Ellie, the nurse who checks on them. I make sure they have their medicines and get to their doctors' appointments."

"You don't look old enough to be a nurse." Most of the women he had seen over the past five years were either on TV or models in magazines. This woman didn't look like any of them. She was athletic, solidly built and pretty, even without the makeup.

He saw the lie on her face before she spoke to correct it. "Well, I will have my degree, in a year. I work for the doctor over in Bailee, and she travels here two days a week, then sends me the other three days to keep the office open. If there's an emergency or someone needs something more than a refill, I call her in by phone."

Yancy straightened. "Well, I care about these folks, too, and I'm telling you right now you're not going to drop in every other week and take advantage of them."

Finally, she smiled. "Fair enough. I'll watch you and you

watch me. Now I have to get back to work. I make the rounds to every house to check their blood sugar and blood pressure."

She picked up her bags and marched back out of the office with her cape whirling in the wind.

And Yancy started doing just what she'd told him to do... watching her.

CHAPTER NINE

Lauren

Lauren sat in the Ransom Canyon High School auditorium while the volunteer fire department chief gave Reid Collins the Hero-of-the-Month award. It looked like an Olympic medal. Everyone yelled while the cheerleaders bounced around shouting, "Reid, Reid, he's our man. Reid, Reid, ain't he grand."

The fact that no one had ever won a Hero-of-the-Month award didn't seem to matter. Neither did the truth about what happened that night at the Gypsy House. When Tim finally got off the painkillers, he told a different story about how he'd been hurt, but no one paid any attention. After all, he'd been on drugs, and Tim tended to tell stories anyway.

Lauren and Lucas, as they'd agreed, said nothing. They let the story Reid told run. And, as Lucas had predicted, his part that night was completely cut from the script.

Reid hobbled up to the podium on his crutches to give a speech that sounded like he'd copied it from Teddy Roosevelt. Everyone cheered, and his parents hugged him.

Lauren had the feeling that when he could drive, if he ever

recovered from his sprained ankle, he'd have all the dates he wanted. Only, he'd never have her, even as a friend, again. The sad thing about it was that he would never know how she felt, and if he did suspect or remember that they'd been friends, he probably wouldn't even care what had happened to make things change.

Winter would age into spring in a few months, but Lauren had grown up a little already. Maybe one of the ghosts *had* whispered to her in the blackness of that old house, because now she knew that people were not always what they seemed. No matter how many awards they gave Reid Collins, the truth hadn't changed. He was no hero.

She watched him pose for the camera and wondered if he was starting to believe his own press.

She walked out as everyone was shaking hands on the stage like they'd bred a wonder in their midst.

Her father's cruiser was in the parking lot. Without much thought, she walked over to it and climbed on the fender to wait for him.

Her pop, the always bossy sheriff, had also changed in the past week, or maybe she finally saw something she'd been too young to notice before. He watched over her like a hawk, but not out of anger or for punishment. That Saturday night had frightened him, she realized it sometime during the fourth or fifth lecture. He was afraid. If he lost her, he'd be alone. Big and strong as he was, she wasn't sure Sheriff Dan Brigman wanted to be alone. That might present a problem when she went away to college.

Lauren considered getting her father to start dating. There weren't many single women around his age that he hadn't given a ticket to or booked into jail. Plus, they might come with children, and she wouldn't wish her father on any child. There was the possibility that her mother might come back; after all, she'd only been gone ten years for her six-month internship.

Margaret Brigman said she still loved him, but she couldn't

live with the man. Maybe if Lauren could scrub him up a bit. Have him wear something besides his uniform. Let his hair grow out. Maybe add a mustache. Maybe change his diet. He only ate from the "B" group of foods: bread, butter, beef and banana nut ice cream. She'd started cooking for herself after she'd spent two weeks one summer with her mother and tried vegetables.

Lauren laughed. She'd begun worrying about her parents— she must be growing up. Funny how wisdom came in big hunks and not little bites. She could almost see the argument she'd have with her pop one day about how it was time for him to move into the home.

"Shouldn't you be in class?"

Her father's voice always made her jump.

"Shouldn't you be at work, Pop?"

"It's hero day," he answered.

"Exactly. Looks like we're both free." As free as I ever am, she thought. "How about we go grocery shopping in Lubbock?"

"We have a good food store here in town. Small, but it has all we need. Why would you want to drive all the way to Lubbock? Traffic. Crowds."

Lauren decided it was worth arguing. "The chicken and the vegetables are both the same color brown here."

While everything else was up for debate, he usually gave in on food matters. "Oh, all right." He tossed his hat in the back of the cruiser. "But we go home and switch cars. I want you driving the back roads every chance we get. Before you apply for your license next summer, we will have logged a thousand miles with me by your side."

Lecturing all the way, she thought, but decided it would be safer to just nod.

Reid and his parents walked by. Mr. Collins called out for the sheriff and Lauren to come over for steaks tonight. "We're having a party for our boy," he added. "Not every day we realize we gave birth to a hero."

Her father looked at her, and Lauren shook her head slightly. He turned back to Davis Collins. "I'll be glad to come, but I have to take Lauren home first. She has to study tonight."

She nodded, backing up her father. They both knew that the men would talk, and she'd spend the evening sitting in a corner with a book. "Maybe next time, Mr. Collins," she answered.

They climbed into the cruiser. "Thanks, Dad," she whispered.

"You're welcome, honey. The whole town may think Reid is a hero for saving you and Tim, but if he had any sense he would have suggested you stay out of that old death trap in the first place."

"I agree." She patted his arm.

Her father covered his big hand over both hers. "He's also a year older than you. He should have known better. I expect you to show more sense after your birthday. Being fifteen and trying something like that is one thing, but at sixteen you'll be almost a woman."

Lauren closed her eyes, praying he didn't start that *growing into a woman in body and mind* talk again. It echoed too many of Mrs. Patterson's words for her father to have thought it up himself.

They were almost home when he spoke again. "Your mother called me this morning. She's coming in next week. She's worried about you, and she's mad at me. That's a hard problem to solve long distance."

"Can she stay with us, Dad? I'll clean the extra bedroom."

He was turning into the long drive down toward the lake when he finally answered, "I guess so, if she will agree to it. She can yell at both of us in the house as easy as she can in public."

"And," Lauren said, grinning, "she won't have far to drag the body if she murders you."

"True. I seem to bring out the worst in Margaret. She wasn't like that when we first married."

"You mean before me?"

"No," he said. "It wasn't you, honey. I think, if anything, it was me. I didn't have enough ambition for her." He was silent for a minute, then added, "Or maybe she had too much for me. Anyway, once the arguments started, neither of us seemed to find a way to stop."

He glanced at her and added, "Margaret would never murder me. Who would she have left to pick on?"

Lauren laughed. "You're right, Pop, you got to outlive her because I'd be the next one she turned on if you disappeared."

Pop smiled. "So if she stays, we hide the guns and knives, just in case."

"Deal." They pulled into the lake house driveway with its wraparound porch and long dock that went all the way to the water.

This was the only home she remembered, and Pop, flaws and all, was the only parent she truly had.

CHAPTER TEN

Staten

The wind blew icy across Staten Kirkland's land. It might be only noon, but he decided to call it a day. Fog was moving in over the canyon rim along his back pasture. With the canyon so close, it wasn't safe to keep working cattle. His men had been out in the below-freezing wind since dawn, and the trucks were all loaded.

With a wave to the cowhands turning their horses toward the bunkhouse, Staten headed over to his home to do paperwork.

If he was being honest with himself, he knew there was another reason he'd stopped work early. Staten wanted to be alone. He wanted to think about Quinn. It had been almost a week since he'd last seen her, but she never quite left his mind.

Most of the time when he needed to think, he'd ride out to the pastures and move among his horses or cattle. The low sounds they made, the click of their hooves over rocky ground, the crackle of the wind in ice-packed trees, all relaxed him. He found his sanity there on his land where the work was never done and he could watch the clouds of heaven pass over and make shadows on the winter grass.

Today he needed to close himself off, to empty his mind so his thoughts could roam.

Once he reached the rambling two-story house that step-mother number two had built but left before she decorated, he made himself a bowl of chili and ate at his desk. His dad had finished the place with furniture bought in room group-ings, but the things Staten loved were the few pieces his grand-mother had sent over from her house a quarter mile away. The old place his grandparents had was still more a home to him than this house. It was still nestled in the breaks with trees on three sides. When his grandfather died, his grandmother had moved to town, claiming she was living with a memory there. Staten never could bring himself to go back inside. The old house had been locked up and empty for twenty years, but it still shone bright in the morning sun.

He shoved aside his half-eaten bowl of chili. He couldn't concentrate on reading stock reports, so he moved to the huge leather chair that had been his grandfather's. There, with the smell of the old man's pipe still lingering, Staten leaned back and remembered last Friday night.

Even in dreams he'd never made love like that. Over the past five years, he and Quinn had learned each other. Or so he thought. Last Friday night he'd learned a few things about her he hadn't known. For the first time he'd felt her hunger for his touch, needing it, almost demanding it.

He'd loved his wife, but somehow in the whirlwind of taking over the ranch and having Randall, they'd grown apart. The love had been there, always, from the beginning to the day she died, but the passion had vanished. He'd filled his days with work, and Amalah had poured her life into projects and spoil-ing Randall. They both had worked hard and shared dreams that all wrapped around Randall.

He remembered always looking forward to coming home and sharing with her, sleeping with her, making love to her, but somewhere passion had slipped away. By thirty they were married, settled, content. Three years later she was ill, and they'd both fought for her life.

Unlike his father, Staten had had only one wife, and she'd died. He knew he could never have that partnership again, and he had no intention of trying.

Quinn wasn't what he wanted in a wife, even if he thought he could marry again. She was too shy. She would hate going to dinners in Austin or Dallas when Samuel Kirkland needed family present. Quinn wasn't a joiner and never attended charity functions, even over in Crossroads. Staten wasn't much good at that kind of thing, either, but he felt a duty to do his part.

What he and Quinn had was special. He told himself it couldn't last. She was just someone to turn to when the pain of being alone got to be too much. She was a friend.

Only, lately what they shared seemed deeper, and he wanted more than an occasional day or two out of each month.

Pulling his cell out of his pocket, he pressed her number and wasn't surprised it took forever for her to answer.

"Hello," she finally said, sounding out of breath.

"Quinn, it's Staten."

She laughed. "I know."

It dawned on him he hadn't planned what he was going to say. In the past five years, they'd rarely phoned each other. "I was wondering what you'd like for supper. I thought I'd come over tonight, if you've no objection, and I could pick something up."

She took a while to answer, then her voice was soft. "I put on a roast about an hour ago, just in case you dropped by. With the weather so cold, I thought you might quit early and head on over."

She knew him well, but he didn't want to impose. "I'll be there. I just called in case you wanted to go out. We could—"

"No," she said. "I don't want to go anywhere."

He wasn't surprised. She never wanted to go out. Once, he'd taken her to a farm-and-ranch show in Abilene and lost track of her. He'd found her an hour later sitting in his truck reading. She'd made no apology, and he hadn't commented on the waste of time. They'd just driven back to her place in silence. That night he'd remembered there seemed to be miles between them. She hadn't taken his hand, and he hadn't suggested staying over. After that night he'd waited six weeks before going back, but when he did, she'd welcomed him without a single question.

"I'll be there before dark," he said and hung up, wondering if she'd even miss him if he never saw her again. She was his rainy-day woman, and he shouldn't try to make her more. Amalah had loved parties and eating out and travel. She'd spend weeks talking about what she'd wear to one of his father's big balls in Austin. She'd loved having fancy lunches with the ladies in the half-dozen clubs she belonged to. Quinn didn't, and, after the drive back and forth to Abilene in one day, Staten never got them confused again.

Quinn would never like things like that. She didn't want to go to the café in Crossroads. What they had was private, between them alone. No one knew he drove the road between his place and hers. He wouldn't have cared, but Quinn wanted it that way.

Drifting off in the leather chair, he was already with her in his mind. At sunset he woke with a start, realizing he was almost late for dinner.

The wind blew him inside when he opened her door without knocking, and Quinn laughed as she caught his hat tumbling in ahead of him.

When she closed the door, he kissed her awkwardly.

She smiled but backed away out of reach. "I'll put the food on the table."

Staten nodded, feeling a bit out of place. Since she'd told him she wanted him to kiss her goodbye every time before he left, something had shifted. He wasn't sure what the rules were anymore. Hell, with Quinn he was never sure what the rules ever were. She never turned him away, but he had no illusion that he was in control. She was his friend. They shared a history since grade school. They had sex now and then, but in many ways he didn't feel as if they were lovers. Not until last week anyway. The way they'd made love that second time was different.

He sat down at her table and didn't miss the fact that she'd taken extra effort tonight. Cloth napkins, a little pot of mums as a centerpiece. "It looks great," he said as she set a platter of roast and vegetables between their plates.

He'd sent her a quarter of beef, freezer wrapped, last spring, and she'd sent him lavender soap. They'd both gotten the joke. She rarely ate beef, and he wasn't about to shower with lavender soap. But she sometimes cooked the meat when he was coming over, and his housekeeper had put the soap in the three guest bathrooms he never used.

"I've been practicing today and thought I'd play for you after supper." She brushed her hip against his shoulder as she filled his coffee cup.

"I'd love that."

When she returned to the table, he stood and pulled out her chair for her. It seemed awkward, new.

"You don't have to," she said, not looking at him.

"I just need to touch you, Quinn." His hand brushed over her shoulder. "I don't know why, but I missed you this week."

"Me, too." She smiled up at him. "Especially when the tractor broke down again."

He took his seat and grumbled. "I know you don't like help, but I'm coming over one day and getting that thing in working order."

To his surprise, she didn't argue. They settled in. He cut her a slice, then filled half his plate with meat. She served the vegetables, giving him one of each, then filled her plate with the potatoes, carrots and celery. As wind rattled the windows, they ate in silence, neither feeling the need to keep conversation going.

His leg bumped her beneath the table, then settled against hers. When she handed him a bowl of cobbler for dessert, he rested his hand on her thigh. She looked up at him, and he saw a fire in her eyes. They'd make love tonight. She must have been thinking about last week, too. They might be in their early forties, but the way they'd made love last time seemed newly born to each.

She stood and put away the leftovers. He simply watched, his hands almost feeling what he saw. The soft flannel of her old shirt. The cotton of her white T-shirt.

Staten stopped his line of thinking. He and Quinn had never been about sex. They were friends first. She'd been there for him when he needed her. They were simply two people who needed someone. They trusted each other. They liked each other.

She took his hand, and they walked to her tiny living room. The piano seemed to take up half the space. He could almost see her as a little girl with pigtails swaying as she practiced. Music would have drifted out the open windows and across her parents' farm.

He leaned back on a couch too small for him and listened as she began to play. They both knew she was giving him a rare gift, and he enjoyed every minute of it. He might not know composers or understand much about music, but he knew that when she played he could hear angels singing.

When she stopped, she turned and smiled. "How did you like that?"

"I loved it, Quinn. You know I did. I wish the world could hear you play."

"It's enough that I play for you. I enjoy that."

He leaned forward, his elbows on his knees. "Oh, I forgot to tell you that the chamber of commerce—"

She laughed. "You mean you, the store owners and a few old women who think they run this town?"

He didn't argue. "Don't pick on me, Quinn. My grandmother made me take her place on the chamber of commerce last year. Claimed at eighty-four she needed a rest from all the decisions they have to make."

"And you never say no to her."

"Nope. She raised me while my dad and his line of wives went to Washington. I figure when she does die, she'll probably leave instructions for how I should live the rest of my life."

"I find it endearing that everyone thinks you're this big powerful rancher, and you still follow orders from her." She moved to kneel in front of him, her hands on his knees. "Your love for her is touching. She's a lucky woman to have you and a smart one for moving to town and not living with you. I'm afraid you'd drive each other crazy."

"Definitely." He cupped her face. "Don't distract me, Quinn, I've got some news. Real news, and that's rare in Crossroads."

Only, she did distract him. She pouted, and he couldn't resist her bottom lip. He leaned forward and kissed her lightly.

"The big news?" she asked.

He brushed his fingers along her jaw. "You know the chamber has been trying to think of a fund-raiser for a year. Well, Miss Abernathy—" he stopped and winked at her "—she was your first piano teacher, I believe. I should thank her for that someday."

Quinn didn't look impressed. "She was everyone in town's first piano teacher. She's also the reason I went to New York to study. She talked my parents into it."

Staten nodded. "Someone mentioned that to everyone at the meeting. Said you might know the pianist she wants to bring in for a one-night concert. Evidently, he is performing in Dallas in March, and she's talked him into stopping here for one performance. We signed the contracts last meeting."

Quinn shook her head. "New York was twenty years ago. I doubt I'd know anyone who's still there."

"Miss Abernathy said he wasn't a student, but a teacher then. When he agreed to come, he asked about you. He had a funny name, Lloyd deBellome I believe."

Quinn pulled away so fast Staten didn't have time to stop her. For a flash he saw the fear in her eyes. She ran to the bedroom and slammed the door behind her.

For a moment he just sat there, having no idea what to do. Then fury rose in him. Whoever this guy was, whatever had happened, didn't matter. All that mattered was that he'd hurt Quinn. She'd done a good job of hiding it from him and probably everyone in town, but that one look hadn't lied.

Staten stood and stormed after her.

He didn't hesitate when he saw the closed door to her bedroom. If it had been locked, he would have knocked it down. His announcement had hurt Quinn, and he'd be damned if he'd leave without knowing why.

Quinn couldn't stop shaking. She curled in a ball and pulled the bedcovers all around her. Staten stormed down the hallway after her and shoved the door open. He was halfway to her bed before he froze. "What is it? What's happened?" His words sounded angry, worried, frightened.

"It's nothing. Go away." She couldn't talk now. He was the last person she'd ever tell what had happened.

He knelt beside the bed. "Like hell, Quinn. I'm not going anywhere." He climbed in beside her and held her as she cried. He might have no idea what had happened with Lloyd deBellome and her in New York, but while she cried he swore he'd make it right.

"How could anyone in the world hurt you, Quinn?" he finally whispered.

Finally she stopped crying and hugged him back. She was no

longer a young girl. She needed to hang on to the one person she knew was safe—him.

He moved his hands over her in comfort. "Tell me what happened, Quinn."

She dried her eyes on his shirt. The clean air smell of him made her smile. She'd always loved the way Staten smelled of the earth and sky and rain and work. Slowly, one long breath at a time, she calmed.

"I'm not going anywhere. Tell me what still hurts you after twenty years." He kissed her cheek. "I wish I could take your sorrow away. I've seen you cry before but never like this. If I could, I would put all your troubles on my shoulders right now. Just tell me, Quinn."

She shook her head. She couldn't. How could she mix such ugliness into what they had? What if it changed the way he looked at her? What if her memories destroyed them? Staten's pain that first night had opened her heart to him. She'd let him into her world like she'd never let another man. She loved the way he always hesitated, always waited for her to make the first move.

He waited now. She knew he was wondering how the mention of a name could be so painful.

She rested her head against his heart and listened to the beat.

Finally, gulping back a cry, she began. "In my last year at the academy I was assigned to a master for private lessons. He would get me ready for my first professional recital. Lloyd deBellome was hard on me from the beginning, telling me I didn't have the talent, pointing out everything that I did wrong and never encouraging me.

"I took the lessons, thinking somehow he was making me stronger, but I hated every minute I had to spend in that little practice room. He was about ten years older than me, and, when he wasn't yelling at me, he was asking me out. Correction, ordering me to go out with him. I was half afraid of him and always said no.

"Finally he insisted, and I went out with him once just to prove that we could never be a couple. I drank too much because of nerves. We ended up in his apartment. We must have had sex, but I don't remember much, only that the next morning I was bruised all over. I collected my clothes and left before he woke.

She took another calming breath before continuing. What was Staten thinking?

"Later, he said I got drunk and fell on the stairs, but I knew he lied.

"At rehearsal he was cold and took every opportunity to touch me. With each hard pat on the shoulder I remembered a little more of what the night before had been like. Sex had been there in the fog, but it was the pain, the times I cried out, that brought him pleasure.

"The next day he told me we would be staying at his place that night, and I said no. He argued through most of my lesson and then seemed to let the subject drop. As I was leaving he said something about how he would give me his special wine again, and I wouldn't care what he did to me. He even laughed and said that in time I wouldn't mind being slapped around or tied down. I might even like it.

"When I shook my head, he laughed and called me a fool for not knowing that pain is only the other side of passion, and I obviously needed both to break out of my shell. He said I would beg to come back to him. I'd beg to be taught how to enjoy the pain."

Quinn felt the muscles in Staten's body tighten, but his hand remained gentle along her back as she continued.

"But I did mind being hurt. I hated him even after the bruises on my body faded. My memory of the night was more like a vague nightmare that still wakes me sometimes.

"One afternoon a month later, he made a pass while he was

supposed to be teaching me. He demanded I respond. When I wouldn't, he started shaking me. I'm not sure what would have happened if someone hadn't accidentally opened the wrong door. He was like an insane man, claiming no one but an idiot would turn him down.

"Once the student who'd interrupted us apologized and left, Lloyd demanded I play an impossible piece even for my level of training. I tried, but I was too angry, too frightened. All I wanted to do was get out of that room. While I tried to play, he threatened me not to ever tell anyone what I'd made him do. He said he'd just deny it, and I'd be laughed at. He said, homely girls always are. Again and again he kept yelling for me to play faster. Nothing I did was right."

She shook as if freezing, and Staten held her more closely, but he didn't speak. He seemed to understand that she had to tell her story all at once or she'd never finish.

"I was crying and playing and shaking from fear. Suddenly, he slammed the piano cover on my hands and swore I'd never learn to play correctly. I wasn't worth his time.

"I stood and ran from the room. He'd broken three of my fingers." She shook as if her sobs were too deep inside to come out.

Staten waited.

She could feel the rage building in him, but his touch was still soft and loving. In a forced whisper, he asked, "Then what happened?"

"I went to the emergency room and waited hours before I saw a doctor. Then, they kept me overnight before letting me return to the dorm. When I got back, my roommate had packed my things, and my parents were on their way to get me. Lloyd had made up some story about me being too mentally fragile to take criticism and I'd been suspended. I never finished college, and I never played again in public."

"I'll kill him," Staten whispered as he pulled her against his chest.

To her surprise, Quinn laughed. "You can't. That happened twenty years ago. He was right about me never wanting or being able to play in public. Maybe he did me a favor by breaking those fingers. I came home and got to spend ten years with my parents before they died. I got to be with my best friend until the day she passed. I've built a good life here. He was wrong about my not playing. I play for you. That's enough."

Staten kissed her hands. He kissed the thin scars on her middle fingers. "But you missed having a career."

She shook her head. "My parents always wanted that for me, and I wanted to please them. If I'd had my choice I would have stayed home, but they'd saved since the day I was born to be able to send me to some grand school. I couldn't disappoint them, but it was never my dream."

"Why were they so set on sending you?" He gently encouraged her to keep talking.

"My great-grandmother had been the best pianist in London in her day. My grandmother always wanted my mother to play, but she didn't have the talent. In me, she thought the family gift would come out. Every teacher, including Miss Abernathy from the chamber of commerce, thought I could make it. Only, no one ever asked me if it's what I wanted."

He began unbraiding her hair. "No one in my family ever had talent for anything but yelling and ranching. While your great-grandmother was entertaining royalty, my great-grandfather was trading a watch for his wife a few miles away in Ransom Canyon. Legend is she didn't speak to him until their third child was born. Family history claims he was from English blue bloods who had disowned him, and she was a captive, part Indian, part crazy."

Quinn laughed. "You Kirklands are a wild bunch. Lucky your father doesn't have to buy his wives or he'd run out of money, or watches."

Staten tickled her, then kissed her. When he pulled away she fought begging him not to leave. She wanted him to hold her until she fell asleep. But he slipped from her bed, then pulled off his clothes and floated a quilt over them both as he climbed back in beside her.

"Mind if I stay awhile, Quinn?"

"Only if you'll hold me." She cuddled against him. She'd told him her worst secret, and he had stayed by her side. For the first time in twenty years the pain of what she'd suffered seemed to be cut in half.

Much later, in the darkness just before dawn, she turned to him, hungry with need. He undressed her and made love to her slowly, with more gentleness than she thought he possessed.

When they finished she cried softly and whispered a thank you.

"You're welcome," he answered. "Thanks for playing for me last night. You're so beautiful when you're lost in the music."

"No."

"Yes, Quinn. You are."

A wind raged outside, but it didn't matter.

"Can we make love again?" she whispered.

"We can," he whispered back. "You make me wish I knew how to be gentle."

"You are, Staten. You always are with me."

He rose above her and stared down at her as if really seeing her for the first time in his life. Then slowly, he smiled and kissed her.

CHAPTER ELEVEN

Yancy

Sundays were always strange days for Yancy. Most of the old folks went to church or off to visit their kids. The few who stayed around seemed to think Sunday was a day for napping. It was also Yancy's only day off.

When he'd first started, the eight old dwarves told him to take the weekend off, but he didn't have anywhere to go, or a car to go anywhere in. After the first weekend in Crossroads, he talked them into letting him work half a day on both Friday and Saturday instead. That way the weekend didn't seem so long.

The first few Sundays he'd been busy working on his box-car-size apartment behind the office. He'd painted the walls, put new linoleum down on the four-feet square of a bathroom, and built a shelf for his hot plate and cans of soup.

Yancy bought every kind of soup the store had. It was nice to know that any time he got hungry he could eat, and there was always a selection. The shelf also had room for a box of crackers and two boxes of cereal. Whenever he ate alone, he made dinner in his room, not the front office. If the old folks saw him eating alone, they'd come over to keep him company, and he'd had all the noisy meals he wanted for a lifetime.

But, on Sundays, he couldn't just stay in his room all day, so he usually went for long walks in the morning, then over to the café midafternoon. The lunch crowd was long gone by then, and the families having dinner there wouldn't be in until later.

Sunday was the only day the café wasn't open for breakfast. Which had turned out to be a good thing, since if it had been, Yancy would have never met the residents of the Evening Shadows Retirement Community that first day.

He made a point to dress in his cleanest clothes. He now had three pairs of jeans and four shirts. The morning had been cold, but by three o'clock it was warm enough to walk across the street without a coat, which he didn't want to get dirty, or a jacket, which he didn't have. The heavy shirt he'd found at the secondhand shop was warm enough.

Taking his usual seat at the end of the counter, he smiled at the petite waitress who worked Sundays. He never asked her name, and Dorothy, the owner of the place, would never waste money on name tags in a town where everyone pretty much knew everyone else. The little waitress was probably about twenty, cute, with a rounded belly that looked like she was stealing a basketball.

If he sat at the end, Yancy could talk to her when she wasn't busy. In a way he felt like a foreigner practicing English. She might not know it, but he was learning to speak.

"Afternoon." She smiled. "I saved you a slice of cherry pie. Figured we'd be out by one if I didn't set one back."

He nodded his thank you. "How'd you know it was my favorite?"

"'Cause when we have it, you always eat two slices."

He glanced at the menu. "I'll have the turkey and dressing plate and one slice of the pie to start, ma'am."

She made out the ticket. "You don't have to 'ma'am' me.

You're in here enough to be a regular by now. My name's Sissy. Call me that."

"Sissy," he said with a nod. "I'm Yancy."

"I know. Mr. Halls told me when he came in last week with his granddaughter. Told me you do a great job."

Sissy went to welcome two truckers coming in.

Yancy acted as if he was reading the menu. He noticed she didn't have a wedding ring on, but she wasn't flirting with him, just being polite. He had five years of catching up to do. If he was going straight, he had to learn how to talk to people. Not too bold. Not too shy.

The café was perfect. On the slow afternoons he could hear every conversation going on in the place. He'd met the owner, Dorothy, when she'd delivered a cake for Miss Bees to take to her Sunday School potluck. Dorothy had told him she did all the cooking at the café, so if he didn't like something he needed to come straight to her.

When he'd said he liked everything, she smiled with pride. She was a woman built to withstand a storm, he thought. She reminded him of a tugboat he saw once. Solid, wide-bottomed and steady moving, with hair that stood straight up, reminding him of a porcupine. Her smile was broad and warm.

As if his thoughts materialized, Dorothy yelled across the pass-through for Sissy to come quick.

The waitress dropped the menus on the counter and bolted into the kitchen. Yancy could hear water rushing. He thought about it a few seconds before standing and catching the swinging door between swings. His thin body slipped into the kitchen.

A pipe was shooting out hot water in an arc as high as his head.

"Need some help?" he said as he moved to the big sink that looked almost exactly like the prison one. Most of the water was tumbling over dirty dishes stacked in soapy water. Before

Sissy or Dorothy said a word, he slid under the wash station and turned off the water.

Dorothy looked down at him, her face red from fighting off hot water. "Oh, thank you!" She turned to Sissy. "We might as well close down. We'll never get a plumber from Bailee on a Sunday, and getting one from Lubbock would cost a fortune."

"I can fix it," Yancy said as he stood, very aware that he was dripping wet.

Dorothy glared at him as if about to call him a liar. "If you can, mister, you'll have a month of Sunday dinners coming."

"With pie?"

The cook grinned. "Sure, with pie."

Yancy ran across the street and got the box of tools Cap had put together for him. When he got back he was shivering in his wet shirt, but he didn't want to take time to change. The kitchen was warm. He'd dry.

An hour later the pipe was fixed, and Yancy was starving. He washed his hands and turned to Dorothy. "You think I could have that first meal today since you're still open?" It was almost the end of the month, and he'd had to count his ones to make sure he had enough money to eat today.

"Sure. You've got four coming. To tell the truth it would have cost me a lot more to call the plumber in Bailee. He charges me seventy-five for just driving over."

Yancy went back out to the dining room, took his seat at the end of the counter and ate his meal. Pie first and last. Sissy told everyone who came in that the café almost had to close, but Yancy had saved the day. Several stopped by to shake his hand. For the first time in his life, Yancy felt like a hero.

When he was leaving, he opened the door for a sturdy woman in a long blue cape. He'd seen her before.

She looked up at him and frowned without bothering to say thank you for opening the door. Her eyes flashed across him as if she were taking mental notes in case she had to identify him later.

"I ain't taking advantage of these people, either, Miss Ellie." He winked. "I did, however, eat all the cherry pie if you're looking for something to yell at me about, and I didn't pay for my meal."

Almost-a-nurse Ellie glared at him. "Folks pay for what they eat around this town. Don't think you can just walk out."

Sissy wiggled her round pregnant belly between them. "He don't have to pay, Ellie. He's got a month of Sunday dinners free for fixing the plumbing."

The nurse settled, but as usual, she didn't apologize. She straightened her back, and Yancy forced himself not to look at her chest. He'd like to see what was under that navy blue cape, but asking her to strip didn't sound like a good idea.

"You here for supper?" Sissy asked the other woman.

"No. I dropped by to bring your vitamins. You left them in the clinic."

"Thanks. I was going to send Harry over to get them."

Ellie glanced at Yancy, as if making sure he wasn't sneaking closer, and then gave her attention to Sissy. "Don't send your brother into the clinic unless he's burning or bleeding. He frightens the patients."

Sissy laughed. "He frightens me half the time. Since he was twelve I make him yell before he enters the house because if he don't, one of the family is likely to mistake him for a bear. I think he's the only sixth grader in town who could grow a full beard."

Yancy wasn't a part of their conversation, but they were standing in the exit. He was afraid to bump into Sissy. She looked like she was about to pop. Though he wouldn't mind brushing Nurse Ellie, he wasn't sure she'd take to the idea. She'd already made up her mind that he was some kind of outlaw. He didn't want to fall into the category of pervert, too.

Finally Ellie turned her fiery green eyes on him and announced, "I'll be watching you. Don't you forget it."

"I'm not likely to forget your threat. It seems to be echoing." He moved closer to her. "Now if you'll excuse me, I've got to be leaving."

Ellie backed against the door to allow him to leave, but he still couldn't keep from brushing her cape. He was as close to a woman as he'd been in five years.

"You smell good," he said without thinking.

"You don't." She wrinkled her nose. "You smell like dirty dishwater."

Yancy hurried out and didn't look back. It occurred to him that maybe she'd been in prison and didn't know what was proper to say, either. Or maybe she'd just taken an instant dislike to him. Or, who knows, maybe she was simply the meanest woman in town. Someone had to be, and, to his knowledge, she was definitely in the running.

Either way, he would be wise to avoid her. At the rate he was going, he wouldn't have to worry about getting involved with any woman in Crossroads, Texas. All the ones he'd met were either old, pregnant or mean as snakes.

CHAPTER TWELVE

Lauren

Lauren Brigman had always been glad February was the shortest month of the year. She hated it. First, the weather was usually crummy. Second, nothing was ever going on in school. And who cared about Valentine's Day. In March she'd be sixteen, so she'd just as soon February got out of the way.

Her father usually got her one of those small hearts with five chocolates inside and a frog or cartoon character on the outside saying something like, *Have a hopping good Valentine's Day.*

Her mother, whom she'd called Margaret since she was five, mailed an expensive card with the usual twenty dollars for every holiday. She always signed *x*'s and *o*'s, but she had no idea what her one child would want on any occasion.

But now Margaret was coming for the weekend, and Saturday was Valentine's Day. At least, Lauren thought she would come by then; she'd already canceled twice, once at the end of January because a storm in Dallas promised a dusting of snow and again in February when she said something came up at work.

Lauren's father had simply shrugged, but Lauren had no trouble reading his mind. Silently he was cussing, knowing Margaret the Great could have driven in if she wanted to, and she was the boss at work, so she could probably have moved her *something came up* to Monday. Crossroads was only five hours from Dallas, but for Margaret Brigman, it always took a Mount Everest effort to get to Lauren.

Work had always been more important than anything else to Margaret. It was important to Pop also. Dan Brigman considered himself the guardian of every person from county line to county line, but Lauren knew his first and last thought every day was saved for his daughter. Even when he wasn't at home he texted her, listing rules and checking in. During the first few years after her mother left, if he had to work late, he'd have Mrs. O'Grady walk over and stay with Lauren or take her back to their place for dinner. The O'Gradys lived a few hundred yards along the lakeshore, so having someone to watch over her was never a problem.

Her mom and dad had separated soon after Pop had taken the job of county sheriff. Evidently, Margaret thought they should move up, which meant a bigger city than Crossroads, Texas. For her, the move to a lake house in the middle of nowhere was definitely down. She couldn't see the beauty in the sunsets on the plains or the colors in the canyon walls as shadows stretched. For Margaret, Crossroads was no more that its name: a wide spot in the road where two highways crossed. A place where travelers stopped for gas or a meal and drove on.

She went off to Dallas to intern with an advertising agency. After all, she'd said, her master's degree *was* in marketing, and how could she practice her skills in a small town? She'd left Lauren's father to manage with a kindergartener and the promise to be back in six months. The internship stretched into a job offer she couldn't turn down, and that slipped into a partnership. The trips home once a month quickly changed to weekly phone calls and apologies.

Pop had done his best when Margaret left, but even at five Lauren had known he was broken. For the first two years she'd expected her mother to come back and fix him. There had been weeks sometimes when they ate nothing but cereal or hamburgers. The house had become a mountain range of piles: work piles, school piles, dirty clothes piles, clean clothes piles. Plus, there'd been ever-growing foothills of shoes, toys and trash that might be needed at some point, like empty boxes and old Popsicle sticks.

Then one day a letter had come. She'd watched her father read it slowly, before folding it back into the envelope and putting it in his work satchel. "Well, honey," he'd started in a voice that sounded forced with calmness. "Looks like it's going to be just you and me. How about we clean up this place and make it right for the two of us?"

They'd redecorated the dining room and called it Lauren's library, and every month they'd driven to Lubbock and added half a dozen new books. He'd let her paint her room, which she did every summer. He'd moved his favorite chair to the porch and sat out there until sundown almost every night. They ate at the kitchen bar or in front of the TV.

They set rules and patterns to their lives. Two trips a year to shop for clothes and once a month for groceries. Lauren became the only kindergartener to pack her own lunch. If she needed anything new, she picked it from a catalog, and he ordered whatever she circled. By age eight she was ordering all her clothes, shoes and supplies that way.

Her mother sent fancy dresses that Lauren never wore and little purses she never carried.

Pop tried to do holidays. He bought the meal-in-a-bag for Thanksgiving that became leftovers all weekend. He stocked up on pizza and frozen dinners for the Christmas break and hung one string of lights on the porch. They always picked out three presents each from all the catalogs that came in December. He'd bring home a tree the day she got out of school and let her decorate it with ornaments she bought at the Dollar Store.

When she was little, he'd take her fishing on the lake. She begged to be left at home as soon as she got old enough to stay by herself. Every Friday night they fought over what movie to watch. He'd burn popcorn and she'd make the sandwiches.

Once a month he found a babysitter and left for the night. It was usually a school night, so she barely missed him. When she was little she used to think he went to see Margaret. Now she doubted that was true. Lauren had never asked him where he went, but he'd only been thirty when Margaret left, so once in a while maybe he wanted to get away to be young again. Maybe one night a month he just needed the load of being a single father and a county sheriff off his shoulders.

Lauren had grown comfortable with her life. She visited her mother for a few weeks during summer break. Margaret would work, and Lauren would spend the days reading or hanging out at the pool at her mom's condo complex while she counted the days until she could go back home. Pop wasn't much fun, but at least he was there.

As far as she could remember, this was the first time her mother had come back to the Ransom Canyon lake house in ten years. On the rare occasions she *came to visit* she usually stayed at a hotel in one of the small nearby towns. Pop always dropped Lauren off wherever she booked the room. The three of them tried dinners out during those times, but it was usually a disaster. Sometimes Lauren wondered how her parents had ever gotten along well enough to make her.

"You got everything you need?" Her father poked his head into what they called the spare bedroom.

She smiled. The sheriff looked nervous, something she rarely saw in Pop. "I got it all. In an hour you won't recognize this place."

"Good. I have to wash down the porch, and I think we're

ready for her. She's had a month to build her case against me
for not taking proper care of you, so I figure she'll be yelling at
me for hours. Try to hide that scar on your leg as long as possible." He smiled. "Oh, and be prepared to take her out to the
old house. She'll want to see where you got hurt."

Lauren giggled, knowing if Margaret saw the tiny scar left by
her stitches she'd be angry, very angry. "I made snacks, so we
won't starve, no matter how long the yelling lasts." Lauren was
very familiar with the fights. Most were over her. He wasn't raising her right. She needed to see more of the world. He should
watch her closer, make sure she did her homework. Give her
piano and dance lessons. Expose her to more than county fairs
and rodeos. The Gypsy House disaster was a forest worth of fuel.

Margaret criticized, but she never offered to take over the job,
either. Her role seemed to be simply to yell at him.

"If it gets bad, Pop, I'll walk down to Tim's place. Since he's
permanently grounded, he could probably use the company."

"Good idea. Have a plan of escape." He smiled, suddenly in
a good mood. "In fact, I might let you date Timothy O'Grady.
With a broken leg, he's not likely to step out of line, and I could
remind him that it really wouldn't be hard to break his other
leg."

"I'm not dating injured boys just to make you happy, Pop. In
fact, I'm not dating anyone."

"Good," he said. "Let's keep it that way until you're in your
twenties, then we'll talk about group dating, or maybe online
dating. That seems germ free, and, of course, I'll be the one
meeting them with you those first few times. Maybe I'll even
go on the first dozen or so dates. After all, it could be fun."

She tossed a new accent pillow at him. "No way."

He caught it, examined the pillow, frowned and tossed it back.
It was the rustic red of the canyon, with lace trim framing it.
He'd let her order a whole bedding set: comforter, pillow and

sheets, even curtains for the room. The place looked almost like the picture in the catalog.

As he turned to leave, she said, "I love you, Pop, I really do."

"I know. I love you, too. We'll get through Margaret's visit. This time, whatever your mother says, she's right. I should have watched over you, told you not to go in old houses. I shouldn't have been working late, so I could have picked you up."

"It wasn't your fault. You let me learn a lesson, that's all." Since that night, things had changed between them. The lectures were still there, the questioning about every detail of her life, the hovering to make sure she was fine, but she saw something else. The love.

The doorbell made them both jump, but Lauren reacted first. "It's only Quinn O'Grady. I asked her if she'd bring some lavender to put in Margaret's room."

He followed her down the hallway. "We ordered flowers delivered?"

Lauren took time to turn around and glare at him. "Of course."

He shrugged. "Of course. That's probably why Margaret left. The house didn't smell like lavender."

When Lauren opened the door, she saw Quinn O'Grady standing outside with an armful of flowers. "I picked a few wildflowers to mix in, Lauren. It's too early for most, but I found a few near the well house."

As Lauren welcomed her, Quinn passed Pop and smiled shyly. "If you'd like, Lauren, I'll help arrange them?"

"I'd be thankful for the help, Miss O'Grady. You're very kind to have brought them by." Pop stiffened. He was back to being sheriff again.

"No problem," Quinn answered with her head down.

Quinn was almost as tall as Pop. They were about the same age, but since he called her Miss O'Grady, she supposed he didn't know her very well.

Lauren thought of adding her to an ever-growing list of possible women her father could date, but Quinn seemed very, very shy and they had nothing in common. Her father tended to yell when he was mad, drink when he was off duty, and smell like fish when he'd been out on the lake more than an hour. Quinn always smelled of lavender, never raised her voice, and barely talked to anyone. If Lauren hadn't done a report on different types of farming in the area, she would have never met the kind woman.

Today, Lauren appreciated the help. Quinn spread her flowers on the table and began to do her magic. In what seemed like minutes, the house smelled like spring. She even helped Lauren finish off the bedroom and suggested rearranging the furniture so Margaret could see the lake from her bed.

"It'll be a beautiful view for her to wake up to," she claimed.

Lauren doubted Margaret would even open the curtains. For her, the only great view was of the skyline of downtown Dallas.

When Quinn left, Lauren found herself wishing she had a woman like her for a mother. She didn't seem to know anything about fashion or makeup or hairstyles, but there was a gentleness about her.

Her father must have noticed it, too, because he insisted on walking Quinn to her car.

Lauren heard him ask what he owed for the flowers, and Quinn replied nothing. "They are a gift to your lovely daughter. She's a great kid."

"You'll get no argument from me," he answered. "Sometimes I wonder if I'm raising her, or she's raising me. I've heard you used to play piano. You wouldn't be interested in teaching her?"

"If I ever teach, she'd be the first in line," Quinn said and smiled at him.

Lauren doubted they were flirting, but at least Pop was talking to a woman. That was progress.

Pop leaned down to her window and said that if she ever

needed a favor that didn't involve where to bury a body, all she had to do was call. He owed her one.

"I'll remember that," she answered as she started her old pickup and turned toward Tim O'Grady's place. "I thought I'd stop in on my cousin and see how her boy is doing. I heard he was hurt."

Pop stepped back and waved, then went around the side of the house to clean the deck.

Lauren walked around the place, checking every detail. They'd cleaned the first weekend Margaret was supposed to come and the second. Now, after the third cleaning, she feared she would scrub off the finish if she dusted anymore. Even after ten years, there were still touches of Margaret in every room.

Apparently when Margaret left them, she'd only taken her clothes. The chest that had been her grandmother's was still in the hallway. Half the books in her father's study must have been her mother's because he never touched them. The nightstands in the guest bedroom, the dishes, the pots and pans had all been abandoned, just like Lauren.

Suddenly, Lauren wished she hadn't fussed so much over Margaret's coming.

But it was too late to take the flowers out or put the old quilt back on the bed. She could hear the hum of a car coming down the drive.

Margaret had arrived.

CHAPTER THIRTEEN

Lucas

Lucas Reyes rode his horse slowly along the sandy breaks that snaked between Kirkland's Double K Ranch and the Collins's Bar W border. He liked taking this way home. No matter the season, there was a beauty about this quarter mile of in-between land where all he saw was nature in every direction, and the sounds were the same as those that must have floated over this land a hundred years ago.

The slender thread of dried-up creek bed wasn't claimed by Kirkland or Collins. A no-man's-land, where outlaws could have roamed in the early days of Texas. The stillness here was like music to Lucus. All he heard were the low sounds of the wild and his own breathing. He wondered if in the big cities people might live their whole lives without ever knowing this kind of beautiful silence.

His grandfather had told him that this path had once been a hidden entrance to Ransom Canyon where in the 1800s tribes and Comancheros traded hostages and slaves from one tribe to the other. Texas Rangers had traveled to the bottom of Ransom Canyon now and then, without their badges showing, so they could pay the ransom on children and wives stolen from early settlements.

Lucas felt like it could almost be years ago tonight, and he might accidentally ride into a campsite that followed no law.

Slowly, as he crossed onto Collins land, he turned his thoughts back to the present.

Mr. Kirkland had hired him to string wire most of the day. Every muscle in his body hurt, but the money was good. He had already saved enough for one semester of college, and, with luck, he would have the next semester's money in the bank before summer. Then he'd start working on a cushion. If he worked part-time during the year, he could cover food and housing on campus, but he'd have to make tuition by working every summer and break.

Every cowboy around knew the Double K was the best place to work. Staten Kirkland paid well, and his ranch bordered the Collins place, so Lucas could ride his horse the few miles home when he finished.

Lucas's father was the head wrangler at the Bar W, Davis Collins's ranch. Lucas and his family lived at the headquarters in a house only slightly smaller than the foreman's place. The Collins family lived half a mile away on a rise that offered a full view of the land they'd owned for generations, but Reid Collins's dad wasn't like Staten Kirkland.

Davis Collins was several years older than Kirkland and ran his ranch from his office. The cattle they raised and horses they trained and sold were no more than numbers to him. On the rare occasion Collins was seen on his land, it was in a four-wheeler. His two sons were far more interested in riding dirt bikes across unbroken pastures than learning the business their family had been in for over a hundred years.

To put it simply, Kirkland was a rancher and Collins was a businessman. If a drought came, Collins would sell off his herd.

Kirkland would haul in feed and keep his best stock to rebuild for when times were better. Kirkland would weather any storm. But Lucas feared that if Reid or his brother didn't show some interest in ranching, the Collins place might be up for sale in ten years.

When he reached the barn, Lucas took care of his horse like his father had taught him, before heading in to supper. It was Saturday night, and he had nothing planned. Maybe he'd ask his papa if he could borrow the old pickup and drive over to see Tim O'Grady. Lucas had noticed that since the accident, Tim and Reid weren't hanging out at school, and to his knowledge, Reid hadn't dropped by to visit Tim. Their friendship apparently hadn't survived the Gypsy House.

The great thing about stringing wire all day was that it gave him time to think. Maybe Tim had seen the light as far as Reid Collins was concerned. Maybe Reid didn't want a constant reminder that he wasn't a real hero hobbling behind him. They'd been friends for as long as Lucas could remember, but football season was over, and Tim was grounded. He would only slow Reid down this last half of their junior year.

After grabbing a bite, Lucas lifted the keys off the nail by the door, held them up and jingled them. His father nodded. With five other kids at home to worry about, his father never asked questions. Lucas often wondered if his dad trusted his oldest so completely, or if he just didn't have the time or energy to ask.

It was almost eight o'clock when Lucas pulled up to Tim's house on the lake. He liked to park down the road a little and walk along the shoreline. Tim's house wasn't big like Reid's, but the O'Gradys were both artists, so it always seemed to be bursting with life and color. Tim's dad taught art, and his mother was a painter. Lucas had no idea if she ever sold any paintings to anyone other than family, but there were so many O'Gradys around this part of the state, they could probably keep her busy.

Tim's mom answered the door. "Evening, Lucas, I wondered if you'd make it tonight."

"I worked until almost dark. Mr. Kirkland ran me off in time for me to ride home before sunset. He said I wander around his place enough after dark. I didn't think he noticed. I've done roundup work several times for his foreman, but the other night when he offered us a ride was the first time I think he really saw me, you know, as a person."

"Do you think he minds you walking his land?" she asked politely.

Lucas shook his head. "I told him I was just watching the night sky, and he reminded me to always close the gates and don't spook the damn cattle." Lucas grinned. "You know, I've figured out that Kirkland thinks *damn* and *hell* are adverbs or adjectives to toss into any sentence."

Tim's mom laughed and turned down the hallway leading to Tim's room.

She didn't need to show him the way. Lucas had dropped Tim's homework off for two weeks after the accident, but he guessed, like Tim, she enjoyed the company.

It didn't take much to know few kids came by to visit Tim. Lucas wasn't really sure why he did.

Mrs. O'Grady grinned. "You boys will have a third person for the visit tonight. I want you both to be on your best behavior. No 'adverbs,' if you know what I mean."

If Mrs. Patterson was the company, Lucas had better think of an exit plan fast. The Baptist preacher's wife could have been the next plague to hit the Egyptians if Moses had needed another one.

"Lauren Brigman walked down from her house just to bring Tim cookies." Mrs. O'Grady relieved Lucas's panic. "She's such a sweet girl."

Lucas heard the laughter behind Tim's closed bedroom door. When he shoved it open, he saw Lauren sitting in the desk chair rocking back and forth like she was on a mechanical bull. Tim had his cast propped on a pillow on his half-bed. They were both staring at the floor.

Tim spotted Lucas and grinned. "Hey, Lucas, look what Lauren brought me."

Lucas glanced down at a box turtle slowly climbing across a shaggy rug. "I was hoping she brought cookies."

When Lauren raised her head her eyes were full of laughter, and he couldn't look away.

"I brought chocolate chip cookies, too. They're in the bag. But, I found this turtle on the way over. Since Tim can't walk around the lake, I brought a lake friend to visit him."

"Tim," his mother's voice came from the hallway. "You are not keeping that turtle." When no one commented, she added, "I'll bring milk to go with the cookies."

All three waited until they heard her footsteps retreating before Tim whispered, "Mom's driving me nuts. If I could get this cast off I'd beat myself to death with it. She's been babying me since I got home from the hospital. If you two didn't come over now and then, I'd go mad, and, believe me, you don't want to see an insane man on crutches."

Lucas winked at Lauren. They'd seen each other at school in passing, different times, different days, but tonight they'd managed to accidentally bump into one another. Neither was paying any attention to Tim as he rambled on about how his mother tried to spoon-feed him.

"What can we do to help?" Lucas finally broke the rant. He took a seat on the other side of the bed, where he could talk to Tim and look at Lauren. "You're in a cast. I guess waterskiing is out, and it's too cold to swim. You'd sink anyway." When no one laughed, he added, "We could watch a movie."

"No, my parents got the bill for all the movies I've rented on cable." Tim frowned. "I can't buy another one. My mom says we've got eighty channels, surely I can find something free to watch."

Lucas shook his head. "It would almost be worth the trouble of sawing that cast off to watch you try to beat yourself to death. At least it's something the reality shows haven't thought of yet."

All three laughed and began to just talk. About everything: school, sports, graduation, movies they hated. The one topic no one of the three brought up was Reid Collins or the night at the Gypsy House. Lucas figured each had their reasons for letting the legend live about what had happened that night at the old abandoned house. Lauren was too shy to go up against Reid. Tim might be foggy about what really happened, and Lucas simply wanted to stay out of trouble. If he said anything, Mr. Collins might let his father go.

It mattered little who'd done what that night, but Lucas would never get to go to college if his dad got fired and he had to help out his family.

After an hour, when the cookies were gone and Tim looked tired, Lucas offered to walk Lauren home. "It's on my way. I'm parked about halfway between your place and here."

She nodded like it wasn't necessary, or maybe she didn't care.

As they left Tim's house, Lucas said, "I don't have to walk you if you'd rather be alone."

"No. It's not that. I just don't want to go back. My mother spent the night last night. She was all nice for a while, even drove me to Bailee so we could get our nails done today, then we spent time going through old photo albums at the house. But at dinner she started arguing over how bad pizza was for her diet as well as mine, and my father jumped right into the fight. From my dietary habits they spun off on why I'm second in the class and not first and how the high school isn't good enough for someone with my mind."

"What did you say?" Lucas took her hand as they stepped onto the damp grass near the shore.

"I said goodbye. Pop and I already agreed I could use visiting Tim as my escape plan." She laughed suddenly. "I didn't really make the cookies. I got them at the bakery, but since my mom freaked out over the pizza, I decided I'd better make sure the cookies disappeared."

They walked for a while in silence. The night held the smell of a storm in the thick air, but he barely felt it. He knew this moment would only last for a short time, and he wanted to remember everything. The wind whipping up off the water. The new moon so thin it looked like a tear in the night's canvas. The feel of Lauren's hand in his as if it were the most natural thing in the world.

He thought of asking her out on a date, but she was fifteen and he was seventeen. Her father, or mother, probably wouldn't let her go. Plus, he didn't have the time or the money to date. "How long do you have before you have to be home?"

"Why?"

"I'd like to show you something, but it will take half an hour."

Her fingers laced with his. "Let's go."

Then, they were running as if every second counted. A few minutes later they were laughing as they climbed into his truck. He shoved ropes, spurs and all kinds of cowboy gear out of the way to clear enough room for her to sit beside him.

"I could always ride in back," she offered.

"Nope. It's a mess back there. Saddles and bloody chaps from working yearlings. I leave it back there so it can air out before I put it in the tack room."

They both laughed again as he piled books in her lap. He slipped in beside her and shifted the pickup into gear.

She ducked low as he slowly drove past her house as if they were running away on an adventure.

Lucas never felt lighthearted, he had too many plans, too much to do, too much responsibility on his shoulders as the oldest child. But at this moment, with Lauren at his side, he was Peter Pan and she was his Wendy. They were flying.

Five miles out, he turned at a back entrance of the Double K Ranch. No one but cattle trucks used the road, and it was too far from the headquarters of the ranch or town for anyone to see his lights.

She giggled as they bounced their way across open land to an old windmill painted in black across a shadowy sky. The stars were out now, the Milky Way sparkling like a cluster of tiny diamonds scattered above them.

He cut the engine, stepped out and offered his hand. "I found this place one night when I was late going home."

They moved over the uneven ground to where a water trough stretched below the windmill. "If you step in something soft, you'll know cattle have been here lately getting a drink, but I don't think this pasture is used much in the winter."

Neither looked down as he whispered, "Listen. It's like a symphony out here." The clank of the windmill as the rusty fan blades turned in the wind did seem like music. Closing his eyes, Lucas heard it all. The slough of the water, the dripping from the pipe. The rustle of the dried leaves. The swish of buffalo grass. The lonely sound of a meadowlark's call.

Somewhere in the stand of trees a quarter mile away, an owl hooted and a hawk's cry sounded on the breeze. This was his idea of heaven.

"I love standing here listening and knowing that it must have sounded just the same for years."

"It's beautiful." She moved against his shoulder.

"I hoped you'd hear it. I come out here once in a while. It makes me feel at peace. Around my house it's never quiet. When the noise gets too much for me, I come here and listen to the quiet. Sometimes when the crowd at school is nothing but nervous yelling and giggling or I'm somewhere I don't want to be, I think of here."

They were silent for a while. He put his arm around her shoulders, and she cuddled against his side.

"You know, Lauren, it's Valentine's Day."

"I know. My pop gave me his usual candy heart."

Lucas pulled her against him and kissed her forehead. "Happy Valentine's Day. If you were older and my girl, I'd get you flowers, not candy."

She laughed softly. "Eventually, I will be older. I'd love to get flowers. Yellow roses, of course."

"I'll remember that."

Then without a word they walked back to the truck.

Neither said a word as he drove back, but her hand rested in his. He wasn't sure how she felt, but for him Lauren was like the windmill place. She felt so right by his side.

When they were close to the lake, she asked, "Why'd you take me out there, Lucas?"

"I wanted you to know about it, so when life gets too much, you'll always have a place to go. Mr. Kirkland probably won't know you're there, and my guess is even if he did know, he wouldn't care. I'll be leaving for college soon. You can have my secret place if you like. Sounds like, with your folks, you'll be needing it."

"You're right, and I'll go out there, too. My mom told me she's giving me her old car for my sixteenth birthday. She said after three years she really needs a new one anyway. I don't imagine Pop will take that well."

"Do they ever agree?"

"No. It's like fighting is the only way they know how to talk."

He turned down the long decline to the lake and her house. "My folks never fight. They don't have time with all us kids. Sometimes I hear them whispering after we've all gone to bed. I imagine they're reintroducing themselves to one another."

Lauren smiled. "I'd love to be part of a big family."

He stopped just before the last bend in the road and turned

off his car lights. "Who knows, maybe someday you will be. You'd better get out here, so it'll look like you walked in from Tim's place."

She leaned closer and kissed him on the cheek. "Thanks for taking me to a symphony tonight."

"You're welcome, *mi cielo.*"

As she climbed out, she asked, "What does that mean?"

"I'll tell you one day," he said.

She shrugged and closed the door to his old pickup.

He watched her until she disappeared around the bend, then he drove home.

When he left here and times got stressful, he'd think of his special place and picture every detail in his mind. Maybe the memory would calm him.

When he visualized, Lucas knew he'd see Lauren there, too.

Lauren slipped through the back door and tugged off her tennis shoes, now covered in mud and sand. The air in the house was warm on her skin, but she could almost feel the frost between her parents. Pop was glaring at the TV. Mom was in the kitchen, checking messages on her phone.

"How was Tim?" Pop asked.

"Better. Says his mother is babying him so badly he's thinking of beating himself to death with his cast."

The sheriff didn't blink. "That would be one horrible crime scene. Tell him to drag his ass over the county line first. I don't want to be the one to have to deal with his body."

She smiled at her pop's sense of humor.

Her mother stood and walked to the doorway. "That's a sick thing to say, Dan. I wonder that you haven't warped the child."

Pop ignored Margaret. "I saw Reyes's old pickup rattle past about half an hour ago. Was Lucas visiting Tim, too?"

Lauren nodded. "Yeah, we figured since he wanted to die, we would throw him in the lake. With that cast he sank like a rock, and bubbles rose for five minutes. Lucas headed back home after the assisted suicide. After all, with Tim gone, there was no one to do all the talking. I had to stay behind and clean up the milk and cookies mess. Wouldn't want Tim's mom to deal with a funeral and crumbs everywhere."

Pop glanced at her, holding up one finger as if to say *wait for it.*

Then he smiled as Margaret fired. "You have warped her with your perverted cop humor. She'll probably be scarred for life. I can just imagine what the breakfast conversation is like around here."

Her parents were so busy bickering, neither noticed Lauren leaving. She walked to her room as an amazing realization hit her. Her father had baited her mother. She'd guessed a long time ago that Margaret loved fighting, and now, apparently, her pop had caught the bug.

As she curled up on her bed, she tried to push the sounds of their voices aside and remember the way the night sounded out by the windmill.

This time in her life, this night, what had happened between her and Lucas all felt so good except for one thing.

She knew she could never mention how she was feeling now to her pop. For the first time in her life she had a secret she'd never share with anyone but Lucas. Just between us, he had said. The way he'd saved her life, the kiss at the hospital and now tonight.

Lauren closed her eyes, knowing she'd never mention Lucas, or the way she felt about him, to anyone. But she'd never forget the way she felt when his hand covered hers.

CHAPTER FOURTEEN

Staten

The last thing Staten had told Quinn when he'd left her place Saturday morning was for her to call him. He wanted her to know he would be there when she needed him, or if she just wanted to talk and have dinner. He wasn't going anywhere just because he learned her dark secret, and he wasn't planning to push to know details.

She had become more to him than just a friend. He now felt protective of her. Hell, it was more than that, but Staten didn't need to think about it now.

When she didn't call, he waited. He would give her space.

After a month, he figured he'd given her enough time. He wanted to see his gentle Quinn again. He wanted her to know that if the past still haunted her, he'd stand near. He needed to make sure *they* were all right. Quinn wasn't an emotional woman. Hell, she'd carried around the horror of what Lloyd had done to her for years. The news that the piano master was coming to her world had upset her deeply. As her friend, he saw it as his job to walk beside her through this. If conflict came, he was more than willing to stand in front of her and fight her fight.

The idea of catching the next flight to New York and flattening the guy had crossed his mind a few hundred times, but he had a feeling that wasn't what Quinn would want him to do.

Staten had tried calling Quinn several times but wasn't surprised she hadn't answered. She didn't carry her phone when she worked outside. The first two weeks of February had been cold, but most of the days were sunny. So the Monday after Valentine's Day, he drove into town to make a few stops, and one of them would be at Quinn's place.

After he had breakfast with his grandmother and ate a few of her leftover Valentine's cookies, his mind turned to Quinn, even while his granny rattled on.

He liked the idea of showing up to Quinn's place in the morning. She'd know he came to check on her, and that was all. They could have coffee and talk.

"Thanks for delivering the magazines, dear." Granny patted him on the shoulder, pulling Staten from his thoughts of Quinn.

Granny ordered a half dozen tabloids every month and refused to have them mailed to her address at the Evening Shadows Retirement Community.

"You're welcome. I needed to be in town this morning for a few errands anyway." He walked around, noticing a new shelf in her kitchen. "You know, you could have the magazines delivered here."

She laughed. "I know, but I like seeing you. The mailman never eats my French toast."

"See you next week." Staten kissed her goodbye and headed over to Lavender Lane.

The need to see Quinn was an ache deep inside him. He told himself he was worried about her, but Staten knew it was more than that. Things were changing between them, and he had no way of stopping what was happening. He liked being in control

of his world. He believed when something changed it was usually for the worse. He had spent a month working hard trying
to keep his mind off her and their new relationship. He'd kept
saying she would call, but she hadn't.

When he pulled on to her place the air was as silent as ever.
It couldn't be much past eight in the morning. Maybe Quinn
was sleeping in.

Staten grinned. He'd like waking her up. They'd be starting just where he planned to end up tonight…in bed. He never
made love to her in daylight. He wasn't sure she'd even be open
to the idea.

As he pulled his truck around back so it wouldn't be seen
from the road, he glanced toward the house and slammed on
the brakes.

The sheriff's cruiser was pulled up close to the porch, where
Staten always parked.

Staten switched off the engine and was out of his truck before the motor settled. He ran, heart pounding, toward the door.
She worked out here all alone. A million accidents could have
happened. She could have been hurt in the fields—snake bites
happened all the time—or she might have been shot by some
idiot popping off rounds at her Lavender Lane sign.

Hell, she could have fallen in her house. Could have lain there
for days, dying an inch at a time.

His boots stormed across the porch, and he hit her door so
hard it rattled off the hinges. "Quinn!" he yelled. "Quinn."

Nothing. No Quinn. No sheriff.

Staten stomped through the house, noticing her phone was
still on the stand charging. For a second he hesitated at the door
to her bedroom. If she was in bed with the sheriff, what would
he do? No, impossible, he thought as he shoved the door open
and saw a neatly made bed.

Just the fact that he thought of her with another man bothered him. It frustrated the hell out of Staten. They'd made no

promises to each other. Hell, they didn't even buy each other Valentine's gifts.

Slowing his pace, he walked back through the house and stepped out on the porch, realizing he'd acted like a fool. The door leaning against its frame was proof. There was part of him that wanted to be considerate and understanding like he guessed women wanted, but some days he knew he hadn't quite evolved that far.

Staten stared at the cruiser, trying to guess what could have happened. She could have been hurt, and the sheriff rode with her in the ambulance. He could have had car trouble and asked her to give him a lift.

That made sense.

A tapping came from the barn, and Staten took a deep breath. Maybe she was simply working on one of the machines. Maybe the sheriff had stopped by to warn her about crime in the area. A woman living alone on a farm needed to know if something was going on. Staten didn't know if she had a gun, but if he had anything to do with it, she would by sundown.

He lowered his hat against the sun and walked slowly toward the noise. Staten was through guessing. It was wearing a bald spot in his brain. If he wanted to worry, he should go back home and worry about how someone had hit one of his bulls last night out on the county road and didn't total their car. That made no sense. The road ran through open range, but the black bull, even at night, still had the right-of-way. Anyone crossing should have been going slow with their high beams on.

The tapping grew louder as Staten stepped into the barn's shadows. Quinn was all right, he told himself. She was simply working on that old tractor. If he ever went crazy and did buy her a gift, it'd be a new John Deere.

"Morning," he yelled, trying not to allow the roller-coaster ride of emotions he'd just stepped off of to show in his tone.

"Morning," a low voice answered. "How are you today, Mr. Kirkland?"

The sheriff straightened from his perch on the tractor. The two men had known one another for years, worked together when need arose, but neither called the other friend. Staten rarely socialized, and Brigman had a daughter to raise.

"I'm fine, Sheriff." Staten removed his hat. "I just dropped by to order some more soap from Quinn. My grandmother loves giving it as gifts." Granny had told him to pick up some if he went by the farm, so Staten didn't consider it a complete lie. "You happen to know where she is?"

The sheriff jumped down. He wasn't as tall as Staten, but he looked like a man who could hold his own in a fight. "I came out to help when she told me this old bucket of bolts wouldn't start."

When Staten didn't comment, the sheriff continued, "She was leaving when I pulled up. Said something about having to go to the doctor this morning. I'm sure she'll be back soon. The clinic never gets busy until school is out in the afternoon." He grinned. "Moms around here probably do what my mother used to. No matter how I complained, she always made me go to school, claiming that if I was really sick the school nurse would send me home."

Staten didn't want to talk to Dan Brigman. He was fighting not to think about what terminal illness Quinn might have. She could be finding out the bad news right now while he was visiting with the sheriff about nothing.

But he couldn't just turn around and run.

He glanced at the tractor. "Did you get it running?"

Sheriff Brigman shook his head. "Got a minute? I could use your help. If you could start it up a few times, I might be able to see why it's missing down here."

"Sure thing," Staten said, wondering why Quinn had asked the sheriff and not him to work on the piece of junk. Hell, he'd offered a dozen times.

Staten might as well help out. The day had started with him

in a good mood, he'd made his grandmother laugh, but from that point things seemed to be going steadily downhill. He had a full day's work waiting back at the Double K. He was wasting time here.

As soon as the engine started sounding right, he planned to drive back through town and see if he could spot Quinn's old green pickup. If she was still at the clinic, he might just stop by and get that flu shot. Ellie, the girl working on becoming a nurse practitioner, ran the place. She'd told him back in September to get the shot. By getting it now, it should be good to the last month of winter and maybe next fall, too.

If he walked in to get the shot, he could casually check on Quinn.

"That does it," Brigman yelled. "She's running smooth as new."

Staten cut the engine and climbed down as the sheriff strapped back on his heavy belt. They walked toward the house side by side.

"Someone hit one of my prize bulls last night," Staten mentioned.

"What was he worth?"

"About twenty thousand before he was hit. About five hundred now."

Dan pulled out his notepad. "Someone ran his car into the back of a couple of thousand pounds on a moonless night. He shouldn't be too hard to find. Even a truck would take major damage." The sheriff jotted down a few notes as he walked. "I'll keep my eye out. Can't help but wonder what a car or truck would be doing on a back county road late at night."

"That makes two of us. It's my land. I'd like to know who'd be barreling across my property." Staten had a fair idea. Rustlers. They'd been growing bolder since beef prices went up.

"You know of anyone who comes on your land after dark?" Brigman asked.

Staten shrugged. "The oldest Reyes boy, maybe. He likes to

look at the stars out where no lights from town interfere, he says. But he's never caused any trouble, and the few times I've seen him, he was walking or riding a horse."

"He drives now." Brigman's voice was low, almost as if he were talking to himself. "I saw him pass my house last weekend in an old pickup."

They reached the cruiser.

The sheriff offered his hand. "Thanks for taking the time to help me out. I owed Quinn a favor."

"Any time." Staten touched his hat with two fingers and headed to his truck.

Twenty minutes later, he was driving slowly down the one main street of Crossroads. If speed-limit signs didn't slow highway traffic through town, the shops on the main street would be nothing more than a blur. As it was, strangers heading south from Amarillo or north from Abilene or west from Oklahoma only saw mostly what *once was* when they drove through. They didn't see the two fine churches that had stood solidly for a hundred years, or the first-rate school, or the little museum that sat back in a wide park of mature trees just east of town. Grade schools for a hundred miles around brought buses to tour the pioneer museum and see the beauty of the canyon that opened up all at once across the plain, flat land.

Staten was proud of what his family had done to put the town on the map. Maybe by some standards it wasn't much, but, like most of the farmers and ranchers around, it was all that was needed. Someday, after he was gone, there'd be a wing built onto the museum to hold all the Kirkland files and papers. His family had kept records further back than any settler. His great-grandfather had even kept a journal of the weather, what he did each day and even his thoughts. They might all be gone, but their story would be there on display.

He pulled himself back to his search. Quinn's old green pickup was nowhere in sight.

He turned around at the rest stop just out of town and circled back. Half the parking spots in front of the clinic were empty, so she would have had no trouble getting a parking place.

He crossed the Country Grocery lot and both gas stations. Maybe he'd simply missed her? It was doubtful she went anywhere else to shop. As far as he knew, she only did major shopping trips for supplies a couple of times a year.

When he left the farm- and ranch-supply parking lot, he decided to go in for his flu shot anyway. Even if Quinn wasn't there, he was six months past due, and with his luck he'd be the last human in Texas to have the flu.

Ten minutes later the nurse's aide pushed a needle into his arm, talking, chewing gum and twirling her shoe with her big toe. "You're late getting this, Mr. Kirkland. Folks your age should have a flu shot."

He had no idea how old she thought he was, and he wasn't about to ask. If he thought he could get away with it, he'd simply ignore her, but she'd probably think he'd gone into shock and yell for Ellie. Ellie Emerson was the nearest thing they had to a doctor in Crossroads most days.

So, to save himself trouble, Staten decided to talk to the gum-chewing rattle-box. "I know I'm late, but I was running errands this morning and thought I'd take the time." He tried to remember what her name tag said. Britney or Binky, he couldn't remember. He refused to look at the tag pinned almost at the point of her breast. "I see the clinic is not busy, nurse."

She giggled. "I'm not a nurse, just an aide. I can give shots and take blood. What kind of errands does a big-time rancher like you do? I love your boots, by the way. What brand are they? Don't you have an assistant on the ranch to run errands?"

He had no idea which question to answer first, so he ignored all three.

When she stared at him, he figured he'd better pick one to answer or he'd be in the cramped room all day until Binky had to go for more caffeine.

Staten answered simply, "I drove out to Lavender Lane to get my grandmother some soap." He almost added that it wasn't the kind of thing he could ask one of the cowhands to do, but he didn't want to talk more than necessary to this woman. Her brain reminded him of a flea, small and jumpy.

"Did you buy any?" she asked as she pulled the needle out of his arm and told him to hold a ball of cotton over the site.

"No. Quinn O'Grady wasn't home."

The bloodsucker giggled as her wiggly shoe flew off her big toe. "I could have told you that. She was in here bright and early. The nurse saw her and sent her straight to Lubbock for testing."

Staten forced calm into his words. "For what?" He kept his tone even by staring at the girl's multicolored toenails.

The nurse's aide slapped a strip of tape over the cotton. "I don't know, and even if I did, it would be confidential. All I did was call the ob-gyn and tell him she was on her way."

Staten walked back to his truck and just sat staring at the dust whirling down the middle of Main Street.

Something was wrong with Quinn. She might be dying. He knew the drill. He'd gone through it with Amalah. First in for a checkup. A simple Pap smear. Then another test. Then another. One day you're fine, just a little tired, and the next day you're fighting for your life.

If he thought he could find her, he'd drive down every street in Lubbock. He couldn't call her. She hadn't taken her phone. All he could do was wait.

Staten turned his truck toward her farm. If he was going to wait, it would be in her house. He wanted to at least be there when she got home, whether the news was good or bad.

On the way back to her place, he swore he almost felt the cold paddles over his chest as the electricity shocked his heart back alive.

The first beats hurt so much he didn't think he would survive. Like it or not. Healthy or dying. Quinn mattered to him.

CHAPTER FIFTEEN

Staten

Staten Kirkland sat in Quinn O'Grady's kitchen for an hour, making several calls to his men. Just because he wasn't there didn't mean that work would stop on the ranch, but his mind didn't seem to be fully in the game.

All he could think about was Quinn. Maybe while he waited at her place, she was getting the news she had cancer. She might be dying, and she'd find out all alone. He knew she'd take the news hard, but in her shy, quiet way she wouldn't let anyone know. They'd think she was handling it well. They wouldn't see that she was falling apart.

Finally, when he could think of no one else to pester, he walked to the barn and collected enough tools to put Quinn's door back on. Now that he had other things to worry about, he realized what a fool he'd been to storm her house. She'd lived out here for years by herself and never had an accident that he knew about. Plus, everyone in town knew Sheriff Brigman was still in love with his invisible wife. People would say things about how the sheriff was trapped. He loved his job, and he still loved a woman who didn't love him.

If Sheriff Brigman had looked out from the barn when Staten had kicked the door in, no telling what he would have thought. Yet, when they'd walked back together to their vehicles, he either hadn't noticed, or simply hadn't commented on the back door sitting beside its frame.

While Staten was worrying about the sheriff's eyesight, he might as well take some time and worry about why the sheriff thought he owed Quinn a favor.

Just as he finished repairing the door, Staten heard Quinn's pickup. If the thing rattled any louder, parts were bound to start falling off.

Sliding the tools behind one of the porch rockers, he waited as she pulled next to his truck.

"Well, hello, stranger," she said as she climbed out. "I wasn't expecting you this morning."

"I gave up waiting for you to call," he admitted.

"I'm sorry. I've had a lot on my mind these past few weeks, and I haven't been feeling very well." She reached the porch but stopped a few feet away as if unsure what to do. "Are you angry with me about not calling, Staten?"

He realized he was frowning, and his fists were knotted at his side. "No." He forced himself to breathe. "I was worried, though. Are you all right?"

She touched his shoulder. "I'm fine, Staten. Don't worry about me. After you left last month, I had some thinking to do. If Lloyd deBellome comes to Crossroads, I'll simply leave town for the night, or maybe I'll go to the fund-raiser and act like I don't remember him. That would crush his ego, and, with you as my date, he's not likely to say anything."

"You'd go with me?"

"I would." She laughed as if she thought he was kidding. "There is no one on this planet who worries about me as much as you do, but we've got to consider that maybe Lloyd stopping by here is for the best. It's time I stopped hiding from a memory. I'm turning over a new leaf. Might even give up some of the farm work and take up a new calling. Maybe remodel this old house. Once I enlarge the living room, I could probably teach piano lessons. I've always thought that would be fun, and Dan said his daughter would want to take lessons if I was interested."

He started frowning again. Something was definitely wrong. Quinn was rattling, and she'd never said so many words all at one time. Plus, she'd tossed the sheriff into the conversation as if they were friends.

It wasn't like her to stay inside, and she'd never once mentioned teaching anything before. Something was wrong, maybe not with Lloyd deBellome coming to town, but with Quinn. She was getting Staten off track talking about piano lessons and not farming. The real problem was obviously whatever had her going to the doctor. Maybe she'd learned she only had a few years to live. That might explain all these changes.

Staten had never run from a fight in his life, and he wouldn't run now. If she had cancer or some other disease, he'd help her through it. "Quinn, tell me what's wrong with you. How ill are you?"

To his surprise she laughed. "I'm not ill, I promise. In fact I'm very healthy. I just had a checkup this morning. I had all kinds of tests run, and there is not a thing wrong."

Her hand spread over his chest. "Can we talk later? I'm starving for food and for you. For the past few nights I've been having these dreams of you making love to me, and I wake up desperately wanting you. I've even thought of driving over to your place and pounding on the door. I'd politely ask if I could borrow your body for a while."

He covered her hand as it rested over his heart. "The door's not locked. Just come on in. You are always welcome."

"I might just do that one night."

He finally relaxed. This was a different Quinn than he had ever seen, but maybe that wasn't all bad. Staten had no idea when that happened to women. Maybe her hormones were out of whack. But he didn't really care. She was happy and saying she was healthy. He could stop worrying.

Leaning over, he kissed her cheek and whispered, "Let's eat in bed."

She tugged him inside and went straight to the refrigerator. While she made sandwiches, she munched on everything she pulled out of the crisper. He watched her, feeling a peace wash over him. Quinn wasn't ill, she wasn't dying. Their life would go on just as before. They were simply getting to know one another better. Feeling more comfortable around each other.

"We've never made love before dark, Quinn," he said as he played with her braid. "Are you sure about this?"

"I know we never have, but for some reason you look irresistible, and I don't want to wait until dark. Would you mind wasting a bit of daylight?"

"Not at all." He undid the first few buttons of her blouse while she took a bite of one of the sandwiches. In the daylight, he swore her breasts looked bigger.

She handed him two glasses of tea and picked up their plate. "Come on, you can undress me while I eat, and when you're finished I'll watch you strip."

"I'm not really very hungry for food."

"Neither am I," she said around a bite. "I want you, Staten."

She carried his sandwich and the few remaining crumbs of hers toward the bedroom. He'd expected her to move under the covers, his shy Quinn, but she didn't.

They made love with a wildness he'd never felt with her. This was a side of Quinn that he had never seen, but he'd gladly get used to. He loved watching her body as his hand moved over her. He'd never seen her in sunlight. Now, when he woke late at night and thought of her, his memories would no longer be in shadows. He took his time memorizing the look of her in daylight as he had learned the feel of her body in moonlight.

When the afternoon sun sparkled across them, she laughed, saying that they'd both be suntanned all over if they did this often.

"I wouldn't mind," he whispered as he kissed his way down her body.

When they both lay sweaty and nude atop her bed, she whispered, "Are you going to eat that other sandwich?"

He studied her, thinking she looked so beautiful with her hair all around her shoulders and her face flushed from passion. "I figured out why you went to the doctor. You've got a tapeworm."

"No, but close. I was planning to call you tonight after I saw the doctor. I've suspected for most of the month, but I found out for sure today. Staten, I'm pregnant. Almost three months."

He took her words like a blow. All the air left his lungs, and he fought to keep from passing out. "What did you say?"

"I'm pregnant." She sat up and reached for his sandwich.

"How is that possible?" It wasn't registering. "Didn't you use protection?"

"Didn't you?" she answered.

He sat up, put his feet on the floor and tried reason. "I thought you couldn't have children. That first night I came over, I asked. You said not to worry."

"Apparently I was wrong. It took five years, but you proved me wrong. I am going to have a baby."

Change, he almost screamed. *I hate change.* "But I don't want..." He couldn't say the words. He didn't want complication in his life. He didn't want to start a family, not now, not at forty-three. He'd sworn he'd never marry again. He'd sworn he'd never love anyone again. She was messing it all up. From this moment on, everything would change. Her two words would finally be the blow that split his mind in half.

But he wouldn't say he didn't want a baby. He couldn't tell that big a lie.

A baby. Quinn's baby. His baby.

She stood and pulled on her jeans and top, watching him as if she'd found a stranger in her bed.

He just stared at her, feeling betrayed. She'd never had a child. She couldn't know how much it would hurt to lose one.

"Look, Staten, this is my baby. You don't have to deal with it if you don't want to. I understand. You didn't ask for this. I can handle it alone. No one has to know it's yours."

Her words sounded rehearsed, as if she'd expected him to react this way when she told him.

"Are you sure it's mine?" he asked, remembering the sheriff who'd been on her property this morning.

Quinn slapped him so hard, his eyes watered, but he didn't move. He took the blow fully, barely feeling the pain.

"I think you'd better leave." Tears ran down her face, but she didn't cry out. "I'm going to the barn. When I get back, you'd better not be in my house, or I swear I'll shoot you in that hole you have for a heart."

Then, before he could take back what he'd said, she was gone.

Staten dressed and tried to piece things together in his mind. Quinn was pregnant, and, of course, it was his. If he'd had any doubt, the slap had knocked it out of him. Also, she obviously didn't want to talk to him anymore. Maybe he'd be wise to follow her orders and leave.

After all, she'd answered another question he'd worried about.

She was armed, and right now her primary target was him.

CHAPTER SIXTEEN

Yancy

Around four in the afternoon Yancy found Cap sunning in the office lobby like an old gray cat. Yancy touched the old guy's shoulder and asked if Cap would drive him the four blocks to the hardware store.

Several of the aging dwarves had cars, most of them rarely used, but Cap liked to drive, so his car looked as if it would start. Yancy had asked him to go with him a few times to pick up supplies and thought, for his age, Cap was a great driver.

"You can just borrow my car, Yancy," Cap said as he tried to snuggle back into his dreams. "With the promise of rain, I wasn't planning on going anywhere."

Yancy tried to think of an answer. He wasn't about to tell Cap that he didn't have a license, and if he didn't go today, Miss Bees and Mrs. Ollie would just be in again tomorrow with their list of repairs in hand. "Cap, I think I can get everything I need, but I might want a little help picking out a new smoke detector for Miss Bees. You know how particular she is."

Cap sat up, mumbling something while he scratched his

goatee. "There ain't nothing wrong with the one she has. I put it in three years ago. A couple of young guys from the fire department came around to check all the batteries before Christmas."

He got up out of his favorite chair in the sunny room and shuffled to the door. He put on his jacket without stopping talking. "You ask me, she hides in her little hallway, where there's no windows, just in case someone's spying on her. Then, she holes up like a criminal and smokes half a pack at a time." He grabbed his blue hat that had *Cap* stitched across the top. "I'll go with you, son. She shouldn't have any complaints when the retired captain of the volunteer fire department picks it out." He always straightened a bit when he reminded anyone of his title.

Yancy grinned. Cap liked nothing more than being on a mission. A few minutes later they backed his boat of a car out of the line of carports built beyond the north fence of the property. It was little more than a lean-to, offering no protection from the wind or cold, but it kept snow off the vehicles in winter.

Cap shook his head. "Miss Abernathy is gone for her weekly trip to the cemetery. She'll get my spot when she comes back, and I'll be on the end again. Last time that happened tumbleweeds about scratched the paint off my whole left side."

Yancy leaned back in the plush seat of what had once been a fine car. As far as he could tell the thirty-year-old Chevy looked pretty much the same all over, so he changed the subject. "Who does Miss Abernathy visit at the cemetery?"

"I have no idea. Near as I know, she came here alone in the early '60s. I asked her once why she never married. She was a fine-looking woman in her day. Always wore four-inch heels and her hair on top of her head, real proper. When she played concerts at PTA, she'd push out that ample chest and keep her nose in the air like she was playing for the gods and not just us mortals." He snorted. "Always reminded me of a turkey."

Yancy knew if he didn't remind Cap of the question, the old

man would go on down first one path, then another. "What'd she say about never getting married?"

"She said she was wed to her music. She was a good teacher, but so was I, and I never thought for a minute that I was married to math." Cap smiled as if seeing something that wasn't there. "I was married to my wife for thirty-two years. When she passed, I filled my time volunteering and teaching. Since the day of her funeral I've never gone back to the cemetery." He looked up with tears in his eyes. "She ain't there. She's gone on to wait for me. I've enjoyed my life, but it'll be a grand day when I walk up to her."

He laughed. "I'm betting she'll act all mad at first 'cause I kept her waiting, then she'll say 'Where have you been, darlin'?'"

Yancy didn't say anything, but he felt it again. The strange sensation that all the people of the Evening Shadows Retirement Community had lived rich, full lives, while Yancy had simply been existing. They had their stories, their children, their secrets. The only stories he had weren't worth the breath it would take to tell them. He couldn't think of a relative he'd claim, and his secrets would stay buried as long as he kept practicing being normal just like everyone else. It was getting easier every day.

A few minutes later they picked out the smoke alarm from the two choices at the hardware store.

Cap stopped to visit with someone he knew on aisle three, and Yancy went in search of nails. He was always running out of screws, nails and duct tape, maybe because he figured that half the things needing fixing around the place only really needed one of the three.

At aisle seven, he began searching for just the right size of nails. Since he planned to put everything on the account, he thought he'd pick up hooks also. With his head down, he heard two men talking as they neared. A drifting conversation not meant for him. At first, he didn't listen. The voices were no more than background noise. But, as they grew closer, he stilled, and that constant tension he had lived with for five years in prison moved over him.

Fear, alarm, a longing to vanish. He recognized the voices, and panic warmed his blood.

"Look, Cowboy, I see your point, but this isn't the place to set up camp. One, it's too small a town. Someone's bound to notice us, and two, I'm not sure I can get all we need."

The second voice was hoarse, as if from a man who'd spent years yelling or smoking. "It's perfect. Less people around, less chance of anyone knowing us. Arlo's got a job at the Collins ranch, and we've got a great spot to stash our load. A month, maybe two, and we'll have taken enough for a real start."

Two men walked past Yancy. He never looked up. Chances were good they wouldn't recognize him, but if they did, he'd be the one in trouble.

He grabbed a few packages of nails and followed, watching them from a distance. The one called Cowboy had been the leader of a gang in prison when Yancy had first arrived. His name was Zane, but no one but a fool with a death wish would call him that. Cons had called him Insane Zane behind his back. He'd taken care of the stock for the prison's annual rodeo. Twice, before Cowboy got transferred, cons had been involved in accidents in the barn. One man had died, supposedly trampled, and another had been paralyzed after falling from his horse. Both had been listed as accidents, but word got around that they weren't.

The other man, shorter and bald, had tried to take Cowboy's place after Cowboy was released, but he hadn't been strong enough to manage the rough cowhands who worked with the prison stock. Yancy couldn't remember the details, but he heard something about Freddie, the bald guy, being in a fight and spending time in solitary. Freddie had the nervous habit of hitting people who got close.

Yancy had hated and feared them both. He didn't want to

be in the same state with either, and now they were both in Crossroads.

"You find the nails?"

Yancy staggered, preparing to run, before he recognized Cap's dry tone. When he turned, the old guy was concentrating on a display, giving Yancy a second to force calm into a body intent on flight.

"Yeah, I found what I needed." Yancy rattled the box of nails. "Thanks for picking out the fire alarm. Now Miss Bees can yell at you when it goes off."

Cap shrugged. "That don't bother me. I'm hard of hearing."

They moved toward the checkout as the two men Yancy had been watching headed through the main door. Cowboy hadn't aged well in the past five years, but he was still good-looking in a rough kind of way, but Freddie was more like the perfect poster child for the death penalty. He had scars across his nose, a permanent sneer on fat lips and one eye that never cooperated with the other.

"You know those two, Cap?" Yancy still hadn't seen their faces close up, but the build and the walk were the same. He had heard both their voices in his nightmares that first year in jail. He wasn't likely to forget what they sounded like.

Cap shook his head. "Nope. The tall one, with the worn Stetson, looks like he works on one of the ranches. I heard somewhere that a couple of the outfits are already hiring for spring. Are they friends of yours?"

Yancy shook his head, almost saying that he had no friends. No one from prison. No one from back home. If he died today, Miss Bees, who didn't even like him, would probably be the only one visiting his grave.

As Cap always did, he wanted to stop at the café on the way home as if their journey had been a long one and not simply four blocks.

Even though Dorothy's place was just across the street from

where he lived, Cap turned into the café lot and parked out front. The old sign had once said Dorothy's Fine Dining, then it had been painted over to read Dorothy's Café. Only as the second paint job faded, the old sign came back like a shadow that didn't match.

Yancy waved at Sissy as they stepped inside the warm café. She smiled at him while Cap slid into one side of the nearest booth and he took the other.

The place always smelled of cinnamon, and Yancy loved taking the time to breathe in the aroma. Though the drizzle had mostly stopped, the day was spotty with fog, and the sweet-smelling air was heaven.

"Afternoon." Sissy waddled over. "You guys looking for breakfast, lunch or dinner?"

Yancy calculated the cost of each in his head. By getting Sunday lunches free, he had extra money for a few meals on weekdays, so lunch sounded good, but the breakfasts were a few dollars cheaper.

"I'll have pancakes," he said.

Sissy didn't ask more. She knew he always wanted buttermilk pancakes with raisins and pecans on top, and he knew if there was any bacon left, she'd toss it on the plate at no extra charge.

Cap ordered coffee and soup. "Whatever kind you got warming on the back burner." He winked.

"We got potato soup today." She turned her head and grinned as a woman in a blue cape blew in. "Come to see me, Ellie?"

The almost-nurse shook her head. "I've come to see Cap. I was passing and I saw his car." She leaned over the table and kissed the old man's cheek. "How's my favorite uncle today?"

Cap shooed her hug away. "Yancy, this is my pesky niece. I'm sure you've seen her across the street. Comes by to poke on us all every other week. She makes the wellness rounds for the clinic."

Ellie didn't look at Yancy. Which was good because he had nothing to say to her. He thought of asking if he could have the hug she'd tried to give her uncle. Something told him she'd probably karate chop his windpipe closed or give him brain damage from that bag she carried slamming against his head. Ellie was no small girl; a blow from her would probably hurt.

"Sit down and have a visit." Cap pointed to the side of the booth where Yancy sat.

She hesitated, then perched on the edge of his booth. "Uncle, did you drive that car of yours? You know you're not supposed to drive until you've had your eyes checked."

"My eyes are fine," Cap said. "Stop worrying. Yancy drove us around today."

Finally, the young woman turned and stared at Yancy with her cold green eyes. She had to be younger than him and she was definitely several inches shorter, but he swore the woman looked down at him. "Is my uncle telling the truth?"

Yancy was trapped. No matter what he said, someone at the table would be mad at him.

"No," he finally answered.

She bounced up. "I knew it." One finger pointed at her uncle. "I'm going to go wash my hands, and, when I get back, we'll have a serious talk about you taking care of yourself, Uncle Cap."

She was gone in a whirl of blue wool. The swinging door that led to the restrooms flapped so hard it hit both walls.

"Why didn't you lie for me, son?" Cap sounded more curious than angry.

Yancy grinned. "I'm more afraid of her than you."

Cap laughed. "Me, too. I'll go tell Sissy to turn in Ellie's lunch order. She'll know what week it is."

"What week?"

Cap slowly pushed himself out of the booth. "One week she's on a diet, and the next week she's recovering from it. She's a sweet girl, my Ellie, but she's bossy like her mother. Wants everyone to follow the rules." Cap's head kept shaking as he shuffled off toward the counter.

Yancy looked out the window wondering if he should "fol-low the rules" and tell the sheriff about the two ex-cons he'd seen, but if he did, he'd have to admit to how he knew them. Yancy had seen the sheriff's car drive by but hadn't spoken to the lawman. He'd like to keep it that way for as long as possible. Something told him that once it got out that his last address was prison, not many people would want him around.

"Scoot over," a voice said from beside Yancy as Ellie slid into his side of the booth.

"I was here first." He meant to say it with conviction, but her leg was pushing against his from hip to knee, and his tongue lost traction.

"Do you mind if I join you and my uncle?" she asked as if she couldn't care less whether he did or not.

"No, Ellie, I don't mind. I'm glad you're watching over your uncle. He's a good old guy."

She seemed to relax a little, but the booth was small and her leg remained next to his. "Thanks for not lying for him. You're right, Uncle Cap is a great man, but he doesn't take care of him-self. The whole family worries about him."

Yancy felt light-headed. He hadn't been next to any female near his age in years, and here she was touching him. Even if it was through layers of clothing, he swore she felt soft. "I'll watch out for him," he managed to say.

"Thanks." She didn't look his way.

He wanted to keep the conversation going. "You smell good."

Now she looked at him and frowned. Obviously he'd stepped over some invisible line. Then she held up her hands. "It's that soap in the bathroom. Lemon coconut, I think."

He blushed and was glad to see she did, too.

He wanted to say that she smelled good all over and then ask, would she mind much if he lowered his hand to her leg and felt the length of just the one resting against his. After all, they were already touching. What did it matter if it was his leg touching or his hand? But he doubted he'd get a sentence out before she drop-kicked him through the open pass-through between the café and the kitchen.

So, he just sat next to her, touching from hip to knee, as he ate his pancakes and listened to her lecture Cap about taking better care of himself.

Yancy lowered his head when the two men from the hardware store came in. Cowboy and Freddie. There was no doubt.

He saw their profiles clearly this time. They were the cons he'd crossed a few times the first year he was in prison. They were both meaner than wild hogs, but Cowboy could fool people because he had an easy smile and a laid-back way of moving that hid his ruthless ways. Cowboy's hair might be longer, but Yancy knew exactly who he was.

"Morning, little lady," Cowboy said to Sissy. "All right if we have a seat at your counter?"

"Of course. I'll take your order in a minute."

Sissy wasn't rude, but she wasn't as friendly as she'd been to Yancy. That made him feel proud. Maybe he no longer looked like a con. Maybe he just looked like a regular guy.

Yancy watched them fold onto the counter stools. They had their backs to him, but he could tell by the way Freddie looked around that he was casing the café. Before he left, the con would know where the money was kept. The real money, not just what they kept in the cash drawer for change. Yancy knew the tricks. All Freddie would have to do was pay with a hundred, then watch across the pass-through as Sissy rushed into the kitchen and pulled a bank bag from somewhere.

Yancy had no proof, but he knew this place was on their list of places to rob in Crossroads. He didn't miss the fact that both their heads turned when Sissy rang up a bill. They would come in fast and hard when they robbed the café. They'd be armed and probably use more force than was necessary. The fact that Sissy was small and pregnant wouldn't slow them down.

He also knew neither of the men had spotted him. Too many years maybe. He'd been nobody, just one more kid in prison for robbery. They'd both always been surrounded by their gangs. He was nothing to them, but for a time they'd been his greatest fear.

When he and Cap left the café, Yancy walked back while Cap drove across to the parking lot. Ellie had left with them, but she hadn't bothered to say goodbye to Yancy even though they'd touched legs for half an hour.

The air was cooler, but Yancy didn't feel it. He'd taken to wearing his flannel shirt over his thermal underwear. It was almost as good as a jacket. Only today he had far more to worry about than the weather.

Somehow he had to keep an eye on Cowboy and Freddie while staying out of their way. A few months ago he wouldn't have cared what they did, but now the old folks were his friends and the idea that someone might hurt Sissy made him sick to his stomach.

He decided if he saw them do one thing wrong, he was going to the sheriff, even if it meant his secret got out. One fact he remembered about every encounter Cowboy had with anyone on the yard; he was meaner than he had to be. Hitting, hurting, maybe even killing. If a bystander got in the way, that wasn't Cowboy's problem. Freddie tended to move in fast and leave anyone bleeding who got too close to him.

The rest of the afternoon Yancy worked on the gutters, keeping watch like a lone sentinel at the palace gate.

Ellie kept circling in his mind, even though he did his best to keep focused. He liked the way she smelled and how she'd felt against him. Something was obviously wrong with him. He was probably some kind of pervert. He could still feel her warm, soft thigh resting against his. A man could lose sleep on just that one thought.

As he worked, he watched the traffic moving through town. Most were people simply passing by, but he was learning the locals one story at a time. When he went in for a cup of coffee, the folks in the sunroom were talking about the ranches around and pointing as their trucks passed by.

The Collins ranch had silver trucks and pickups. "Think they're uppity," Mrs. Ollie said without missing a stitch. "Old Adam Collins, Davis's father and Reid's grandfather, was like that, too. Always wore an expensive Western hat but never had any manure on his boots. I swear Davis buried the old man in thirty-year-old boots that had never touched dirt."

Mrs. Kirkland pressed her lips together so hard they disappeared, but didn't comment. If she had stories about the men who had been her next door neighbors, as ranches go, she wasn't saying.

"Looks like the plumber got a new truck," Leo added as if anyone cared.

They moved on to a conversation about students who'd grown up, and Yancy went back to watching the traffic as he worked.

The Kirkland ranch trucks weren't as fancy as the Collins ranch vehicles, but every one Kirkland owned had two K's on the driver's door. They were back-to-back mirror images. Double K's. Yancy thought they kind of looked like stars or maybe a real stiff spider. Maybe, if he ever met Kirkland, he'd ask him what the K's looked like to the man who owned the ranch.

Twice, Yancy thought he saw a suspicious one-ton truck go down the street. No markings and whatever logo had been on the driver's side looked to have been spray-painted over. The guy driving wore a cowboy hat low on his forehead. Yancy couldn't see his face for the shadows, but it could have been Cowboy. Whatever they were doing in town was keeping them busy.

He shook off the nervous feeling. Maybe he was wrong. After all, he hadn't gotten a real good look at the two men except for a moment, and it had been almost five years since he'd seen them. What were the odds that three men from an Oklahoma prison could end up in a small town in Texas? And if they were here, it was no business of his.

Yet that night Yancy couldn't sleep. About midnight he put on the long, black wool coat Mr. Halls had given him and went outside.

The town was asleep, and the air so still he heard his own breath going in and out. Crossing over the road, where the night's shadows were deeper, he walked with no particular destination in mind. He moved past the high school and tried to remember one good thing that had happened when he spent time in classes at any one of the dozen schools he had attended.

His mom had moved around, living first with one relative, then another. She'd start a new job and he'd think they'd be fine, then she'd begin drinking, and before he knew it, they'd be moving again. When she finally ran out of relatives, they'd lived in hotel rooms and dumps with men she always wanted him to call uncle.

By the time he was fourteen he was staying out all night. She never noticed. Never asked about school. Never offered him lunch money.

One night he just didn't come home. After that he never went back to school. He didn't care what happened to her any more than she probably cared where he was. He ran the streets with other kids no one wanted. For a few years, he felt wild and free. Then he was caught stealing. Once trouble found him, it never let go for long. Serving time became the norm between vacations of freedom.

As he walked past what Cap had pointed out as the Gypsy House, Yancy heard the eerie sound of branches scratching against the roof. He stood perfectly still and stared. The air was calm, but he swore he heard the branches clawing over the top of the house.

The house seemed out of place along the two-lane road. It was still within sight of town, but no longer a part of it. Years of weathering had turned the outside to the color of dirt, but the way the windows sagged left dark holes just like blind eyes watching him from the crumbling home.

Crossing the road, he walked through the twisted trees to the remains of the homestead everyone called the Gypsy House. Nothing moved. He heard no sound to indicate that anyone, or anything, had caused the sound, yet he swore he'd heard branches scraping. As he stood close he heard the whirl of the night air circling through the rooms from one broken window to holes in the roof. For a moment he swore the house was breathing.

It crossed his mind that the house was luring him closer, and he couldn't help but wonder if it had done the same to the kids who got hurt there. Maybe the house hadn't wanted them.

Maybe it wouldn't want him if he stepped any closer. Maybe it would. Folks called it the Gypsy House, and one of the old-timers had asked if he had Gypsy blood. Maybe he did. Maybe the place was calling him home.

His mother used to tell him, when he was growing up, about a town called Crossroads where she had to live with a crazy old grandmother one summer.

He'd always thought she made the story up, but now, staring at the house, he wondered if this could have been the very house his mother feared.

Turning, he hurried away. The wind was whipping up, and he needed to head back. He had a full day of work to do tomorrow. He needed sleep.

As he crossed the road, he swore he heard the sound of branches move over ancient tiles on a roof, rotten and caving. The pull to go back and look closer was strong, but Yancy forced his steps to put distance between him and the old house. Ghosts and hauntings were for children. He was a man of twenty-five. He would not give in to fear.

"I'll come back," he whispered. "It's nothing but an old house. There are a lot worse things to fear that are real. I'll come back and prove it one day," he swore, and he knew he would.

CHAPTER SEVENTEEN

Staten

Staten Kirkland didn't remember much about driving back from Quinn's farm. He must have gone a hundred through town. There didn't seem enough air in Texas to breathe until the cliffs of Ransom Canyon rose before him, and he knew he was almost home. His always-pessimistic thoughts were piling up in his brain.

She wasn't a young girl barely out of her teens as Amalah had been. What if Quinn died during delivery or lost the baby? Hell, even with a healthy baby they'd be living on Social Security before the kid could graduate from college.

But no matter how the worries stacked up, a tiny part of him knew that he wanted to be involved in his child's life. He wanted this baby. He felt as if he'd just awakened on Christmas morning and been given a gift he didn't know to even ask for. A wonderful gift that came with a bucket-load of worry and a ton of excitement.

Quinn would be a good mother, no doubt about that, only Staten had no idea what kind of father he might be. He was no longer in his twenties. He had hardened so much, he might not have enough love to spread out over all the growing-up years.

Might not be an option anyway. He may have slammed the door on any chance he had by asking if she was sure it was his kid. Staten swore for a few miles. He should write a manual of the dumbest thing to say when a woman tells you she's pregnant. Apparently, he was a natural-born expert.

Think. You've got to straighten this out. All he had to do was talk Quinn into speaking to him again. Right about now the mother of his future child was probably plotting to murder him.

What had she said? *This is my baby. I'll take care of it. People don't even have to know it's yours.*

Damn, he didn't care if the whole country knew it was his. It *was* his. In six months he'd be a father again, and damn it, he planned to do it right.

Hell, he thought, *I have six months to stop saying damn and hell.* Women didn't think much of a man who cussed around newborns. Which made no sense. They didn't understand a word you were saying anyway.

CHAPTER EIGHTEEN

Quinn

Quinn walked the rows of plowed earth surrounding her house. The lingering smells of lavender and the warm rich dirt blended. She was home. This land. This place. She'd grown up here. Her child would grow up here.

She hadn't had time to think about how Staten would react to her news. Part of her didn't believe it was possible until a few hours ago. Her periods had never been regular. The few other times she'd been late, she'd simply waited, but this time was different. When she'd missed her cycle, Quinn had hoped that she could dream it might be true if only for a short while.

For once she'd wanted to be selfish and keep it to herself. Over the years she'd watched her friends who were pregnant. She wanted the private kind of joy of knowing every moment of every day that you carried life inside you.

Staten had never mentioned love or a future between them. If he'd wanted more than what they had, surely he'd have voiced one thought about it. But the way he'd acted, all angry and sharp, hurt her. It was like she was trying to force him into something.

Quinn smiled through her tears. She wanted this baby, her baby. If Staten didn't want to be part of that, it didn't change anything.

Staten

Staten felt as if his brain might explode. Too much joy, too much sorrow in this life. He handled it the only way he knew how. He moved all feelings aside and tried to concentrate on work. That was the way his grandfather had taught him, and he'd practiced it religiously. Tonight he'd think of the right thing to say to Quinn, but right now he had problems he had to deal with.

When he crossed the cattle guard onto the Double K, he decided to take the county road. The land would relax him, help him get all the details of his life in order.

The bull that someone had run into last night would be gone, but, who knew, the guy who had hit his prize stock might have returned to the scene of the crime. Maybe it wasn't rustlers. It could have been a drunk on the wrong road. Maybe the drunk hadn't realized what he hit. If he just drove off, he might try to retrace his path.

Staten's men would have hauled off the bull, but maybe somewhere there would be a clue. Besides, Staten decided, he was in no shape to carry on a conversation with anyone, so going into headquarters didn't sound like a good idea.

For the second time in his life he was about to be a father, and right now, if he told anyone, Quinn would probably be even more angry than she already was at him.

This wasn't something that she could keep secret long. He didn't care who knew, but there were a few people he needed to talk to before word got out. His granny, for one.

Two miles up the county road, he spied the sheriff's cruiser parked up on the hill half a mile away.

Staten pulled his truck alongside Sheriff Brigman and leaned out the window. "Can I help you, Sheriff, or are you just out for a stroll?"

"I thought I'd see if I could spot anything strange. Right now a dead bull is the only clue we've got to your destruction of property claim."

Pulling his truck off the road, Staten joined the sheriff. He almost argued that a dead bull was a hell of a lot more than just destruction of property. Every man on his ranch carried a rifle or handgun in his truck. If they'd seen whoever hit the bull racing away from the crime scene, shots would have been fired. To the man, they all rode for the brand and would protect his property.

"What are we looking for exactly?" Staten asked. He wasn't in the mood to act normal, but maybe trying would calm him down. Part of him wanted to turn around and race back to Quinn, but reason told him he needed to get over wanting to murder the driver first.

"Tire marks," the sheriff said, breaking into Staten's worries. "Maybe something that blew out of the bed of the truck. Broken glass. There had to be damage done to whatever, or whoever, hit him. To hit a bull hard enough to kill him, the front of any car or pickup would be smashed to pieces. I've seen what a deer can do. A bull must have done a great deal more." Brigman glanced over at Staten. "Did you ever lose a cow like this before?"

"First, I didn't lose a cow, it was a prize bull. And second, of course I've lost both cows and bulls, even calves. The boys and I are guessing we've taken a hit on half a dozen since fall, all to rustlers. That's over twice what we lost by this time last year."

"Would they show up at the sale barns? The brand inspector is surely watching for them."

Staten shook his head. "Most end up in the freezer by morning. Once they're slaughtered, they're gone. Now and then a small-time farmer will steal a few head and mix them in with his own. They breed with his herd, and as long as he doesn't sell them, chances of someone spotting a brand is slight."

An old pickup rattled down the road toward them. Staten knew from the sound that it belonged to Reyes, the head wrangler on the next ranch. He'd seen Lucas drive it around town and into headquarters last month to pick up his pay. Funny how the boy had been nearby and on the ranch for a while, but kind of off Staten's radar until the night the kids got hurt at that old house near town. Ever since, he'd made a point to talk to the tall, lean Reyes boy every time he saw him.

Sheriff Brigman moved closer to Staten. "I asked one of your men to have Lucas Reyes drive his truck over here. You said once that he comes on your land, so he's my most likely cattle-killer. Correction, bull-killer."

Staten frowned. "Lucas didn't do it." He'd watched the kid work stock. He knew too much to barrel across open range at night. His father had worked for the Collins operation for years. Lucas was raised on a ranch, and, legal or not, like most farm and ranch kids, he'd probably been driving since his feet could reach the gas pedal.

Quinn crossed Staten's mind. In about six months she'd have a son or daughter. Whichever didn't matter, but Staten wanted the baby to feel born to the land the way he always felt. He wanted his offspring to grow up on Kirkland ground.

He almost laughed aloud. Not much chance of that happening with Quinn not speaking to him.

Lucas pulled up, jumped from his truck and headed right to Staten. "You need me out here, sir? I was planning on finishing that fence in the west pasture before dark."

Staten didn't like the idea of Lucas thinking he had any part of this interrogation Brigman was about to launch into. He liked Lucas. There was a real intelligence in his eyes, and he didn't back away from hard work. "The sheriff is asking me questions, and I thought you might lend a hand. I told him you like to come out in this back pasture after dark. We were hoping you might have seen something if you were here last night."

"I haven't been out here for a few nights, Mr. Kirkland. If I ever did see something, you'd be the first to know."

The boy was still looking directly at his boss, not the sheriff.

Brigman moved closer. "Exactly what night were you last here, Lucas? Two, three, four."

"It was Saturday night, Sheriff Brigman."

"Before or after you visited Tim O'Grady?"

Staten didn't miss Lucas's surprise, but he didn't hesitate. "After."

"Did you see anything out of the ordinary?" The sheriff moved between Staten and the kid. "Like someone who shouldn't have been on this land."

"No, sir."

"Were you alone?" Brigman snapped.

For a blink the kid glanced his direction, and Staten saw the boy panic, then Lucas straightened his shoulders as if preparing to take a blow straight on.

"Yes, sir," he said. "I always come out here alone. With five brothers and sisters, I like the silence of this back pasture, and Mr. Kirkland doesn't mind that I walk across this corner of his land."

Staten had never considered himself a mind reader, but he understood his men. He knew the cloth they were made from. Lucas was a hard worker. The other men liked him. Staten had seen them kid him about still being wet behind the ears one minute, then turn around to help him the next. He'd also seen Lucas help others, even working overtime to make sure they got their job done.

Staten would bet his ranch on two facts. First, Lucas Reyes hadn't killed the bull. Surely, even the sheriff could see that there wasn't a dent in Reyes's truck. And the second fact he knew beyond any doubt was that Lucas Reyes had just lied to a county sheriff.

Since the sheriff looked as though he had more questions and Staten figured the discussion was over, he slapped his hand on Lucas's shoulder and said, "Walk with us. We're looking for any clue that would tell us who could have plowed into my bull."

"Yes, sir." Lucas joined Staten on the other side of the road from where the sheriff walked. "What exactly are we looking for?"

"Glass, a fender, anything. Rain's coming in tonight. If we don't look now, a clue might be washed away."

Lucas smiled. "Whoever it was must have been going fast or was a complete idiot. Probably drunk or on drugs if he missed a bull."

"I agree," Staten said. "You wouldn't happen to know anyone who fits the description?"

"No, sir." Lucas hesitated then added, "It could be someone wanting to test how fast a car would go. Everyone knows these back roads aren't likely to have radar on them."

"Good point." The sheriff kicked at dirt as if he thought he might dig up something. "Could have been kids. They steal a car, go for a joyride."

Lucas glanced at Brigman. "You have any stolen cars turned in?"

"No. If it was just joyriders, we would have found the wrecked car. They always leave it somewhere along the side of the road once it runs out of gas."

"That leaves someone testing out a new car," Staten said to himself, thinking he knew of one person who'd gotten a car early last week for his birthday. Reid Collins. Only, Staten wasn't going to suggest anything to the sheriff. Brigman would have to figure that out on his own, and he would. After all, he and half the county had been at the kid's birthday party.

Staten saw something shiny and knelt. Broken glass. Could be a headlight, but it was small, only a sliver.

Brigman joined him. "Looks like they missed this piece. See

the markings in the dirt. Someone swept the ground here. Probably cleaning up the wreck. A drunk wouldn't do that."

"Blood," Lucas yelled from ten feet in front of them. "Leading off that way."

Staten walked the blood trail. What happened was obvious. The vehicle had hit the bull where they found the glass. The bull had managed to wander off, bleeding for another hundred yards, before it died.

Brigman got a call and rushed toward his cruiser. "I got to take this," he yelled.

Staring straight at the kid, Staten said, "I don't think you had anything to do with this, Lucas, but I need to ask. Were you here last night?"

"No, sir." Lucas met his stare.

"Then tell me why you lied to the sheriff about being alone out here a few nights ago." Before Lucas could think about his answer, Staten added, "I don't plan on telling anyone, but this is my land, and I need the truth from my men. The whole truth."

Lucas took a slow breath and met Staten's gaze once more. "I couldn't tell the sheriff I wasn't alone the last time I was in this pasture. I was with his daughter." He didn't look away when he added, "We weren't doing anything, sir. I just wanted to show her my favorite place to watch the stars."

Staten nodded. "You were wrong to lie, but I guess I might have done the same if I was facing my girlfriend's father and he was armed."

Lucas grinned. "She's not my girlfriend. At least not yet. We're just friends."

Staten turned back to the road. The sheriff shouted that he had to get to town.

As they watched the cruiser pull away, Staten issued a low order, "Take care of the west fence before dark."

"I will, sir, and thanks."

"For what? I'm a man of my word, Lucas. You be that, too."

"I plan to be."

Staten could almost see the future. This kid was going to make something of himself. "I've got more than twenty years on you, son, but let's shake on something. We'll never lie to each other. Between you and me, it'll always be nothing but truth."

"Deal." Lucas offered his hand.

"Deal." Staten shook on it. "Now get to work."

As the kid ran off toward his old pickup, Staten remembered how he used to say that Quinn and he were just friends. They'd gone far beyond that now, and he'd better find a way to mend a few fences, too, or this stubborn bull of a man would be walking his own blood trail alone until death took him.

CHAPTER NINETEEN

Quinn

Quinn stared in the mirror, looking for any signs that she was pregnant. Her breasts were a bit bigger and her tummy slightly rounded. With her height and slim build she could probably carry a child unseen into the fifth or even sixth month.

She could handle three months of listening to folks ask questions. The answers were simple. Of course, the baby was hers. Yes, she knew who the father was, but that wasn't anyone's business. She planned to raise the child alone right here on her farm.

In the days waiting for Staten to call, she'd figured out a few things during the silence. She might be shy and like keeping to herself, but she was strong. She could do this. She could have the baby and raise it herself.

She'd thought of making up a story about how she'd had an old boyfriend show up for a few days, and she'd thought they might rekindle their love. But, she'd realized that they weren't meant to be together. He'd already gone his own way, she'd say. He wouldn't be interested in a baby, but she was.

Quinn laughed. No one would believe such a ridiculous story.

She never had an old love, and, with her luck, the kid would look exactly like Staten.

Maybe she should leave for six months or so and come back with a ring and a kid. But there would be people who would do the math and realize she'd been pregnant when she left. Also, it was time to plant. She couldn't leave the farm now.

This was the twenty-first century, not a hundred years ago. No one cared where the father was, and everyone who loved her would love the baby. She wasn't rich, but they'd never go hungry.

Just as she finished dressing, someone pounded on her door. Quinn didn't hurry. She knew who it was. The only surprise was that he'd taken two weeks to come back.

Walking through the house she saw Staten standing just beyond the screen door. Quinn found herself slowing so she could take him in for a moment longer. He was big, well-built, powerful-looking. His face was as cloudy as the storm rolling across the sky behind him, but even now she thought him the handsomest man she'd ever met.

When she reached the door, she didn't open the screen or invite him in. "If you've come to tell me to abort, you're wasting your time. No matter what the argument, I wouldn't."

He braced the sides of the door frame as if it were strong enough to keep him out. "You know I wouldn't do that, Quinn."

She did know. She knew him better than anyone alive. "Then why are you here, Staten?" Quinn needed to hear the words.

"I want to be in your life." He paused as if he thought one sentence might work. When it didn't, he continued, "I miss you. I need to help you with this baby or at least be around if you need me."

She still didn't move.

"I can't handle the thought of losing you." He pushed away from the door, walked a few feet, swore, and came back. "I don't know the words to say. I can't sleep. I can't eat. I'll be dead in a week if you don't let me come in."

He looked so sad, she unlatched the screen.

He stepped one foot inside and waited, his hat in his big hands.

Quinn remained close. She wasn't afraid of him, she never had been. "I know what you're saying, Staten, but you hurt me too badly."

"It was the shock of it all." He took a deep breath. "I hate not talking to you. You're the only friend I have, Quinn."

She smiled. "I've no doubt. Folks say you're hard as rock. Leaves me wondering if you'll be any good for a baby."

"I'll try. Truth is, I don't know much about babies. Amalah's mom moved in when Randall was born, and Granny drove over to help out almost every morning. Between working hard to get the place going and trying to stay out of my mother-in-law's way, I don't remember much from birth to the day he could talk."

He met her gaze. "I'd try harder if I had another chance. I swear I would."

Quinn shook her head. "I don't want to hurt you, Staten, but I need time to think. We're not two kids. I didn't plan this, but now it's here I want to experience every minute. I don't want to make a decision that I'll end up regretting."

He gave one jerk of a nod. "I understand. Do you want to know what I want?"

"No," she said softly. "Not yet, maybe not ever." She guessed he'd suggest marriage and her moving over to the ranch. She wouldn't fit in his world, and he'd never fit in this place. Or, he might not suggest they marry, and somehow that would be sad. He'd never said he loved her, but she knew she mattered to him. Maybe that's how it would be with the baby, too. He'd come see their child. The kid would matter to him, but there would be no love involved, just a duty to take care of his responsibility.

Kirkland men tended to marry outgoing women. For a hundred years, Kirkland women had taken leading roles in running the town and socials. The library was named after his great-grandmother. Kirkland money kept the museum going.

His grandmother had run the chamber of commerce for years. Even Amalah had chaired several charities before she became ill.

Quinn wasn't the wife for Staten, and she never wanted his sense of duty to force them both into something they couldn't live with.

"Can we talk?" Staten carefully set his hat on the back of the nearest kitchen chair as if testing the waters. "Not about the baby, but just talk. I've missed you."

"Me, too." She hadn't really realized how much until she'd seen him standing at the door.

"We could go into town for breakfast. I could buy you a cup of coffee if you've already eaten. It looks like rain, so we won't get much done today anyway." His low voice rumbled, echoing the distant thunder.

She thought of all the times he'd offered to take her out and she'd said no, but somehow, this time it seemed right. "If I go, will you promise we won't talk about the baby?"

"If that's what you want. You have my word."

She lifted her jacket from the hook by the door and walked out of her house without bothering to lock up.

He followed her to his truck and opened the passenger side for her. "Need any help?"

She swung up. "No, thanks."

They drove toward town talking of the weather. Both lived by the seasons. It was the last thing they checked at night and the first thing they checked in the morning.

When he passed the high school, he recalled a few things that had happened when they were in school. Amalah and Staten had been seriously dating by the time they were all three juniors. Quinn swore she'd heard every detail of every date her best friend had with Staten.

"Remember the time Amalah fell when all the cheerleaders were building a pyramid? I think it was the last football game of the season."

Quinn grinned. "I was in the band. It was halftime, and we were playing the school song when I saw her tumble. I stopped playing and ran out of line, but I couldn't get to her."

"I was huddled up listening to the coach when I heard some-one scream and turned to see her falling. I thought my heart would stop when she didn't get up. I wanted to pick her up and make sure she was all right, but she had a crowd around her."

"After the game she laughed at us both for overreacting." Quinn smiled. That was one of the few times she'd felt sorry for Staten because she knew exactly the fear he'd felt. In an odd way they shared Amalah. Over the years her loss was something they also shared.

He covered Quinn's hand with his. "She loved us both, you know."

"I know. She had shone so bright during those years. I always felt like a shadow next to her. I was never jealous, you know. I wouldn't have wanted her life, and I'm guessing she wouldn't have wanted mine."

To her surprise he shook his head. "No, Quinn, you're wrong. You had talent. Real talent. Amalah once told me she wished she could play like you, and she was green when you got to go to New York to study. Miss Abernathy used to brag on you all the time. She'd say you were the brightest, shining star to ever grow up around here. Amalah was proud to be your friend, but I think she would have traded if she could have."

"Sure. Some star." Quinn shrugged.

"You're just as bright, whether you play in New York or just for me. If you decide to teach, I think you'll be great at that, too."

They pulled up to the café. He rushed around and helped her out of the truck. Neither bothered with opening an umbrella or even pulling up their hoods. The gentle rain made both smile.

"Staten," she whispered as they hurried inside, "don't let me eat any bacon."

He raised an eyebrow and then seemed to figure it out. "Right."

The café was long past the breakfast crowd, and the waitress was new, so they ate in peace. He told her about the mystery of his murdered bull, and she talked about how she planned to change up her fields some this spring. She even planned to lease out the back forty acres of her land to the farmer behind her. "The lease will probably pay me more than any profit I could make growing lavender off the land."

If anyone had been there to listen in, they'd simply think that two old friends were having breakfast together. A farmer and a rancher talking about their problems with the land.

When the waitress brought the breakfast plates, she commented that Dorothy piled on extra bacon. "She said when she saw you, Miss Quinn, she remembered you always ate double the bacon when you came in with your parents several years back."

Quinn thanked the waitress. Without a word Staten ate the bacon on both plates, making her smile. This hard businessman was doing his best to be charming.

He drove her home and walked her to the porch.

She said goodbye twice and thanked him for the breakfast, but he just stood there blocking her way into the house.

When she could think of nothing else to say, she just stared.

"I'm not leaving." He set his hat down on the railing. "I have a promise to keep. I'll kiss you goodbye first, then I'll leave."

Since she was the one who'd made him promise, she couldn't complain. She just waited.

He took his time moving closer, placing his arms at her waist and tugging her against him. Then, tenderly, he kissed her.

Quinn felt herself melting as the kiss deepened. There was something about how he held her just right, making her feel needed and cherished.

When he finally ended the kiss, she didn't step away. His hands moved over her back, and she wished this one moment might last forever. His words came to her low and loving. "I want to undress you, Quinn. I don't want to talk or even think. I just want to hold you."

She understood all he wasn't saying. Change was coming and like it or not, for better or worse, what they had would never be the same. She'd been his shelter for five years, and he'd been her rock.

Without a word she took his hand and led him into the house and down the hallway. She stood in the shadows of the cloudy day and watched him slowly undress her. Silently he moved Quinn onto the bed and turned her on her side while he untied her braid. Then he lay beside her, letting his hand move over her hair and down her body.

The air was damp and cool, so they cuddled under the covers when they began to make love as if for the first time...as if for the last time. A pure kind of loving without words. No agenda, only showing each other how much they cared.

As she drifted to sleep in his arms, she felt his hand spread wide over her abdomen.

Hours later, when she woke, he was gone. She tried to recall the last moment before she'd fallen asleep. Had he leaned down and kissed her tummy, or had she dreamed it?

Quinn spent most of the week drifting from project to project while she waited for Staten to return. She had no doubt he would.

Her mind kept going back to the few words he'd said and the way he'd touched her. She knew there were a hundred things to do, a hundred decisions to make, but the memory of the way they'd made love wouldn't seem to leave her mind.

He'd kept to his word. They hadn't talked about the baby. The time would come when they would have to, but for right now, there were enough days left before the world changed to just enjoy being together.

★ ★ ★

A little before dark on Saturday night Quinn got a text from Staten.

Got invitation to Lauren Brigman's birthday party at the lake next week. I'm not going unless you are.

Quinn laughed. She liked Lauren; they'd become friends, but Quinn had no idea why Staten would be invited.

I'm going.

Good, he texted back. I'll drop by later tonight and we can talk about what I'm supposed to get a sixteen-year-old.
Sounds good, she answered. Supper? Or Dessert?
His answer came back in a blink.

YOU!

She held her breath during the long pause, then he added, I loved holding you while you slept. Any chance we can do that again?

A river of unsaid words ran between them, but for now the place where they were was enough. He wasn't pushing her or trying to talk her into anything. He was giving her time and letting her know how he felt about her.

Thirty minutes later when she called his cell, thinking he'd be on his way, a stranger answered.

"Kirkland's phone, this is Jake Longbow," a voice rusty with age said.

"Jake," she laughed, remembering the ranch hand from years ago when she and Amalah used to ride horses out on the Double K ranch. "This is Quinn O'Grady. I'm trying to reach Staten."

There was a long pause, then Jake said, "He ran out and

jumped in his pickup when we heard gunfire a few minutes ago. Tossed me his phone and told me to call the sheriff. I called the county office, and the sheriff didn't even bother saying goodbye to me. Sounded like he dropped the phone and started running."

Quinn took a quick breath. Probably only hunters. They tended to ignore posted signs. "Jake—" she tried to sound calm "—could you have him call me when he gets back?"

"Will do, but if he's wanting the sheriff, he's planning to press charges this time."

Quinn hung up the phone and picked up a blanket. She'd watch the sunset from the porch and pray Staten called.

CHAPTER TWENTY

Staten

The last light of day played along the jagged edge of Ransom Canyon as Staten raced toward the far pasture that bordered the Collins ranch. For him the colors of sunsets across the wide horizon reminded him of Quinn's music. Whenever she played, he thought of his land, ever changing, through the seasons, through the years. Some would describe the terrain as desolate and barren, but if he lived to be a hundred he'd love the views every day.

As much as he loved the land, he hated the sound of gunfire rattling across the calm air. One shot after another seemed to clatter off the clouds and echo through the canyon, warning that trouble was coming to call.

Over the years, Davis Collins had opened his place to friends wanting to hunt, and he also offered leasing rights to companies he didn't know, but Staten never considered doing such a thing even if the money was good. Most of the hunters were respectful, following all the rules, keeping to the property boundaries. But some were drunks and careless, dangerous men who only handled a rifle a few times a year. They'd cross at the sandy ravines and step over low fences without really being aware, or caring, that they were on someone else's property. Some hunted at sunset and shot at eyes in the darkness, not aware that the eyes looking back were those of a cow and not a deer. Most of the drunks even left their kill in the field. With the Bar W over-hunted, they moved onto neighboring land. Staten planned to at least act as though he was pressing charges this time.

Once, he'd questioned Davis about the hunters, and Collins had sworn no hunters crossed property lines. Staten had only two choices, call the man a liar or walk away. He'd walked away, knowing that getting along with his neighbor was more impor-tant, at least until he had proof.

As Staten bounced toward the back pasture, he saw the Reyes pickup turning onto his land and heading straight toward him.

He smiled. Lucas, he'd bet. The kid might live on the Col-lins spread, but he'd made a hand for the Double K. Staten was more impressed with his skill and brains every time they worked together. Reyes had raised a good boy. Though the boots of a cowhand fit him now, Lucas would go on to greater things, and Staten planned to be there watching.

"Mr. Kirkland," Lucas yelled out his pickup window as he pulled alongside. "I heard shots. They had to be from near here."

Staten slowed to a stop. "Hop in my truck, Lucas. We're li-able to run into one another out here once it gets dark."

Lucas pulled off the road and cut his engine. In a blink he was climbing into the big cab of Staten's truck.

"Wow, Mr. Kirkland, this place is big enough to be a mobile home. You got a microwave in this thing?"

"Nope, but I'll order that next time."

Lucas settled in, knowing that if they crossed pasture lines he'd be the one hopping out to open the gates. "How can I help? I know this is your land, but I think of it as my special place and I hate the thought of someone out here bothering it."

Staten nodded. "I know how you feel. I like knowing you're

out here watching the stars, but I'll be madder than hell if I find out that someone cut fence to come in. So just listen, kid. If trespassers are still on this section, we'll hear them." Staten turned the truck off the road so they'd travel more quietly on grass.

Lucas's voice was high with excitement. "You think it's rustlers? My dad says they've hit the Collins place twice lately. Maybe a dozen head in the past month.

"Jake said you've been having trouble with them, too. They wouldn't come out this early, would they? It's barely dark. My guess is they'd feel safest cutting fence and rounding up cattle long after midnight."

"Breathe, kid," Staten ordered. "It's not rustlers, it's idiots. Drunk hunters or, worse, high ones. I was thinking they might have come from the Collins place and crossed over at the ravine."

Lucas shook his head. "Dad said at supper that the whole family has gone down to check out colleges for Reid's older brother, Charley. If they're not home, the guest quarters should be empty."

"Charley bright enough to go to college?"

Lucas looked over at him, and Staten had his answer without Lucas having to say a word.

"No surprise. I've watched him grow up. IQ and shoe size seem about the same. Collins is putting his bet on Reid to take over the ranch, but I don't know. Any boy dumb enough to talk you three kids into going into that death-trap Gypsy House might want to run for office. He's got persuasion skills and no brains, just like my old man."

Lucas laughed. "What makes you think Reid didn't try to talk us *out* of going in that night?"

Staten lowered his speed along with his voice. "I thought about it. You and Lauren both have too much brains to do something like that after dark, even though you'd been carrying flashlights. Only she's fifteen, so she might have just wanted an adventure. Tim always seems to be following Reid, never lead-ing. That leaves you, Lucas. Why'd you go in?"

Lucas was silent.

Staten turned to look at him in the low light of the dashboard. "I'm guessing you went in to watch over your friend Lauren."

The kid didn't say a word. He didn't have to. Staten read the surprise in Lucas's face.

"Don't worry about it, Lucas, we all do foolish things, take chances when we should have hesitated, and sometimes the end result turns out to be great." Quinn walked through Staten's mind. They'd been foolish not to use protection at their age, but who knew, it might turn out all right. The idea of shar-ing a child with Quinn was settling in his mind. After all, they weren't that old. Lots of people started families in their forties these days.

Lucas pointed toward a stand of elms scattered along the creek. "Something moved over there by the water." Half the trees had died during the drought, leaving barkless white bony skeletons strewn among the live trees.

Staten slowly turned the truck so the lights flashed across the rocky ground near the water. "Pull my Colt from the glove compartment and follow me," he said as he lifted a rifle from the rack behind his head.

Side by side they moved down the rocky slope. A young deer, not yet full grown, lay jerking in the mud. Staten smelled the blood even before he saw it. "Keep your eyes open for anyone. If they're hunting for food, they'll be tracking the animal. I want to know they're near before they see us."

As Lucas stood guard, Staten lowered to his knee beside the doe. She didn't try to pull away when he placed his hand on her side and felt her heart racing.

Slowly his eyes adjusted to the shadows, and he made out her wound. She'd been shot in the head, but the bullet hadn't killed her. Another wound, halfway down her back, left a gaping hole so deep it looked like someone had hacked a chunk out of her.

"How is the deer?" Lucas whispered though the silence.

"Dying and in pain." Staten moved his hand along her neck as if making one last attempt to calm her. "Easy now, girl."

Lucas had been raised on a ranch. He knew what had to be done without Staten having to say the words. He passed the rancher the Colt.

One lone shot rang through the night. The deer stopped moving. The men didn't make a sound. Staten's hand moved once more along the deer's neck and whispered, "Jake Longbow always says the same thing when a wild animal dies. *Go. Run with the wind in a place of no pain.*"

Lucas took the Colt back as Staten shouldered the deer. "Sounds almost like a prayer."

Slowly, Staten stood and passed his rifle to Lucas. "Let's put her in the truck bed. I don't want the coyotes getting her."

Lucas carried both the Colt and the rifle back to Staten's pickup. After the rancher covered the animal with a tarp, both men stood watching the night. Someone was out there who didn't belong.

"They're waiting for us to move on," Staten finally whispered as he shoved his rifle back in its place. "I can feel them."

"What are we going to do?" Lucas walked a few feet away from the truck and into the grass without making a sound.

Staten followed. He knew the sounds of his ranch. He'd recognized the rush of quail, the gobbles of wild turkey, the tapping of mule deer when a small herd crossed the road. He also had no doubt that whatever happened, Lucas Reyes would stand by his side now, but he had no idea what they were about to face.

"The sheriff's on his way. First thing he'll do is order a block on the county road. If they think they can't go out that way, they'll have to cross open land. Unless they know this section of pasture far better than I think they do, they'll pick the easiest route and that will be straight past us. If we wait, they'll be heading our way soon."

"We're going to confront men with guns out here in the dark?"

Staten barked a laugh. "I didn't live to be forty-three by being that dumb. Chances are slim they'll even see us. They probably left their trucks in the shadows of the elms. Once they pass us, we'll follow them. I know this area well enough to drive it without headlights."

"Oh, I understand. Good plan, Mr. Kirkland. I wasn't much on the 'Gun-fight at the O.K. Corral' idea."

Staten chuckled and pulled the rifle from the rack once more, and they moved forward to the shadow of a cluster of mesquite trees. There, they'd wait. The night wind rustled over the tops of tall buffalo grass. Staten forced out slow breaths, thinking that he could feel trouble coming and wondering if that was how men had felt on this land for hundreds of years. Bones and weapons had been found at Yellow Creek and at the south bend of the Red River miles northeast. A dozen cavalry men had died at Antelope Peak little more than a hundred years ago. Maybe their cries still circled high in the air like smoke from a long spent fire.

He widened his stance and waited. An uneasiness galloped over his thoughts. He couldn't hear it or see it, but he could feel it in his blood.

After fifteen minutes of silence, Lucas whispered, "You think we missed them?"

"Nope."

"Maybe you should call the sheriff and make sure the road block got set up?"

Staten swore. "I would if I hadn't left my phone back at the barn. Any chance you've got one I could borrow?"

Lucas shrugged. "I'd let you if I had one."

"A teenager without a phone? Impossible."

The sound of an engine silenced them both. They stood still, their shadows blending with those of the trees.

Staten held his breath as the grind of a motor grew louder, but underneath the roar of what had to be a truck was something else—a smaller motor. A car, or maybe a small pickup. For a few minutes they seemed to be traveling together, then the smaller engine veered off and grew fainter. Maybe going another way? Maybe slowing down to see if the truck made it?

The starless night revealed little but finally, as foggy as a day-old dream, came a lone truck moving across the night no more than shadow on shadow.

"There he goes!" Lucas jumped from the trees and started running for Staten's truck.

Staten reacted like a parent reaching for a child who darts into the street. If he'd been three feet closer he could have stopped the boy. Now all he could do was join him.

If they were lucky, they'd make it to the truck before the smaller engine came into view. Once inside, he'd wait for the second car to pass before following.

Lucas ran full out, fast and light.

"If we're lucky," Staten whispered just as his luck ran out.

Pain, like lightning volting from his shoulder, hit him out of nowhere. Time slowed and didn't pick up until he heard the sound of a round being fired. He waited a second, expecting to hear the bullet fly by. Only it didn't. It had already hit him.

Staten's strong body crumbled. His face hit the cold ground as fire raged through his shoulder. The Colt tumbled from his hand as all feeling seemed to leave his arm.

As he jerked, Staten swore he heard Jake Longbow whisper, *"Go. Run with the wind in a place of no pain."*

Helpless to move, Staten watched Lucas make it to the truck before the shot registered. He glanced back, and to the kid's credit, he didn't hesitate as he reversed his route.

"Get down!" Staten yelled, knowing it didn't matter if he

was hurt. Whoever was out there knew exactly where he and the boy were.

Lucas dropped and spider-crawled toward Staten.

"Are you hit?"

"Stay down, kid. They'll come closer. Fire off two rounds toward the moon. That should slow them down and bring any of my men within hearing distance running toward us."

Staten fought to keep from passing out. "If you hear movement coming toward you, fire again, high. If it's my men coming in to help, they'll be yelling." Staten felt like an elephant just sat down on his head, but he had to stay conscious long enough to make sure Lucas would be all right. "If someone shoots back," he said weakly, "lay down and wait until you've got a clear shot, then aim for their legs. Even if you miss, it'll slow them down long enough to…"

Lucas

Lucas moved closer to his boss, feeling around for the Colt. For one panicked moment, he thought he might not find it or remember what to do.

"Mr. Kirkland." He touched the rancher's arm. "Where are you hit?"

When Staten didn't answer, Lucas grabbed his boss's shoulder intending to shake him awake, but warm blood met his touch. He had his answer.

Fighting down fear, he moved his hand over the wound. Left shoulder. High. Not close to the heart but too much blood.

Pressing the wound with one hand, Lucas spread his fingers through the dirt near Kirkland's side. One sweep. Two. He touched the butt of the Colt. It took Lucas a few agonizing seconds to grip the gun without decreasing the pressure over the wound. He didn't know if he was doing any good, but it was the only thing he knew to do to possibly stop the bleeding.

Lucas held the gun as far away as he could and fired two shots in the air.

The whole world went silent. He leaned over Staten. "Don't die." His voice came fast and angry. "Don't die on me. I don't know what to do."

Spreading out next to him, Lucas hoped whoever was out there couldn't see them for the weeds and tall grass. He waited, knowing that as soon as it was safe he'd be able to carry Kirkland to the truck, only right now he couldn't seem to stop the tears dripping off his chin.

He went over what Staten had told him to do. If men move in silently, shoot at the ground in front of them. Lucas wasn't sure he could shoot at a man, any man. He'd done target practice, but he'd never shot at a living thing.

The low sound of an engine came again through the silence.

Lucas raised the Colt and fired two more rounds.

The rattle of a truck seemed to turn right toward them. Maybe whoever was out there firing at them planned to run over them both, now that they were down. A hit-and-run right in the middle of a pasture. Or, maybe the men at the headquarters had heard the two shots.

As the truck light flashed toward him, Lucas raised the Colt and prepared to fire.

Just as he aimed between the headlights he heard shouts and two rounds of gunfire coming from the truck.

They were Kirkland's men. He shook with relief. "They're here, Mr. Kirkland. They're here."

Dropping the gun, Lucas sat up, waving them in with his free hand.

Within seconds the men were out of the truck and surrounding them. One flashed a light over Staten. Blood covered his chest now, as well as the front of Lucas's shirt.

"Give me your shirt, Phil," Jake Longbow ordered. "We'll tie up his shoulder as best as we can."

One of the cowhands ripped the buttons as he yanked off his shirt and dropped to help lift the boss while Jake tied a knot directly over where Lucas's hand had been applying pressure.

"Let's get them to the hospital!" Jake yelled. "Load them in the back of my pickup. A couple of you men crawl in with them to make sure they don't fall out. I'll be driving like I'm running from hell."

Lucas tried to tell them that he wasn't hurt, but no one seemed to hear. They were too busy asking questions and swearing and making threats to whoever did this.

Men pulled rifles and flashlights from Jake's truck, planning to walk the mile-long pasture to make sure no one was on the property.

The smell of hay and leather surrounded Lucas as he sat in the back of Jake's pickup, back to the cab. His heart was still pounding double-time when he watched the men lift Kirkland in beside him and brace the boss with horse blankets and saddles. Men sat at the four corners while Lucas knelt beside Kirkland. When he lifted Staten's head and used his hat as a pillow, the boss came to.

His deep blue eyes were clear, even though his voice was barely more than a whisper. "Lucas, call Quinn," he said. "Tell her I may be late."

"You got it, boss," Lucas answered. He guessed Kirkland was talking about Quinn O'Grady since she was the only Quinn he knew in town. He'd had no idea that she and Kirkland were even friends, but he'd follow orders.

Lucas fought down a smile. They were a hell of a lot more than friends if she was the one person Kirkland wanted him to call. He thought of asking if one of the men had a cell phone, but decided maybe he should make *this* call in private.

CHAPTER TWENTY-ONE

Quinn

Quinn ran through the hospital doors at full speed. A message had been left on her phone over an hour ago. Some kid saying Staten had been shot and was at the hospital in Lubbock. No details.

When she'd heard it, she had dropped her quilt and grabbed her keys. All the way to the hospital she'd thought of how mad she still was about what he'd said when he found out she was pregnant. How could he think that there would be another man in her life?

Only now, if he died, what did being angry with him matter? She still loved him, still wanted their baby. The thought of facing the years ahead without Staten in her life was too much to bear. She needed him. Wanted him to share the joy of a child with her.

The memory of the touch of his hand across her abdomen almost a week ago returned so strong she could still feel it. One caress he'd made when he thought she was asleep, that was all she needed to know. The last night they'd shared had been about them, whether it was a beginning or an end between them she wasn't sure. But the caress had been about the baby. He wanted the child. That was a beginning. Staten Kirkland was a hard man who rarely showed any emotion, but he wanted the baby that grew inside her, and he wanted her.

Could she be happy with that? Was it enough to build her life around?

If Staten lived, Quinn made up her mind that she wouldn't—couldn't—deny him. He was an honest man who wouldn't offer what he couldn't give. Somehow they'd work it out. Together or apart they'd both raise the child.

"May I help you?" a man in a white coat whom she took to be an orderly asked when she passed her second set of swinging doors.

Quinn didn't take time to look at his name tag. "I'm looking for Staten Kirkland."

The man began shaking his head.

Quinn continued, "He was shot on his ranch earlier tonight. I think it's been about two hours ago since his men brought him in."

"Oh, the rancher. He's in a private room on the third floor. Can't miss it. The men who arrived with him are all still here."

Without another word the orderly hurried off down the hallway while Quinn moved to the nearest set of elevators. When she stepped off on the third floor, she froze. Twenty men, most dressed in chaps, boots and spurs, circled the waiting room. None looked to be waiting patiently. Their shirts were dirty. A few looked bloody, and all seemed a bit lost. Their Western hats sat, crown up, along one wall of the open area.

They all stared at her as if she was a newly arrived alien. Quinn rarely left her farm, but she knew a few of the men. Marybeth's oldest son—Quinn had decorated the venue for his parents' anniversary party. One tall man who'd been the groom at an outdoor wedding where she'd dressed all the pews with lavender bouquets. A few were volunteer firemen. She'd seen them at the Fourth of July parade. And Jake Longbow, who'd welcomed her when she used to drive out to the Double K to pick up Amalah for their days out. He'd always hollered, "Where you ladies off to?" and they'd name some wild place like the beauty parlor and then ask him to come along.

Jake Longbow had aged since she'd last seen him at Amalah's funeral. Twelve years had passed since she lost her best friend. A lot more than Jake Longbow's face had changed over those years.

He gave her a sad smile. "Quinn?" he said slowly, as if not sure she'd know him.

"Yes, Jake. How is he?" When he didn't answer, she added, "How is Staten?"

Jake answered straight out, then. No sugarcoating, no lies. "He's in surgery right now. They're taking a bullet out of his shoulder. That's all we know. The emergency room nurse said once he's cleared from the recovery room they'll bring him up here, but since then nobody's told us nothing." Worry dripped from every word.

She nodded. "Is it all right if I wait with you?"

Jake put his bony arm around her and directed her to a row of chairs. "Sure, honey. You wait right next to me."

If anyone thought it strange that a woman living on the opposite side of Crossroads on a lavender farm would be worried about the owner of a huge ranch miles away, they didn't comment.

After a few minutes, a tall, thin kid of about seventeen sat down beside her. The blood on his shirt had dried, leaving Quinn to guess that it wasn't his blood.

If the blood wasn't his, then she knew without asking that it had to be Staten's.

"I was with him when he was shot," the boy whispered. "He asked me to call you and say he'd be late."

She smiled. "I was about to start cooking spaghetti. I'd just moved inside when I noticed you'd called." Even as she said the words she thought how crazy they sounded. Staten was in danger, and she was talking about her plans for dinner.

"I'm Lucas Reyes. I remembered you from a research paper Lauren Brigman did last year. Your farm looks like it should be in a magazine. It's so beautiful in the spring."

"Lauren's a friend of yours?" Quinn was only half following the conversation. Her eyes never left the door to the right.

"Yeah."

"Are you going to her birthday party next week?"

The kid shook his head. "I have to be at freshman orientation that day here in Lubbock. You know, they'll show all upcoming freshmen the campus and probably tell us all about college life. I doubt I'll make it back to town in time for the party."

"So, you're going to Texas Tech." She smiled. Everyone who grew up in Crossroads dreamed of getting away to school or a big city, but in truth most stayed and started families. They farmed, or ranched, or worked for one of the oil companies. Those who did break free often returned to retire. Funny how the very place you can't wait to leave is, in the end, the only place you want to go back to.

Quinn tried to think of something to do besides storming the double doors and making a fool of herself. She wanted to ask Lucas what had happened, but she wasn't sure she could bear to hear the details. If it was bad, and it must have been, she might start crying in front of all Staten's men. She had a feeling he wouldn't like that.

She'd wait. She'd ask Staten as soon as she saw him. As soon as he was out of surgery, as soon as the doors no longer barred her way.

Glancing at Lucas, she asked, "What are you getting Lauren for her birthday?" She had to think of something to say. The men around her were pacing, talking about working night shifts, talking about getting back to the ranch. They were no longer just cowhands. They were guards, soldiers in a war.

One man suggested they do what cattlemen did a hundred years ago during the Remington Blockade. One man, one rifle, one mile. If trouble rode your way, you fired, and all the others came running after they relayed the shot. It had stopped diseased cattle from climbing the caprock a hundred years ago and infecting West Texas ranches.

"I hadn't thought about a present," Lucas said, breaking into her dark thoughts. "I guess I should bring something if I do make it to the party. She'll be sixteen, and for a girl that's a big deal, or so my little sisters tell me. I turn eighteen three days after her birthday, and my folks are buying me a saddle. I'll probably be working every break I get from college, so a good saddle will come in handy. Somehow I don't think that's something a girl would want."

Quinn realized Lucas was doing exactly what she was, trying to keep his mind off what was happening beyond the double doors.

The elevator doors opened, and a mob of men in suits rushed out. Among them was a tall man, looking like an older version of Staten. Quinn recognized Samuel Kirkland, even though she hadn't seen him since she'd been maid-of-honor at Amalah and Staten's wedding. Staten's father had made an appearance that day at the last minute as if the whole affair was about him. A senator from a small town is everyone's friend. When he'd been working the crowd, the bride and groom had seemed nothing more than props. People had stood in the receiving line not to congratulate the young couple, but to shake hands with a senator.

Quinn remembered hearing that Samuel and his second wife stayed the night at the ranch so they could do a photo shoot the next morning. Staten once said that Samuel's third wife looked just like the second so they wouldn't have to redo the photos.

Quinn shook her head. Funny she should think of something

so meaningless at a time like this. Thoughts kept drifting in her mind like snapshots in a mixed-up album. Staten had stood behind her for the class picture in the third grade. He'd helped her with her science project in middle school. When her parents died, he'd dropped everything and managed her farm until she could sort through all the paperwork. He'd always been there. She wasn't just the friend of his wife. Quinn was his friend, too.

He'd talked to her about his dad liking to be *from* the area. When she'd mentioned it to Amalah, she'd said she'd never heard him talk about his dad much. But he'd talked to Quinn.

She knew that Staten still went to Dallas when his dad was back from Washington. But when Samuel came home to see Staten, his father snuck in and out and never stayed overnight at the ranch. His fourth wife said she didn't like the bugs and the wind at the Double K. She claimed the smell of cows made her gag.

Somehow, over the years, Samuel Kirkland's image had outgrown the man. Staten had once laughed and said his many stepmothers married a senator but had to sleep with his dad.

She watched Samuel Kirkland now, still playing to the small crowd of yes-men and reporters.

Jake Longbow rose and went to the senator, filling him in on what little he knew. The suits on either side of Staten's father were all on their cell phones.

"You have a cell?" she asked Lucas. "Your parents might be worried."

"Nope. I borrowed my cousin's office phone to call you. She works down on the first floor." He was silent for a minute before smiling. "I doubt my parents even noticed I wasn't there for supper. My dad always figures if I'm working late at the Double K, someone will make sure I get a meal."

Jake came back to Quinn, looking as if he'd been trying to communicate with a squirrel. "The senator is gettin' ahold of the hospital administrator so he can find out what's goin' on.

All he found out was that it'll probably be another hour or more before we know anything."

Quinn watched the room. Cowboys on one side, suits on the other. She knew it would just be a matter of time before someone asked her what she was doing there. The only woman in a room of headstrong men.

"Lucas, would you do me a favor?"

"Of course," he answered. "Anything."

"Come with me downstairs to get something to eat."

The kid stood and offered his arm. "I'd be honored."

With few people noticing, they slipped out the stairway door and walked down two flights of stairs to a small cafeteria. She bought a pizza with the works and French fries on the side. Then, when he hesitated, she ordered him the same and insisted on paying for his.

Half an hour later he laughed, claiming he'd never known such a slender woman could eat so much. "My mom never sits down for a meal. She just nibbles while she cooks, and chases kids, and cleans up. She's round as a butterball. Maybe if I got her to sit down and eat she'd lose weight."

Quinn smiled. "Does her weight matter to you?"

"Not a bit," he answered. "She's huggable size."

The love for his family was obvious. Quinn liked the idea of raising a child who would love her like that.

There was something about the young man that set her at ease. Maybe because she guessed he was one of the shy people in a world of talkers, and she knew he was making a true effort to help her relax.

When they went back to the waiting room, nothing had changed. Still cowboys on one side pacing and suits on the other playing with their cell phones.

Jake limped over to tell them that Staten was doing fine in recovery but no other news. A nurse had let the senator go in for only a moment to see his son. The doctor was with the senator, probably filling him in on the surgery.

Quinn sat in the back by the windows. If she could have managed to be invisible, she would have been. She didn't want to be just waiting, and she couldn't leave.

When Samuel Kirkland walked out of the double doors, he looked shaken. Cameras flashed but his usual bright smile was gone.

All were silent.

He stood in the center of the room and cleared his throat. "Thank you all for coming," Samuel said as if they'd all just dropped by. "My son and I want to thank you for your concern and prayers. He'll be out of recovery in a few minutes. Wants to see all his men, but I'm not sure he doesn't need rest more."

One of the cowhands faced Senator Kirkland, but it was the foreman who spoke. "We all understand how you feel, sir, and we'll keep our visit short, but if Staten wants to see us, we're going in." He hesitated a moment before continuing, "We've got trouble at the Double K, and unless you're planning to take over, we need to be getting our orders from him."

All the cowboys nodded and reached for their hats. One by one the worn Stetsons and Resistols disappeared off the floor, and the low sound of spurs shifting circled through the room as the cowboys moved toward the double doors.

Quinn didn't miss the shocked look on the suits' faces. They were all yes-men who followed whatever the senator said. For a moment Quinn realized she was looking at two different kinds of men, and not one of them would trade sides if they had the chance.

"I would take over," the senator announced, "only, now I know my son is going to be all right, I have urgent business to take care of in Washington. I'm sure he has plenty of help running the ranch. My place is helping to run the country." He straightened to his picture-perfect posture for the cameras.

The cowboys weren't listening; they were disappearing one by one behind the swinging doors.

Quinn looked at Lucas. "I don't want to go in with the others, but I'm not staying here with that man. Could you come down to the cafeteria and get me when everyone's gone?"

"Of course," he answered. "Mr. Kirkland will want to see you. When he told me to call you, it was an order, not a request. I'm guessing he'd rather have seen your face when he woke up from surgery than his father's."

Quinn looked back at the senator. He was preparing to talk to the reporters who'd gotten an anonymous tip that Senator Kirkland was in town on a family emergency. "Staten hates the press. He told me that even when we were kids."

Lucas laughed. "I know he must hate reporters. The first time I was stringing wire for him he told me if I ran out of posts, just hammer in any reporter that stepped on the property."

Quinn smiled and kissed the kid on the check. She could see that he respected his boss, and if he'd been the one Staten told about her, then the feeling went both ways.

Half an hour later Quinn walked into Staten's hospital room. She'd never expected to see him like this. Some people just seemed strong enough to face any storm.

Lucas stood next to the bed. He looked up and saw Quinn at the door. "Miss O'Grady is here, Mr. Kirkland."

Staten's low voice answered, "Thanks for taking care of my lady, kid. I owe you one."

"Anytime, sir." He nodded once to Quinn and picked up his hat. "I'll be outside the door for a few minutes making sure you're not disturbed."

Quinn slowly moved closer to the bed.

Staten's eyes were closed and a bandage wrapped around his chest and shoulder. His left arm was tied into the bandage so he couldn't move it.

She laid her hand over his heart and kissed him gently.

His eyes slowly opened. "I was hoping that was you and not the nurse." His right hand covered hers. "When I was shot, all I could think about was making things right with you, Quinn. I didn't mean what I said, and if I have to apologize every day for the rest of my life, I will. You just got to talk to me. Let me be part of your life. However you want it to be. I'll—"

"You're forgiven, Staten. You don't have to keep apologizing. I figured out what you must have thought when you saw Dan over at my place fixing my tractor. I did a favor for his daughter, and he insisted on paying me back. We're friends, that's all."

She smiled down at him and realized sometime in her forgiveness speech he'd fallen asleep. Maybe all he needed to hear was that he was forgiven.

"I love you, Staten. I think I have all my life." She whispered her words to her sleeping man, knowing that she might never say them when he was awake. "The nurse says you'll be out for the rest of the night, but if you don't mind, I think I'll sit with you awhile."

An hour later she was almost asleep when she heard him whisper her name. She moved to the side of his bed and brushed her fingers along his jawline.

"Quinn," he said without opening his eyes. "Don't give up on me."

"I'm right here, Staten." It wasn't a promise, but a fact. She'd been close to him always, even when he had no idea she was there.

CHAPTER TWENTY-TWO

Yancy

Yancy Grey realized something was different the moment he walked into Dorothy's Café. First, most of the tables were full, and it was supposed to be the dead time between lunch and dinner. Second, if he didn't know better, it looked like someone had called a town meeting. Businessmen, farmers, shop owners and cowboys were packing the place like it was Sunday morning after a wild Saturday night, and Dorothy had the only coffee in town.

One look and Yancy started backing away. If there was trouble boiling, he was usually the one it spilled over on. In life's lineup he guessed he was the only one with a Pick Me sign on his forehead, so he'd better be moving on.

"I saved you a place at the counter." Sissy grabbed his arm. "You won't want to miss this."

Yancy thought of screaming that he really, really *did* want to miss this, but by the time he pulled free of the round little waitress, he was halfway across the room.

Looking over the crowd, he saw Cap and Leo right in the

middle of the mob. "We got to do something," Cap demanded, slamming his fist on the table so hard spoons jumped.

A man with a badge, the sheriff Yancy had avoided every time he'd seen him, held up his hand as if blocking Cap's suggestion. "This happened outside the city limits. It's a county problem. I've already called in backup, and a Texas Ranger is sitting up in my office as we speak. A man's been hurt. We'll get to the bottom of this."

One cowboy in the back yelled, "Your ranger is a brand inspector, Sheriff Brigman. We're not talking about a cow being shot."

The sheriff corrected. "He's a ranger first. We think Staten Kirkland walked into a crime scene last night. He was shot because he was at the wrong place at the wrong time."

"Crime scene, hell, he was walking across his own land," an old cowboy yelled before spitting a brown stream of tobacco into a cup.

"That better be a paper cup, Jake Longbow, or I swear there's about to be another crime scene right in my café," Dorothy shouted from the pass-through.

"It was, honey-pie," Jake yelled back, not seeming to care that half the town was listening.

Several men fought down laughter. Jake Longbow had been courting Dorothy longer than most of the men in the room had been alive.

"What's going on?" Yancy whispered to Sissy.

"A big-time rancher was shot last night. You've met him, Mrs. Kirkland's grandson? Word is there's not one clue. Could have been drunk hunters, but they'd have to be real drunk to mistake a man like Staten Kirkland for a deer."

The sheriff stood on a chair. "All right, everyone, calm down. I called you all here to help. Someone was on the Double K Ranch last night, and the odds are somebody saw something. We're asking those who can to help us walk over the section of land. We might just get lucky and find a shell casing or something."

"This is starting to sound like an episode of *CSI*." Sissy giggled. "Only I don't think they have a ranch unit. Most folks in America probably think crime only happens in big cities like on TV."

Yancy tried to listen to what was going on, instead of to Sissy, but he smiled at her, so she wouldn't know he was doing his best to ignore her.

Everyone, including Leo and Cap, was willing to go out and help. Yancy didn't want any part of this. Too recently he'd lived on the wrong side of the law and this didn't feel right, but if he didn't volunteer, someone might ask why. He had to think. He had to do what a normal man would do, even if the ex-con jitters were threatening to take over.

"Do we go on horseback?" Jake Longbow asked. "I can have a dozen mounts saddled and ready at the Double K's headquarters in no time."

"No. It's a nice day. We walk. We'll need a few riders to move back and forth, but any man riding needs to stick to the road as much as possible so he doesn't contaminate evidence." Brigman pointed to another man with a badge. "Load up two or three evidence kits we can strap to saddles." He turned to the rest of the men. "We meet at the cattle guard coming on to his ranch from the north in two hours." The sheriff climbed down and began talking to Cap and Leo.

"Evidence kits," Sissy whispered. "We're into big-time crime now."

"Sounds like it," Yancy admitted. The urge to run was strong, but he was too far from the door, and he didn't want to look like a coward.

By the time Yancy worked his way over to Cap and Leo, both were busy taking down names.

"Sheriff left us in charge of keeping up with who goes onto

the land. What time they walk on or off. It's an important job, or he wouldn't have taken us out of the field," Cap said after he noticed Yancy standing beside him. "It's a big responsibility, but we can handle it. Leo and me will have to stay at the gate in my car to make sure we don't miss anyone."

"Mind if I ride out and lend a hand with the walking?" Yancy asked, feeling like a fish offering to cut bait.

Mrs. Kirkland's grandson was always polite to him when he stopped by. Even took the time to tell Yancy he thought he was doing a great job around the place. If Yancy was going to step into being normal, now seemed a good place to start.

"No, we don't mind. The sheriff needs all the able-bodied men we can find." Leo shook his head. "This isn't going to be an easy case to crack. Did I tell you that I once thought of being a forensic investigator? I could have done it, too. Read all about blood spatters and beetles aging in dead bodies. They say the average criminal makes a dozen mistakes while he's commit-ting a crime. All we need to find is one."

Yancy was starting to consider this an educational field trip. If he failed at this normal stuff and went back to a life of crime, he'd know what not to leave behind.

Cap interrupted Leo. "Tell us about it in the car. We need to get up there." He turned and yelled, "Dorothy, load us up a couple of thermoses and some fried pies if you got them."

"Will do." She laughed. "This is just like the days when you were captain of the grass-fire division over at the fire de-partment. You always ordered me around when an emergency came."

As most of the men moved out, a lanky cowboy limped to the counter. "You better not be ordering my Dorothy around, Cap."

Dorothy stepped through the swinging kitchen door with three thermoses. "Oh, hush, Jake, this is official ordering and nothing more." She set two containers in front of Cap and handed one to Jake Longbow. "This one's for you, Jake. Bring it back when all this police business is over."

Jake grinned. "It might be late, sweetie-pie."

"I'll be up waiting." She turned to the others. "You all be careful."

All three men nodded and headed out.

Yancy left a dollar tip, even though he hadn't had time to order anything. There were half-empty cups of coffee everywhere and water glasses spilled across tables in the rush to get out. If Cap would have waited on him, Yancy might have stayed to help Sissy clean up, but the old guys were ready to march.

Two hours later a slow-moving army began to walk across the far pasture of the Double K. The day was warm, but the earth didn't lend itself to straight lines. Mesquite trees, rock formations and ravines where water flowed every time it rained were all in the way. Every man walked the mile from fence to fence, with a stick in his hand and his eyes alert and focused on the ground. No one knew exactly what they were looking for. The sheriff just said they'd know it when they saw it.

Yancy saw more piles of manure than anything else. Weeds and cactus brushed against his jeans. The warm sunshine brought out a few spiders and bugs he'd never seen before, but he didn't find anything that looked like it didn't belong to nature.

It took him over an hour to walk the first mile, and then he had to move fifty feet over, turn around and walk back. Only now, the sun was in his eyes and he couldn't see the next step, much less any evidence. He almost tumbled to the bottom of a dry creek bed, and when he managed to climb out, he was relieved to find a stretch of flat, treeless pasture.

Three quarters of the way back to the road where Cap's boat of a car was parked, Yancy noticed something shiny next to a cluster of rocks about a foot high. Beyond the rocks there was a ridge where someone hiding out would have a clear view of the road—a clear shot at a man standing in the pasture below.

Having been told to call out and not touch anything unusual, he tried to brush what looked like a spent shell an inch away from the rock.

It rolled the wrong direction, and the stick was too thick to fit beneath the rock. He didn't want to shout if it was nothing. The sheriff or the ranger would simply rush over and probably yell at him for wasting their time.

Leaning down, Yancy slipped his hand into the slice of an opening. Once under the rock, he could wiggle his fingers, so the opening must widen.

He pushed deeper, digging dirt away until his hand was almost completely under the rock. He'd just brush whatever the shiny metal had been out into the sun. He wouldn't pick it up. As soon as he saw it might be a clue, he'd yell.

Pain suddenly shot up his arm, and Yancy jerked his hand away as he yelped in panic and fear.

The men on either side of him came running, asking questions.

"I thought I saw a spent shell, but it rolled under the rock." Yancy stared at blood dripping from his first finger. "When I reached to get it, something bit me."

"We'll get that shell out of the hole," a cowboy smart enough to be wearing gloves said as he slapped Yancy on the back. "You go over to Cap's car. I'm betting he'll have a first-aid kit. Bites are nothing to mess around with."

Yancy did as he was told. All the way to the car, he stared at his finger, dripping blood like the leaky pipe in Mrs. Kirkland's sink. It didn't really hurt that badly, but the thought that something bit him freaked him out. Mosquitos or flies were one thing, but something big enough to take a hunk out of him was serious.

Five minutes later, when he reached the car, Leo and Cap took over as if they were handling a major emergency.

Just as he settled onto the fender of the car to wait for them to find the first-aid kit, a tiny little Volkswagen pulled up. Ellie Emerson, Cap's niece, jumped out, looking all serious in her almost-professional nurse manner.

"Glad you're here, Ellie," Cap yelled from the back of his car where he and Leo were tossing things out while they searched. "We got us an emergency here."

With her cape flying, she rushed to Yancy.

He tried to smile but must have looked brain-damaged, because she held his chin and stared into his eyes. "Where's he hurt?" she asked as if he wasn't conscious. "Any sign of blurred vision or vomiting?"

Yancy thought about yelling back that his ears hurt, but Cap beat him to the answer. "Figure it out, Ellie. We're busy. I know the kit is in here somewhere."

Lifting his first finger, wrapped with Cap's questionably clean handkerchief, Yancy gave her a hint. "Something bit me."

"Spider, snake, prairie dog?"

"I don't know."

Examining the wound from every angle, she gave her diagnosis. "If it's a snake, we need to get you into the clinic, but this doesn't look like a snake bite."

"You seen a lot of snake bites?" He swallowed hard and fought to keep his eyes from crossing.

She met his gaze. "Two. Both were puncture wounds about half an inch apart. This looks like something was planning to have you for lunch."

"Then you're the expert. I was simply on the menu."

Ellie managed a half smile as if she wasn't sure if he was kidding or not. "If it's a spider, you'll be dead before we can make it to the hospital."

Now he gave a half smile, having no idea if she was joking.

The wind whipped up, circling her cape around her plump little body. "Get in the backseat of this car. We don't want any dust in the wound." She pushed on his shoulder, almost knocking him off the fender. "If you feel faint, let me know. If you pass out, we'll have real trouble getting your long body inside."

He followed orders, thinking she had the worst bedside manner he'd ever seen. But she sure did smell good.

She climbed into the other side with her bag in one hand and a first-aid kit probably older than Yancy in the other.

There wasn't much room in the backseat. She had to put her bag behind her to get close enough to him to work. "I can clean the wound." She captured his forearm between her elbow and her breast as she began wiping the blood off his finger with a square of wet tissue she'd pulled from a sealed packet.

Yancy felt light-headed. Every time she breathed, something very soft pushed against his forearm. He leaned his head back and closed his eyes. He'd never told anyone in prison that he'd never touched a girl. They would have thought it a great joke. But, between age fifteen and twenty he'd been in and out of reform schools or on his own. The few girls in his world weren't the kind he wanted even if they'd been dumb enough to want him. So, when the guys talked about women, he'd played along, retelling stories he'd heard in other places.

"Are you all right?" Ellie pressed closer as she lifted one of his eyelids.

"I think I'm dying," he whispered.

"If a prairie dog bit you, you've probably got rabies. That could kill you if we don't get you to a doctor. I've heard rabies shots are no fun to take."

Cap leaned in the open window. "Give him some water and see if he starts foaming at the mouth."

The rusty voice of Jake Longbow came from somewhere behind Cap. "Looks like he stuck his hand in a prairie-dog hole. Dunk the wound in alcohol and tape it up. He'll be fine."

"But—" Ellie began.

"No buts. Prairie dogs don't carry rabies. Unless he starts running a fever, he's fine."

Cap bristled. "How do you know, Jake? You're not a doctor, and my Ellie is almost a nurse."

"I've been bit or stung by every kind of animal, insect and plant on this place. I finally just started biting them back."

Ellie grinned, and Yancy thought she looked pretty but he wasn't about to say anything. He had a feeling she was only slightly more friendly than the prairie dog.

Five minutes later with his finger professionally bandaged, he stepped from the car and almost collided with the sheriff.

"You Yancy Grey?" the lawman asked.

Yancy almost answered *Yes, boss* like he'd had to answer to the guards. "I am." He straightened and looked at the sheriff. After all, he was just a normal citizen, nothing more.

"Well, Yancy, you did a good job. Besides that mad prairie dog, we found a spent shell the trespassers may have left there last night. We also found several cigarette butts and a few footprints. You've just found us our first evidence."

"Glad I could be of service." Yancy said what he thought he should say. "Where can I help out now?"

The sheriff shook his head. "How about you call it a day? If Ellie can drive you back to town, the rest of us will finish up here."

Yancy thought that sounded good. A moment later, when Ellie told her uncle that she planned to check on Yancy every two hours to make sure he didn't develop a fever, he thought it sounded great.

Climbing into her little car, he tried to think of something to say as she drove back to town like a maniac. He hadn't driven, even illegally, in five years, but he had no doubt he could do better. At one point he started putting together his obituary. *Man survives wild animal bite only to be killed in car crash.*

He reached over and touched her arm.

"You feeling sick?" she asked without slowing. "All kinds of infections could set in. A few might even kill you."

He slid his fingers along her arm until he reached her fingers. "Would you mind if I held your hand?"

"Of course. Part of nursing is offering comfort."

He thought about asking if comfort extended to other body parts, but he decided he'd never get that lucky. After today he'd probably never get this close to her again.

Ellie insisted on walking him to his one-room place behind the office. "Now, you rest, and I'll check on you in a few hours."

He lay down and let her put a quilt Mrs. K had given him all the way up to his chin.

On one crazy impulse, he rose to his elbow and kissed her cheek, then backed away waiting for the blow.

To his surprise she finished tucking him in and walked away without saying a word.

From the two-inch opening in his door he heard Ellie tell the old folks that he was resting, but they should watch him closely.

"I fear he may be delirious," she said as if giving a medical opinion. Then in a lower tone he barely heard, she added, "And I think I like it."

CHAPTER TWENTY-THREE

Staten

Dawn still whispered along the horizon as Staten Kirkland stood staring out the window, dressed and ready to leave the hospital. He had about all he wanted of being poked and patted on. He had never been a man who gave or accepted comfort easily, and he didn't want it now.

"If Jake doesn't get here soon, I swear I'll start walking," he said more to his reflection in the glass than the nurse babysitting him.

The woman in green scrubs looked nervous. "We can't do that, Mr. Kirkland."

He thought of reminding her that there was no "we" in the room. She hadn't been shot, she didn't have a ranch to run, and he saw no point in talking to her.

"Like hell I can't." His boots echoed off the tiles. His spurs jingled slightly, a tiny reminder of who he was and what he needed to do. Staten was ready to go back to work. "I wasn't sick when I walked in here, and I'm not sick now." The girl was so thin he could probably blow her out of the way without much effort.

He hated the square room with all the stainless steel and thick glass. He hated the smell of the place. He hated the way things beeped and rang all day and night. He felt as though they'd stuffed his bear of a body into a rabbit cage.

Jake Longbow slipped around the door about the time Staten was thinking he'd simply pick up his parting gifts of a bedpan and small pink water pitcher and leave. Walking home might take days, but it would clear his head. He had a ranch to run and a woman he cared about who needed him, even if she didn't seem to know it. As soon as he figured out what the right thing to do was, he planned to tell Quinn. Problem was, she still didn't want to talk about the baby.

"About time you got here, Jake," Staten snapped when he saw the old ranch hand offering his lopsided grin to the nurse.

Jake didn't take offense. "Doctor said they'd release you about nine o'clock. I figured I'd better get here before seven."

"You were right. I've been waiting since five."

Before Staten could make his escape, the doctor appeared in the doorway. He was young, probably an intern, but he didn't look intimidated. He simply smiled. "Morning, Mr. Kirkland. I figured you'd better be my first patient today. I got a dad who, I swear, could be your twin."

"Does he ranch?"

"No, he runs a law office, but you two would get along." The doctor handed him a packet of papers. "I won't keep you. Here are your discharge forms and instructions on what you can and can't do. That shoulder has to heal, and you can't hurry it no matter how much you try. Only remove that sling to take a shower, and then keep your arm as still as you can. When you come back in two weeks, we'll evaluate your progress."

"I don't need to come back. I'll be well by then," Staten said. "The nurse showed me how to put the sling on. How about I wear it until I don't need it anymore?"

"All right." The doctor didn't argue, obviously seeing any

discussion would be pointless. "Try to stay out of the way of any bullets. You were voted the least likely patient we'd ever want to see again."

"Is he being funny, boss?" Jake asked.

Staten walked out the door. "Probably not."

They stopped at the pharmacy and waited in line for pain pills Staten probably wouldn't take. Half an hour later, when they passed through Crossroads, Staten insisted on stopping at the sheriff's office.

Brigman's office was on the main road through town. There was no sign on the front, just a five-point star with a circle around it carved into the door. County offices were downstairs and a courtroom on the second floor.

A reception area in front split off into four offices. One for the sheriff, one reserved for Texas Rangers, one for the coroner and the last one for the justice of the peace. His job must be very peaceful, because no one in town had seen him for months. A receptionist, long past retirement age, was the guard at the gate. She looked old enough to have dated Davy Crockett when he rode into Texas heading for the Alamo.

"Morning," Staten said with a nod. "Sheriff in?"

The woman pointed them to the only open door, then giggled as Jake winked at her.

Jake pointed one finger at the coffeepot. "Mind if I have a cup, Pearly?"

"Not at all," she answered. "I'll make a fresh pot in case you stay around."

Staten tried not to notice the exchange between the two. They might be just being polite, but he swore an undercurrent was weaving through the conversation, and the receptionist was developing bedroom eyes behind her bifocals. He didn't want to know what was going on between the two. In his day, Jake liked to brag that he'd shoved his boots under many a bed and left every lady smiling.

Dan Brigman stood when Staten appeared at his door. The sheriff motioned him over to a table near the window. The entire six-foot surface was covered with maps.

Brigman looked tired, and Staten couldn't help wondering if he'd slept the past two nights. If the bullet that hit Staten had been two inches over, Brigman might be dealing with a murder. It didn't sit well with Staten that he'd be the victim.

"Fill me in, Sheriff." Staten fought from cradling his left arm with his right. There was no use wasting time with small talk. Both men knew why he was there.

With Jake and Staten leaning over a county map, Dan Brigman explained every fact they knew about what had happened the night Staten had been shot. "I have two witnesses who saw an old one-ton truck on the road between your back gate and the county line, but my men watching the main road since your bull got hit said no truck passed them. Since one of the witnesses was sober, I think we'll have to list the sighting as a clue. Only problem is, do you have any idea how many one-ton trucks are registered in this county?"

"There are a few back roads that turn off before the spot where you posted your men. Anyone traveling those would have to know where he was going or they'd be lost for hours driving from one water tank to another."

"Some aren't even on this map," Brigman agreed and moved on. "The shell that Yancy Grey found on your land is pretty common, probably used in half the rifles around. But, if we find the weapon that shot you, we can send it in for testing."

Jake leaned back to spit in his empty coffee cup. "Weapon didn't shoot him, Sheriff, a man did."

The sheriff nodded at Jake and added, "Since you said you heard several shots earlier, we may find where he was standing when he wounded the deer. I'm pretty sure Yancy found the spot where he stood to fire at you. If the same man shot both you and the deer? Probably not, since the slugs we dug out of the deer didn't match the one the doc dug out of you, Staten. There could have been two hunters out there. One looking for game and the other looking for you."

"Hold up a minute. We're talking about a pasture, not the Two Step Bar over in Bailee. What are the chances there would be two men out there at the same time?" Jake thought for a moment, then added, "Or maybe it was a woman firing at you, Staten. You pissed off any stepmothers lately?"

"No," Staten answered. "Me and the latest one gave up talking about two years ago. She told me she was going to have some work done, and I told her to be sure and record it because I'd bet a hundred dollar bill that she's never seen work in her life."

The sheriff choked down a laugh and continued with every detail they'd found that might be a clue. The cigarette butts, the footprints made with shoes, not boots. "From the looks of it, one man climbed out of his car or small truck and waited until you moved out of the shadows, after the truck you saw passed by. He must have guessed you'd want to tail the truck.

"We think the car pulled off the road behind trees, and the shooter found a place where he had cover from three sides. After the shot, he turned around and left through the north gate. That might be why you or Lucas didn't see another vehicle."

Staten didn't like the idea that the shooting had been premeditated. He'd rather have thought it was simply an accident.

He paid attention to every detail as the sheriff continued. "The tracks we found near the spent shell were not that of a truck with any weight. Which explains the two engines you heard. One driving past you, one turning off waiting for you to step out so he could get a clear shot."

"So, you don't think it was just bad luck." Staten took the news cold, without feeling. "If someone was waiting, willing to make a long shot, then the odds were good he knew what he was doing. You think they were out to shoot me."

"You, or one of your men." Brigman scratched his head. "It

doesn't make sense. Rustlers don't go after trouble. They want to sneak in and out."

Staten had heard enough. He'd gladly face trouble head-on, but he'd have to think about this. He had no idea if the shot was meant for him, or for anyone who'd driven out to check on the shots fired earlier. All he knew was that at least two people were on his ranch who didn't belong, and apparently both were armed.

By the time Jake got him home, Staten was exhausted and would have even gone back to the hospital to sleep.

He wasn't surprised when Quinn met him at his own front door. She hadn't been over to his place in years, but he knew she'd want to make sure he was all right. In his experience women were like that, even with men they were mad at.

His lady might be quiet and shy, but she had a stubbornness about her that sometimes made him smile.

Jake saw him to the front door and walked away, complaining he should have left his boss in town. "If he keeps complaining, Quinn, just hit him in the head. He's already brain damaged, so I don't see that it would do any harm."

Staten put his good arm over Quinn's shoulders and leaned on her just a bit as she walked him to the couch in his big office. She felt so good against him, he knew she'd be the only medicine he'd ever need.

"I'm guessing you're not going to let me put you to bed." She laughed.

"Not unless you're going with me," he answered.

"But you will rest."

"I will." When he leaned against the pillows she'd already stacked, he relaxed for the first time since he'd been shot. "You going to be here when I wake up?"

She kissed him. "It'll take me all day to pick this place up. Your house is so dark and closed up. Cave dwellers must have built it."

He nodded. "Stepmother number two. She hated the ranch and didn't want a single view interrupting her décor." He didn't

add that when Amalah died, he and Randall had taken everything upstairs that they decided they no longer needed, and then
they'd lived in the two downstairs bedrooms, the office and the
kitchen. When papers and supplies piled up, Staten didn't care.
At least he knew where everything was.

After his son died, he stripped away all that had made the
house a home. Somehow he wanted a shell to live in. A cell. A
hole, where feelings would never find him again.

Five years later, his office was stacked with paperwork. He
quit using the cabinets in the kitchen and started just stacking food on the counter. Saved time. He had no idea what was
upstairs, where Randall's things had been moved. He rarely
climbed the stairs to the four bedrooms on the second floor.

The space that had been Randall's bedroom downstairs was
completely bare. He'd go in there now and then and stand thinking that the room reflected his soul, barren and scraped clean.

Only now, when he was weak and exhausted, Quinn had
stepped into his colorless world.

"Do whatever you want, Quinn, just be here when I wake
up," he whispered, half-asleep. He didn't care if she took a match
to the big house. It was no longer a home.

Eight hours later, he woke to the smell of heaven. Quinn had
cooked. She was still in his house. He sat up, one pain at a time,
and pulled her against him as soon as she came close.

"Feed me," he whispered after he kissed her.

She laughed and helped him to the kitchen table. He was on
his third bowl of stew when he noticed that he could see the
kitchen counters.

"You cleaned up. You weren't kidding."

"Do you mind?"

"Nope."

She handed him a pill, and he took it without arguing. Then,
she walked him to the bedroom and undressed him for a change.

"Stay with me," he asked, wanting her close.

"I can't, but I'll come back tomorrow. When I drive out, I'll tell Jake to send one of the guys over to sleep on the couch in case you need something in the night."

"I won't," Staten said. He thought of arguing about what difference did it make if they slept together here or at her place. But he knew that it did matter to her.

She left before he thought of any words to say. They needed to talk about the change coming, but she wasn't ready yet. He knew he'd have to respect her choices or he'd lose her completely.

In the silent house he thought he should have told her that she'd been his every thought when he was on his way to the hospital.

They both seemed to be fighting for their world, their relationship to remain the same, but it couldn't, it wouldn't.

In less than two weeks Lloyd deBellome would be in town for the concert. She had to make up her mind if she was going to go to the fund-raiser and possibly face him, or run and avoid him. Either way, Staten planned to be by her side.

Thanks to Miss Abernathy's visit at the hospital, he knew more than he ever wanted to know about the master pianist. Lloyd was starting a world tour beginning in Dallas next week and covering the globe. He had agreed to play at Crossroads free, only charging expenses. Of course, this concert would bring him publicity and goodwill for his tour, but that wasn't the reason he agreed.

She quickly mentioned that the expenses included having his classic BMW shipped to Dallas from New York and a first-class plane ticket. But, after all, he needed his car so he could drive to Crossroads. Miss Abernathy explained that he loved the car and needed to drive it one last time before he left for Europe.

Staten didn't care what the guy did as long as he stayed out of Quinn's life.

If he bothered Quinn, he wouldn't have to worry about the tour. He'd be headed back to New York by ambulance.

CHAPTER TWENTY-FOUR

Lauren

"I'm sixteen," Lauren whispered to the mirror in her bedroom. "I'm finally sixteen."

The day was windy and still cloudy, but she didn't care. Tonight was her party. A birthday party on the beach, or it would be if she could call the mud around the lake a beach. Her father had borrowed picnic tables from the Baptist church and ordered a big cake. He'd dug out a pit six inches deep and three feet around and banked it with rocks for a big bonfire.

He'd even offered to decorate the tables, but she decided she'd do that herself. In two hours people would start arriving. It wouldn't be a huge party like Reid Collins had last month, but that didn't matter. Her dad planned to let everyone roast their own hot dog and she'd made sure she'd bought all the toppings.

She'd invited several adults, too, so, hopefully, her father would talk to them and not interrogate her friends. She had simply made a list of all the people who weren't criminals that her father had talked about in the past few months. Lauren wanted him to have a good time, as well.

Her pop sat on the deck blowing up balloons when the door-bell rang. Lauren squealed. She wasn't dressed yet in her new jeans and jacket. The kitchen had no decorations, and the fire wouldn't be started for another hour.

The bell sounded again, and she had no choice but to open the front door.

There, in a business suit, was her mother, looking totally out of place.

"Hello, sweetie," she squealed as if she were the grand prize of the night. "I thought I'd surprise you for your birthday."

Lauren forced a smile. In truth she was surprised Margaret remembered her birthday. Usually a card arrived sometime in March, but never close to the day. "Come on in," she managed, then added, "Please, don't fight with Pop today."

Her mother had the nerve to look hurt. "I'm not here to fight. I'm here to celebrate my baby girl growing up."

Tears welled in Lauren's eyes. All year she'd thought about this day. If her friends saw them fighting, they'd probably feel sorry for her or make fun of her parents. Just this one night she wanted the world to revolve around her.

Margaret looked worried. "I shouldn't have come. This was a bad idea. Just let me get your gift out of the car and I'll go."

Now Mom was making her feel bad. Lauren shouldn't have let her feelings show. She should have just let Mom come in and ruin her party.

Before Lauren could think of what to do, her father appeared and caught up with his ex-wife halfway to her car. "Stop making this all about you, Margaret. We'll be glad to have your help around here. She's your daughter. You should be here. But, Lauren's right, no fighting today. Whatever you've decided I'm doing wrong this month will just have to wait until the night is over."

Margaret opened her mouth to argue, then snapped it closed.

Lauren watched in shock as Margaret released her trunk and

got out a small box and her purse. Pop pulled out a suitcase and said, "Your room's still ready. It may be a little dusty."

"That's fine." Margaret lifted her chin. "I'm not here to be any trouble. I'm not a guest, Dan, I'm here to help with the party."

Pop walked past Lauren and whispered, "That'll be the day. Trouble's walking in, and I'm dumb enough to carry her suitcase."

Lauren grinned. Her father usually let Margaret walk all over him, but today he'd refused to let her do the same to his daughter. She was proud of him for standing up, and she was also proud of Margaret for bending just a little. Maybe the party wouldn't be so bad with both of them here.

An hour later she had to escape. Her parents were trying to kill each other with kindness. Margaret offered to help him do everything, and he praised her for her efforts, though decorating was not her mother's strong suit. Together her parents had managed to make the picnic tables outside look like they'd been taken hostage by clowns.

Lauren walked up the beach toward Tim's house. She wasn't surprised to see him sitting on the deck, his nose in a book. The joker had become a bookworm since he'd broken his leg.

"You coming to my party?" she called.

"Of course. Can't wait. You're my only social life."

She climbed the steps and leaned against the deck railing. "It's no big deal. Just a birthday party. My dad had Dorothy make the cake in the shape of Cookie Monster because I used to love him when I was four. When my mother saw it she freaked out and thought candles would help make it more sixteenth birthday-looking. They didn't help. Other than that, the food will be good."

"I don't care about the cake as long as we can eat it. Yours is the first party I've been to this year," he said.

"Why didn't you go to Reid's last month? Everyone was there."

He shrugged. "I don't know. Reid and I stopped hanging out. Maybe I'm not as funny as I was before the accident. He hasn't dropped by to show off his new car. Guess he's afraid to drive down the hill."

"You're still my friend, Tim."

"Thanks. To tell the truth, I'm in no hurry to see him, either. I'd just as soon sit on the porch and read a book." He frowned at her. "Did you ever have the feeling that we grew up that night at the Gypsy House?"

"Yes," she admitted. "It's like I looked the same the next day, but inside I was different."

"Me, too."

"Promise you'll come tonight," she begged.

"I promise. Mom's driving me over." He looked up and stared at her.

"What?"

Tim seemed to struggle with his thoughts, then said, "Don't go out with Reid if he asks you. Promise me."

"Why?" She hadn't planned to, but it seemed odd of Tim to warn her.

"Just don't. If you mean it that I'm your friend, take my advice."

She smiled, making light of how serious he'd turned all at once. This wasn't the Tim she knew. "All right. I promise."

On the way home along the water's edge, Lauren wondered why Tim felt the need to warn her. Reid was so popular he wouldn't be seen with her anyway. Plus, if they did go out, she could handle him, football player and all. Being a sheriff's daughter had its advantages. She'd been trained.

The shadows had grown long, and she could see the twinkle lights come on at her place. Amazingly, Pop had gotten them up and working. They made the deck look like a fairyland.

She was sixteen. Sixteen, with her whole life in front of her.

There was magic in the air tonight. Like she was stepping into a new world, waking up as the cocoon began to crack open.

When she reached the bottom of the deck stairs, Lauren glanced up and saw something that froze her blood.

Her parents were just above her with their lips locked together. They weren't hugging. It looked like somehow their mouths had accidentally touched and stuck together, but their bodies were fighting the attraction.

This could mean nothing but trouble. Lauren whirled around and made it two steps before she slammed into someone.

"Reid!" she managed to say before he pulled her farther down the path, away from the lights.

"What are you so mad about?" he asked, laughing at her. "Your little party not going like you want it to?"

She could smell beer on his breath. "Reid, you've been drinking. Are you drunk?"

"I'm older then you, Lauren. I always will be, so stop talking to me like I'm a kid."

"You're not old enough to drink." She slapped his chest as if he needed waking up.

"What you going to do about it, birthday girl? Tell your daddy?"

Suddenly Lauren felt trapped. If she told Pop, all hell would break loose. Reid had to have driven here. He might not be falling-down drunk, but he was on his way. If he showed up at her party drunk, her father was bound to notice.

"You can't come to my party," she ordered, pushing Reid a few feet farther away from the deck.

"Why not? I brought a bottle to add to the lemonade. You won't even taste it, but you'll feel it. It'll make everyone happy."

"No!" She shoved again.

Reid caught her arm. "Forget the party, Lauren. Go for a ride with me. Just me and you."

"No," she answered, feeling suddenly sorry for him. "Why

do you keep asking, Reid? We're not alike. I'm not your type. After the disaster at the Gypsy House, I'm not even sure we're friends."

"Sure you are," Reid insisted as he grabbed her arms and tried to pull her close. "You know you've always been nuts about me." He leaned in to kiss her. "I'll prove it."

Lauren reacted just as Pop had trained her. She jerked her knee up, slamming Reid hard between his legs.

To her surprise, he crumbled.

While he gulped for breath, she said politely. "Thank you for coming to my party, Reid, but I think you'd better go."

She walked away, wishing she could tell her pop how great his lessons had worked. But she never would. She wasn't even mad at Reid. She knew he didn't really like her; he was simply wanting one more girl to join his fan club.

The thought crossed her mind that maybe the reason her parents didn't touch when they kissed was because one would likely hurt the other. It must be a kind of hell to be attracted to someone you hate.

As parties went, Lauren rated hers a B. Nothing bad happened. Everyone laughed and talked. Most of the popular kids didn't show up. Most of her friends did. Reid would have probably been disappointed to know that no one missed him.

Her mother gave her something she might use for once—a diary. Obviously Margaret had lost the argument to give Lauren her old car. All the other gifts were great. Staten Kirkland and Quinn O'Grady, surprisingly, arrived together and gave her a phone with a whole year's worth of usage free.

The rancher and Quinn didn't fit together, but somehow they seemed to be a couple. Lauren decided it must be a full moon or something because strange people seemed to be pairing up. Quinn and Staten. Her mother and Pop. Reid and—no wait a minute. That one was not happening. Not tonight. Not *any* night.

She worried that Pop might think she didn't need a phone, but he said he wished he'd thought of it. Then he listed a few rules. She knew he'd think of more later.

At ten, everyone waved goodbye. Her parents were talking as they did the dishes, so Lauren walked out along the beach. She was sixteen. She had expected to feel different today, but she felt pretty much the same.

Halfway between her house and the O'Grady's place, she noticed Lucas's old pickup parked on the lake road.

When she strode near, he climbed out of the cab. Even in the moonlight he looked different. The boots were still there, but tonight he wore a regular white shirt, black slacks and a red pullover sweater. For a moment, she thought, he looked older.

"I'm sorry I missed your party." He walked slowly toward her. "I just got back from Tech. It's like a whole other world there. In a few months I'll be stepping into this bubble where everything is different."

She laughed. "You sound excited."

"I am."

He took her hand, and they moved to the tailgate where they could sit and watch the night sky. "I wish I could have been here with you. Or better yet, you could have been there with me. The campus is beautiful, and you wouldn't believe the library. There is a bookstore right in the middle, and the place is so big I'll have to hop a bus to get from class to class."

"I wish I'd been there, too. The party was fun. Tim made everyone laugh for the first time since his accident. My folks got along for a change. Mr. Kirkland gave me a phone, and he barely knows me."

"Funny, he gave me one, too. Said it was for my birthday in three days, but since I was going to be on the road today, he wanted me to have it early."

They pulled their new phones out and clicked them together, then laughed.

Lucas flipped his open. "I haven't used it yet because I didn't have anyone I wanted to call, until now."

"You don't even know my number."

"Tell me," he said.

She ran through the numbers she'd just learned, then said, "Aren't you going to put my number in or at least write it down?"

"I got it," he said. "I won't forget."

The phone suddenly became her favorite gift. "When you leave, we can keep in touch."

"Sounds like a plan. You can tell me what's going on here, and I can tell you about college."

She bumped his shoulder. "You know for three days I'm only a year younger than you, so you'll have to stop treating me like a kid."

He put his arm around her. "Deal. You're no longer a kid." He hopped off the back of the truck and disappeared. Thirty seconds later he stood in front of her with one long-stem yellow rose. "I had to stop at three florists on the way back to find this. Happy birthday. No matter how old you get, *mi cielo*, for three days we'll only be a year apart."

"We're almost the same age." She'd looked up what he'd called her in Spanish and knew it meant *my sky*, but she was too shy to ask him to explain why he called her that.

Laughing, they walked back to her house. Just before they reached the lights, he leaned down and kissed her. Her first real kiss. Not a light touching of lips or a quick peck in greeting, but a long, curl her toes, real kiss. She wrapped her arms around his neck and leaned in, wishing this one kiss could last forever.

When he pulled away so he could see her, Lucas laughed. "You know, we can only do this for three days. After that, you'll be too young for me."

"Do it again," she whispered. "I don't want to forget."

He kissed her again, hugging her so tight she knew he felt as she did. Neither wanted these few minutes to end.

Finally, he pulled away, and without a word he disappeared into the night. If she wasn't still holding the rose, she might have believed she'd dreamed him.

They weren't dating, or falling in love, or promising to be best friends. In August he'd be in college, and she'd be a junior in high school, but they would talk. Mr. Kirkland had no idea what he had started.

Somehow thinking about the next few years didn't seem so bad. Whenever she was alone, she'd think of Lucas, and if he got too rushed at college, maybe he'd remember her and the way they watched the sky.

Lauren walked in the back door and smiled when she didn't hear her parents screaming at each other. The night had turned from good to great with one rose, and nothing, not even their fighting or Reid trying to make a pass or getting a Cookie Monster cake would change that.

"Did you have a good time, sweetie?" Margaret asked.

"I had a great time. It was the perfect party." She kissed them both on the cheek. "Oh, one thing, I've decided I'm going to Tech when I graduate, and I plan to graduate early, so start saving."

Pop looked shocked. He glanced at Margaret. "Man, they sure do grow up fast."

Lauren laughed. "Maybe you two should consider having another kid so you'll still have something to fight about."

To her surprise her pop looked like he was considering the idea. Then, Margaret jabbed him in the ribs with one of the forks for roasting hot dogs.

Lauren backed away as they both tried to out-yell each other on which thought her idea was the worst they'd ever heard.

They were still yelling when Lauren fell asleep.

CHAPTER TWENTY-FIVE

Yancy

The wind howled all Monday morning like a pack of wolves, holding back the spring. Yancy Grey usually liked working outside, but today he'd found one excuse after another to stay indoors.

After a breakfast of leftover donuts, Yancy tackled Miss Bees's to-do list. Like Miss Abernathy, Miss Bees had never married, but unlike Miss Abernathy, she didn't have a kind bone in her body. She'd taught physical education for forty years after playing semi-pro baseball right out of college. She had a wall of trophies and ribbons to prove it. From the looks of her place, she'd played baseball, golf and hockey. Worn sticks and bats and clubs occupied every corner, and she used them as walking canes. Their prominent display was probably her way of burglar-proofing the place.

She limped around her house, pointing with a golf club at every crack in her walls. Most only needed toothpaste stuck in the cracks, left to dry, and one brush of paint to complete the job. But she felt the need to instruct him, to tell him to be careful and inspect everything he did.

"Mind telling me why you're in a bad mood today, Miss Bees?" he finally asked.

"I'm not in a bad mood," she shouted as if he'd suddenly gone deaf. "You don't want to see me in a bad mood, believe me. I'm a woman who keeps her temper under control. I've only lost it a few times in my life and then only with good reason."

He believed her completely. If this was happy, Yancy wasn't sure he would live through mad.

As soon as he finished, he headed back to the office feeling like he needed to be vaccinated to make sure he didn't catch what she had.

The old folks must have heard the wind, too, because Leo was the only one to wander out to sit in the glass office in front of Yancy's rooms. When the mailman walked past, Leo started talking without looking up, like one of them chatty snowmen stores put out around Christmas that were movement activated.

"I've heard tell," Leo began, "that when the wind whines like this, death is riding in. The Apache have a legend about a dark spirit who walks the night in the space between winter and spring. He holds back the warm air for as long as he can. At first he's strong and not even the bravest of the brave can fight him and win, but eventually, he ages and can no longer stand against the changing seasons. When he finally turns his back and rides away, he'll take the breath of whoever stands near."

The few rusty red hairs on Leo's head seemed to stand on end. "So this might be a good day to stay inside, Yancy."

"I don't believe in Apache legends. Plus, you probably made that up, Mr. Leo. In the two months I've been here I've learned not to believe a word you say."

Leo smiled. "You're smart, young man. Only you might want to remember that even an honest man lies now and then, and a liar sometimes accidentally tells the truth."

Yancy just nodded, then decided to skip his usual lunch of soup and head over to Mr. Halls's place. With the wind whipping up dirt, he couldn't paint outside, but he could paint the old principal's living room. It had taken him two days just to move out all the books. Once the walls dried, they'd be putting them back, and no one would notice the paint job. But Mr. Halls wanted it done, so Yancy agreed.

He needed something to keep his mind off Ellie. Cap's niece hadn't been by but once all day, and the last time she'd checked on him, too many people had been around for them to say anything personal to each other, even if he could think of something personal to say.

She had checked his prairie dog bite and told him he didn't have to wear the bandage anymore. She hadn't even patted his hand or anything. That woman could be downright irritating when she was all professional-like.

Apparently, when he didn't develop rabies, she lost interest in him. If he wanted to keep a girl like her, he needed to come up with some symptoms.

By six that night his back ached from painting and moving books around. He went home planning to clean up and eat at the café. He was too tired to even open a can of soup.

He decided to stretch out on his bed and relax, only he fell asleep. Dreams of wild prairie dogs chasing him and howling like the wind outside finally woke him. It was almost nine, but Yancy didn't want to go back to sleep.

After pacing the dark glass office, he decided to take a walk. The wind had finally slowed, and it wasn't too cold. Yancy strode out of the side office door and stood in the shadows, thinking about Leo's legend. He'd never really had much he believed in, but he sure didn't believe a dark spirit rode the wind.

Slowly, wishing he'd brought a stick along or one of Miss Bees's bats, he moved to the side of the road. The gas station was still open, but not a single car was parked out front. When he finished his walk, Yancy thought he might go inside and buy one of the burritos. Nothing the gas station sold was worth eating, but it was fast, and this time of night they sometimes had two-for-one sales on the burritos.

As he moved in the shadows, he saw the truck he'd thought might belong to the con called Cowboy pass by. Yancy watched as it turned off the highway and circled around to the back of the gas station where a dozen or more trailer homes were.

The trailer park was blocked from view by a line of storage buildings. Yancy crossed the deserted street and moved behind the station.

It wasn't too hard to find where the truck had parked or the two cons he'd hated in prison. All he had to do was follow the cussing. From his vantage point between two dark mobile homes, he saw the men unloading something from the truck to the trunk of an old car. It looked big enough to be a side of beef or a body. Each claimed he was lifting the heaviest part.

Yancy had no idea what they were doing, but he'd bet it was something illegal. Freddie, the bald one, mentioned something about Arlo not doing his share of the work. Cowboy didn't argue about that but muttered that all this would be over by the end of the month, and he'd never have to look at him or Arlo again.

The wind kicked up, sending old bags and trash whirling through the lot. Yancy didn't think the dark spirit would get him, but he wasn't so sure that the two cons wouldn't track him down if they caught his scent. Somehow they were linked with the recent trouble at the ranches. He could feel it.

Retracing his steps, he noticed the café's open sign was still blinking. Hunger drove him toward the lights.

Several people were in the side room Dorothy had labeled Private Dining as if it were a fancy place that didn't get the same paper napkins the front part did.

When he tried the door it was unlocked, so he thought he'd see if he couldn't get a quick meal.

As soon as he was inside, Sissy stood up from the booth where she'd been sitting and welcomed him. "Dorothy's already shut down the grill, but I could make you a cold sandwich and chips if you're hungry, Yancy. Coffee is left over, but it's free."

"Sounds great." He wasn't particular. "Any kind of sandwich would be fine." He pointed to the back. "What's going on?"

"The chamber of commerce moved over here to eat while they talk about the details for the upcoming event. Ain't you heard? We got us a real big-time fund-raiser. They're talking about making thousands of dollars."

Yancy had heard Miss Abernathy talking about it. A famous pianist was coming to town for one night. She said folks from as far as Abilene and Lubbock would come to hear him. The old piano teacher had talked every one of the residents at Evening Shadows into buying at least one ticket as well as volunteering for the event.

Sissy handed him a coffee cup. "Have a seat with Ellie and I'll bring your plate." She waddled off to the kitchen rubbing her tummy as if it were a crystal ball hidden under her top.

He moved to the last of the booths. "You mind if I sit down?"

Ellie wasn't frowning at him, but she didn't look happy to see him. She seemed to be simply studying him, as though he was the new lab rat.

"I don't mind." To his surprise, she moved over so he could slide in beside her.

Yancy had no idea what to say. She didn't ask about his finger, so he guessed that subject was done.

Finally, she broke the ice. "My Uncle Cap bought two tickets for the fund-raiser. You want to go with me? He told me he'd buy two so long as he didn't have to go. He claims he'd rather do parking-lot duty than listen to music that isn't country."

"I've never been to a recital."

"Me, either." She frowned at him. "Do you want to go or not?"

"I'd like to, but I don't have a car. I'm saving up for one."

She had that strange look about her again. As if she were trying to figure out what planet he was from. "I can pick you up, but if we eat anything, you have to pay, because it's a date."

"Do folks eat at recitals?"

"Popcorn maybe," she said.

He'd have to dip into his savings, but he figured it'd be worth it. Smiling, he moved a little closer until his leg brushed against hers. "It's a date."

She grinned. Ellie may not have had many dates, but she'd had more than him. She sat with him while he ate, and Sissy sat across from them talking about how her body was falling apart now that she was pregnant. Yancy barely kept up with the conversation.

When he paid for Ellie's Coke and walked her out to her car, he felt as though he was walking into a normal life with his head up.

He held her car door open, and when she climbed in, he kissed her cheek. "Good night," was all he could manage, though he thought about adding sweetie or honey. Somehow that just didn't fit Ellie.

"Good night," she answered. "See you next Saturday night."

As she drove off he couldn't stop smiling. He had a date.

Yancy had a pure moment of joy before he turned around and saw Freddie and Cowboy staring at him.

His perfectly normal life was about to end. This was worse than Leo's Apache dark spirit.

CHAPTER TWENTY-SIX

Staten

Staten waited in Quinn's tiny living room for her to finish dress-ing. A cool spring breeze drifted past her open back door and made the old house smell new. He hated the whole idea of this concert from the beginning, but never as much as he did right now, dressed up in his best suit and boots. With his arm still in the sling, he felt as if he'd be useless to Quinn if trouble came.

"You don't have to go," he yelled at her closed bedroom door. "You've nothing to prove to anyone."

No one around knew what had happened to Quinn when she'd studied under Lloyd deBellome, and Staten knew that was the way she wanted it. They all thought the pianist to be a great and gifted man. If Miss Abernathy called him *special* one more time, Staten swore he'd do his best to choke her with one hand.

Despite the hunger to flatten the guy and break not only his fingers but every bone in his body, Staten wished this night would just be over, and they could all go back to forgetting Lloyd existed. Quinn was the only person who counted. He wanted her safe and happy. Keeping her away from Lloyd seemed the best way to do just that.

Only Quinn had decided she wanted to go to the concert. No, not the concert, he reconsidered. She wanted to face Lloyd. She wanted to be done with the man who'd changed her life, crushed her dreams and sent her into hiding from all strangers for twenty years.

His shy Quinn had something to prove to herself, and Staten planned to stand beside her. He didn't mind that she was shy. Hell, he couldn't think of more than a dozen people he liked to be around, but he didn't want her frightened.

"I have to go," she called from the bedroom. "He's asked Miss Abernathy if I'll be there, and I have to show him I'm no longer afraid of him. He's nothing to me. No more than a rabid dog I once encountered in the woods of Manhattan."

Staten knew she was behind the door giving herself a pep talk. Maybe if she kept talking long enough they'd miss the concert.

His arm and shoulder hurt from doing exactly what the doctor had told him not to do. If she'd just say the word he'd strip off his Sunday clothes and cuddle up in bed with her, but he knew she had made up her mind. He was so proud of her strength.

"Well," he said, "if you're going, I'm going with you. I plan to be right by your side all night, so don't think I'm backing out if you're going."

"I know you will be beside me," she answered. "I'm count-ing on it. But remember your promise. You will not attack him in any way. This isn't about you, Staten. It's a demon I have to fight on my own."

"What if he attacks *me*?" Staten could only hope.

"He won't. Lloyd would never fight. He is very proud of his appearance. I remember him saying that he was born to per-form, blessed with his long aristocratic nose and beautiful hands."

Staten swore under his breath. He had no choice but to go along with what Quinn wanted. Mad as he was that someone had hurt her, if he did the wrong thing, it might hurt their re-lationship. The possibility of what might be between them had been building inside him since she'd told him she was pregnant. Lloyd deBellome would be here for a few hours, but Staten wanted Quinn in his world for the rest of his life.

They'd been dancing around all the important conversations they needed to have all week. Nothing had been settled about the baby or what either planned to do about it. All he knew was that she wouldn't stay with him at the ranch. If he couldn't get her to spend the night, he didn't have much chance of get-ting her to move in.

The baby was a Kirkland. He or she should be born on Kirk-land land. Only, he wasn't about to say that out loud.

He remembered how his granny used to quote Eleanor Roo-sevelt. *We must all, at some point, do the one thing that we believe we can not do.* Maybe facing Lloyd was Quinn's one thing, just like letting her make this call about their child was his.

He knew this night was going to be hard for her and he al-most claimed he wasn't feeling up to going. Only, Staten guessed she'd just get the sheriff or someone else to go along with her. His shy Quinn was showing the first signs of having a backbone, and he was so proud he couldn't, wouldn't rain on her parade.

"I'm ready," she said as she emerged from the bedroom. "And, like it or not, Staten Kirkland, you're my date."

He watched her walk toward him, more beautiful than he'd ever seen her. The weight she'd gained with the pregnancy rounded her slim body to perfection and the cream-colored silk pantsuit she'd bought to wear tonight hugged her in all the right places. One strand of midnight pearls hung from her high neckline.

"You're beautiful," he whispered, loving the way her long hair swayed straight down her back in one shiny waterfall. How could he have known her all his life and not seen the full beauty of Quinn until this moment?

"I didn't dress this way because of Lloyd or the fund-raiser. I want everyone to know tonight that I'm stepping out of hiding. I want them to know I'm with you, Staten."

"I'd like nothing more," he admitted and realized just how much he meant every word. "But, Quinn, folks aren't going to realize we're together tonight because all anyone is going to see is you."

He offered his arm, and they walked out into the cool breeze of spring. Staten couldn't stop staring at her.

They drove to the concert both lost in their own thoughts. Staten couldn't help wishing that the evening was over, and they were on their way back to her place. He wanted to hold her.

When they pulled up at the high school, a hundred cars and trucks were already there. One spot on the loading dock behind the auditorium was roped off for Lloyd's classic BMW. Since the spot was empty, Staten guessed that the guest of honor hadn't arrived yet. All Lloyd had to do was pull up and walk into the back of the auditorium. That way he wouldn't have to mix with the locals. His granny and Miss Bees seemed to be guarding the back door just in case some fan rushed in. Which wasn't likely. Most people in town couldn't name a single famous pianist.

The faculty lot was roped off for valet parking.

Staten pulled into the line and waited his turn. He recognized several men with the volunteer fire department sitting like pigeons on the loading dock beside the back door, waiting for the rush of cars needing to be parked.

Retired Captain Fuller smiled at him from behind a card table. "Five bucks to park your car, Staten. All proceeds go to the fire department."

Staten helped Quinn from the truck, tossed his keys to one of the firemen and handed Cap a twenty.

The old man frowned. "I don't make change."

"I didn't figure you did, Mr. Fuller." Staten might be over

twenty years out of high school, but Cap would always be Mr. Fuller to him.

Staten and Quinn walked into the front of the school and along a wide foyer to the open doors of the auditorium. Ransom Canyon High had been built in sections. The main wing and the cafeteria were there when he and Quinn went to school, but the auditorium had been added years later along with the new gym. Both were colorfully walled with a tile mosaic of the canyon.

"You all right, Quinn?" he whispered as they handed over their hundred-dollar tickets. Quinn had a death grip on his good arm, so he wasn't sure.

She nodded slightly, too nervous to speak.

Wanting to help, he pulled one memory of their high school days. "Remember when we had a Howdy Dance down the hall in the cafeteria our senior year? You dressed like Raggedy Ann with your hair up in dog ears."

She smiled. "I turned my head and dipped my hair in your drink, then panicked and slung red soda all over everyone around us." She laughed. "Everyone suddenly had freckles."

He nodded. "I didn't mind. When we danced later I thought of asking if you'd do it again. That was the funniest thing that happened all night."

He looked into her warm, loving eyes, thankful he'd found a memory they alone shared. Leaning close, he whispered, "Ready?"

"Ready," she answered.

They hadn't made it to their seats in the third row before Miss Abernathy waylaid them. "You must come backstage to meet our guest when he arrives. He told me he's been longing to see you again."

Both Staten and Quinn shook their heads, but the dear piano teacher insisted. "Don't worry, we're keeping it very private. I've got Miss Bees at the stage door with orders to let no one in but Master deBellome. She brought a hockey stick and a bat to make sure." Miss Abernathy checked her watch. "I'm afraid you'll only have time for a quick hello. I really thought he'd be here by now. It's almost time to open the curtain."

Staten looked at Quinn and waited. She was calling the shots tonight.

Quinn shook her head slightly just as Miss Abernathy was pulled away by an emergency. It seemed one of the church buses was unloading and blocking the spot for the honored guest.

Once she was out of sight, Quinn let out a long-held breath. "I can do this. I can listen to the music, then leave. If I have to meet him, I'll simply act as if I don't remember him."

"Me, too," Staten whispered. "It won't be too hard a job for me. The sooner the bastard is out of my state, the better."

The crowd began to fill up the auditorium. Staten counted down each minute. In five minutes it would start. In forty minutes it would be over. They'd clap and walk out, and it would all be finished.

He laced Quinn's fingers into his and held on tightly, trying not to think of what the man who was about to step on the stage had done to this woman he cared about. He'd drugged her, then raped her, then beat her, and when she'd refused to allow it to continue, he'd broken her fingers.

Staten felt his breathing quicken and his muscles tighten. Hard as he tried to stop it, hatred rose in his chest.

Hope that the guy wouldn't show up sprang into Staten's thought. It was ten after eight. Maybe he wasn't coming? Even the firemen were in the auditorium in the back row. The only person not here tonight was Lloyd deBellome.

Miss Abernathy showed up again at Staten's side.

"It's past time to start," Staten said, hoping the little piano teacher would suggest calling the whole thing off.

Miss Abernathy looked as if she might start crying. "The master just came in, but he refuses to begin until he sees you, Quinn. He says you were very special to him."

Staten shook his head. He wouldn't put Quinn through that.

Panic rose in Miss Abernathy's voice, and she began to hiccup out in little squeals. People in the audience were getting restless. "Quinn, please come backstage for a moment. I can't deal with this. I had no idea he'd be so temperamental. He…he yelled at me. Called me names no one has ever called me."

To his surprise, Quinn stood. "I'll see him, but Staten is coming with me."

They moved across the front of the stage to where the sheriff stood guarding the entrance to backstage. He pulled the curtain aside and started to speak to Quinn but stopped suddenly as if he'd seen a ghost and not one of his friends.

Miss Abernathy and Quinn moved behind the curtain, but the sheriff gripped Staten's arm when he would have passed.

"Wait a minute, Staten," Dan Brigman whispered. "I don't know what's going on, but I'm not letting you pass. Hell's breaking loose backstage with our guest, and something tells me seeing you won't help."

Staten tried to jerk away but was aware that most of the audience could still see him. "I'm going with Quinn." His words came out fast and hard.

Dan's grip didn't lessen. "If ever a man had murder in his eyes, it's you. I'm not letting you pass until I know what's going on."

Staten knew he only had seconds. He didn't want to fight Dan. The sheriff wasn't the problem.

The truth was all he had time to tell. "Lloyd raped Quinn when she was in college. He broke her fingers, making her quit any dreams of being a concert pianist, and now the bastard won't play until he sees her."

Dan stared at Staten and seemed to read all he wasn't saying. "If you assault him, I'll have to arrest you. It's my duty."

"I understand."

To his surprise the sheriff released his arm and let Staten pass behind the curtain.

Quinn was standing in the center of the stage. A huge baby grand piano was between her and a tall, thin man with salt and pepper hair streaked back from his high forehead. His features were sharp, like a hawk's. Long nose, lifted eyebrows, hollow cheeks.

"Of course you remember me, Quinn," he said in a harsh whisper as if he'd just been insulted. "I noticed your last name is still O'Grady. Apparently, you never got over me." Lloyd deBellome grinned as if he shared a private joke with her.

Staten looked around. Miss Abernathy was nowhere in sight. Lloyd must have sent her on an errand. Somehow deBellome had planned to get Quinn alone, and he thought he'd won. Only he didn't see Staten to his left ready to storm in if the guy moved one step closer to Quinn. The master couldn't have seen the sheriff behind Staten, either, or the two ladies standing in the open doorway at the back. All his focus was on his prey.

"I'm afraid I don't know you, or want to." Quinn's voice was surprisingly strong. "I recall very little about my time in New York. It was a dark period in my life with nothing worth remembering."

Lloyd deBellome laughed. "I remember you. How you tried to fight at first. How you curled into a ball when I began to discipline you and how you passed out, making the ending to our little mating rather boring. I've looked for you for over twenty years. You were the one that got away. The one I couldn't control. The one I couldn't make scream or beg. I thought I'd lost you forever, but your old piano teacher told me where you were. One call from her and you're in my life again."

Staten took a step, and Dan grabbed him from behind. "I've changed my mind, Staten. I've heard enough. I'll hold him for you if you decide to pound on him."

Staten nodded, knowing he'd honor Quinn's request as long as he could.

"You are nothing to me, not even a memory." Quinn stopped

Staten with her strong words. "You're nothing but a sick, mean, old man."

A slow smile twisted Lloyd's face. "How about we talk about this over a drink after the concert? I'm stopping over tonight in Lubbock before I fly out tomorrow. I'll make great money on this tour, and I might be talked into letting you tag along. It could prove very interesting."

Quinn turned away, not even bothering to answer him.

Lloyd did what Staten had been waiting for. He took a step toward her. Almost dragging the sheriff with him, Staten blocked the pianist's path. His right hand doubled into a fist. One blow was all he needed to rearrange the master's face.

Quinn glanced back and raised her hand, silently stopping him for a second. She'd done what she'd come to do. She'd won. There was no need for him to hurt Lloyd because the man could no longer hurt her.

In that one lost moment, Miss Abernathy seemed to fly in from the wings. The woman who'd told everyone in town how great Lloyd was now looked like an old avenging angel about to rain all hell down on the man.

The curtains began to open as Lloyd snapped, yelling that he was leaving this nothing town and all the crazy hicks who lived in this middle-of-nowhere place. He swore these people wouldn't know great music if they heard it. It would be a waste for him to play. He was meant for the palaces of Europe, not the crossroads to nowhere.

Miss Abernathy told him to get out, but Lloyd kept yelling, telling everyone in the audience what a waste of his valuable time it would be to play for people who were no more than clods on the earth.

Yancy Grey and a few others stood up and started arguing with the master, claiming he looked ridiculous in his monkey suit and long hair.

Miss Abernathy must have become aware of the fact that her

concert might develop into a wrestling match at any moment. She ran out the back door crying. She passed Miss Bees, who was waving her hockey stick at the master, calling him every name she could think of.

Staten pulled Quinn backward into the curtains and hugged her tight. "I'm proud of you," he whispered. "I'm so proud of you." He didn't care about the concert or the riot going on.

She smiled up at him. "Do you think we should save Lloyd before this crowd lynches him?"

"No. He's digging his own grave. Give him time."

Staten kissed her gently, then rushed with her to the back door, where a terrible pounding noise had started.

The moment he saw what was happening, Staten froze.

She peeked around him. "What are those ladies doing?"

The pounding was as steady as a heartbeat as Miss Bees swung her golf club against the BMW. "It's good for working off your anger. Try the bat, Beverly. I've already broken the hockey stick."

Miss Abernathy raised a baseball bat and whacked the taillight out, then giggled "You're right. I feel better all ready."

Lloyd must have heard the pounding for he rushed through the open door and started screaming. Apparently the sheriff was already outside in the shadows just watching. Lloyd demanded the officer do something. While the pounding continued, Dan pulled out his notepad to record the complaint.

Staten closed the heavy door to the outside and smiled. The demolition might still be going on, but no one inside would hear it. "We owe these people a concert, Quinn. Play for them the way you played for me the other night. They deserve to hear a real master play."

"I can't," she whispered as he tugged her to the piano.

"Ladies and gentlemen, we don't need to bring someone in to play beautiful music. We have our own gifted pianist." He sat her on the piano bench. "Maybe, just maybe, she'll play tonight."

Quinn didn't move. She just sat perfectly still and stared out at the packed house.

Staten waited for her to start. He knew he was taking a big risk, but it was for her. Nothing would remove the horror of what Lloyd had done to her like proving that he hadn't taken her gift from her.

He waited.

Quinn seemed frozen.

Everyone in the auditorium was silent. They'd all heard Miss Abernathy talk about how Quinn had a great talent. They knew the story about how she'd quit school and returned without giving a reason. They all knew she refused to play in public.

No one in the seats beyond the footlights made a sound.

Taking a deep breath, Staten pulled his arm from the sling and moved to the huge piano. With his big hands on the side, he spun the baby grand around, then he took Quinn's hand, tugged her to her feet and moved the stool so that her back was to the audience.

When he lowered her back to the bench, he whispered, "Play for me, Quinn. Play only for me."

Dragging a folding chair onstage so that Quinn could see him and he could see all the people behind her, he waited.

Finally, she straightened her back and lifted her hands to the ivories.

Complete silence greeted the soft music drifting through the air. Slowly it grew until her melody filled every inch of the huge space, circling around everyone in the room.

Staten crossed his arms and leaned back in his chair. He never stopped smiling as she played.

Deep inside him all the wounds he'd refused to let heal vanished. One shy lady with her gentle ways and magic had coaxed his heart into beating again.

CHAPTER TWENTY-SEVEN

Staten

An hour later, Staten and Quinn sat in the sheriff's office trying to keep their hands off each other while the sheriff tried to sort out everything that had happened at the concert.

All Staten wanted to do was hold Quinn, but the twenty people crammed into the office and the reception area were in his way. She'd stood up to her demons and won. She'd played just for him, leaving no doubt in anyone's mind that she was gifted or that Quinn O'Grady was his woman.

"I need to talk to you," he whispered.

"I know. Me, too, but we can't leave all these people." Quinn grinned. "I'm afraid this is worse than splashing red soda on everyone. The sheriff looks like he's thinking of resigning his post. He keeps glaring at us as if he thinks all these people going crazy is somehow our fault."

"How could it be our fault? We're the only two in the room who didn't want deBellome here in the first place. If Miss Bees and Miss Abernathy hadn't heard what Lloyd said to you, I could have handled him quietly. I would have only broken a few bones."

Quinn nodded. "Everyone knows Miss Bees has a temper. But I've never known of a time where she's actually hurt anyone, or damaged property. With a swing like hers, she should go pro."

Staten grinned. "She sure damaged that little car. It'll have to be towed."

"I was shocked when Miss Abernathy joined her. In a few minutes they turned from two senior citizens into Butch and Sundance."

He glanced over at the piano teacher. Miss Abernathy was in handcuffs and smiling. Everyone who walked by got the whole story about how one of her students was a great pianist. She told everyone she always knew Quinn had it in her. The dear seemed to have forgotten her own criminal activity during Quinn's concert. Miss Abernathy's back was straight and proud, and she didn't seem to mind that her silver bracelets were connected and locked together.

She may have only been able to hear the last few minutes of the concert because she and Miss Bees were busy. But she had no doubt that she'd heard a master play.

"We stopped when the sheriff threatened to lock us up," Miss Bees said to Leo when he passed her a cup of coffee. "I've got a temper, and I didn't like that guy one bit. He seemed to think his car was more important than one of my students, and I won't stand for that."

All the teachers in the room nodded their agreement.

"Leo says we're going up the river," Miss Abernathy whispered loud enough for most of the room to hear. "Oh, Miss Bees, I don't think I'll do well there."

"Well," the former physical education teacher said with her head up, "all I got to say is they'd better have clean sheets. I'm not sleeping on bedbugs."

Yancy Grey and Ellie were down the line of folding chairs

from the two delinquents charged with destruction of property. "They don't have bedbugs, Miss Bees. They spray the cells down."

"How do you know that, Yancy?" Miss Bees yelled. "You done a world tour of the prison system, have you?"

"Nope," he said. "I'm just guessing." Yancy tried to go back to talking to Ellie.

Miss Bees wasn't finished. "What are you two doing here anyway? Yancy, you and Ellie haven't done anything wrong. Go home."

"We're witnesses," Yancy said. "I'm just a regular citizen here to do my duty."

Ellie shook her head. "I didn't see anything but that funny-looking guy fall down the stairs."

Staten had been watching them and decided the trip to the sheriff's office was simply part of their first date. Ellie had had to help get deBellome in the ambulance, but Yancy was tagging along. The two could have left the office, but they seemed to think this was an after-the-performance party. All the others who lived at the Evening Shadows Retirement Community must have a pack mentality.

Dan Brigman stood on a chair. "All right, everyone, I need silence."

Everyone agreed to give him the floor.

"First, if Mr. deBellome presses charges, I'm going to have to arrest several of you."

"For what?" Cap yelled from his seat near the door. "All we did is throw out the trash after he tumbled down the stairs."

Everyone laughed except the sheriff.

"Miss Abernathy, did you knowingly and willingly destroy property?"

The old piano teacher smiled. "I did my best."

The sheriff shook his head. "What about you, Miss Bees? Why'd you go along with such a crazy action?"

Miss Bees puffed up. "I didn't go along with anything. I'm the one who started it. I guessed the idiot would hurry out if he thought his car was in danger. Besides, he's the one who gave me the idea. When he strutted in late to his own concert, he pointed one of his long fingers at me and told me to make sure no one touched his car, like I was working for him."

Dan looked as if he was aging by the minute. "Look, ladies, I think we can work this out without charges being filed. I can't imagine the famous Lloyd deBellome wanting it known that two ladies like yourselves got mad enough to do damage. The press would love that story."

He raised his voice and continued, "What I need to know is which one of you tripped the pianist on the back steps leading off the dock? I was trying to stop Miss Bees from taking another swing while he was yelling that a few of you men were standing in his way." The sheriff pointed to Cap, Leo and Mr. Halls. "The next thing I knew he was tumbling down the stairs."

"Where is the bastard anyway?" Cap shouted. "Why don't you ask him?"

Dan glared at Cap. "You know where he is. Ellie and Yancy loaded him in the ambulance. He's on his way to the hospital with a broken nose and a busted knee and who knows what else. I suspect a few of his wounds may have occurred while all of you were rushing in to help him up." The sheriff pointed his finger from one senior citizen to another.

Staten swore that everyone looked guilty, even his granny.

"Now, back to my questions. When the dust cleared, all you folks from the retirement community were standing around. Anyone of you, except Miss Bees, could have tripped him. So, who did it?"

The room was silent for a few seconds, then Mr. Halls shouted, "What'd he say?"

"He wants to know which one of us tripped the bastard," Cap yelled.

The old principal, dressed in one of the suits he'd once walked the hallways in, stood. "I tripped him with my cane," he shouted. "I'm the leader, so I'll do the time."

"No, you didn't," Mrs. Kirkland announced. "I shoved him over with my walker. I was the one closest to him."

Staten would have told his granny to stop lying, but he wasn't too sure.

One by one, each resident stood and confessed. Even Miss Bees claimed she swung her golf club, when the sheriff wasn't looking, and did the deed.

Mrs. Butterfield, who hadn't been following the conversation, stood with the others and said whatever it was, she was sure she was guilty. Mrs. Butterfield never talked much, but apparently she didn't want to be left out. She also offered to bring pies to serve at the trial if someone else would provide the plates, napkins and forks.

Dan gave up. "Yancy, help these folks to their cars and see they all get home. We'll sort this out in the morning."

"But..."

"No buts, Yancy. You're my deputy as of right now. Get all these criminals home."

Yancy didn't look too happy but seemed to cheer up a bit when Ellie offered to help. One by one Staten watched the old folks leave. They were fighters, rabble-rousers and heroes. He could see why his granny had wanted to live with them. Even at twice his age, they were far more fun to be around than he must be.

When they were gone, Dan collapsed in his chair. "I can't arrest any of them."

Staten shook his head. "You going to bring them in one at a time and interrogate them?"

"Nope. It would be a waste of time." The sheriff propped his boots on his desk. "I'll drop by and visit with Lloyd tomorrow. When he finds out we had several witnesses to what he said to

Quinn, he'll drop any charges. He can't prove someone actually tripped him, and his insurance will probably pay for his car being vandalized."

"Sounds like he's getting off easy," Staten said.

Quinn shook her head. "There were enough reporters there that word will get out about him refusing to play."

Dan nodded. "I think I even saw one getting tape of them loading him up. He was cussing the town, the state and old folks. I wouldn't be surprised if someone didn't record him shouting at the audience. It'll be all over the news by dawn."

Quinn added matter-of-factly, "He'll have to cancel some, if not all, of his tour to recover. He's so vain I can't see him playing at all until his nose heals. The promoters will probably replace him and sue him for breach of contract."

"So, you're saying his career is over?" the sheriff asked.

She nodded. "Maybe so. If he was young, he might outlive the way he acted, but not now. If the school in New York gets wind of how he yelled and cussed onstage, he'll lose his teaching job, as well. I'll bet Miss Abernathy will make that call first thing in the morning."

Dan looked at Quinn and changed the subject. "I'm sorry I was out back and didn't get to hear you play."

She laughed, suddenly nervous. "If you had been inside, there's no telling what Miss Bees and Miss Abernathy would have done."

Dan leaned forward and took her hand. "If you ever play again, I'd love to hear it."

"I'll invite you." She smiled. "I promise."

Staten felt a shock of pure jealousy for the first time in his life. If it had happened when he'd been a teen he would have been ready to fight, but at forty-three he knew if he said anything, he'd only look like a fool. Dan Brigman was Quinn's friend, and he was just being nice. Or at least he'd better be *just being nice*.

Staten stood, took Quinn's free hand and started toward the

door. "If you don't need us, I think Quinn and I will call it a night."

Dan's grin was almost wicked. "I knew you two were a couple when you knocked her door off the frame that day I was in the barn, but I guess everyone in town knows it after tonight."

Staten didn't slow as Quinn said, "What day did you knock my door down?"

"Thanks, Sheriff," Staten yelled back, knowing he'd have to come up with an answer fast.

"Anytime, Kirkland." Dan laughed.

Quinn walked up the steps to her porch, leading Staten into her little house decorated in a style he would never fit into. She couldn't stop smiling, even when she finally turned to him.

Staten puffed up like a bear ready to fight. "If you won't come back to the ranch with me, I'm staying here tonight." Staten stood his ground. "There will be no leaving you alone tonight, Quinn."

She lifted her chin. "You're putting your foot down, are you, Staten?"

"Nope. I'm putting my whole body down next to you. I don't care if we talk or make love or just go to sleep. I'm going to be with you tonight, and that's the way it is."

"I kind of like that idea myself. It won't be easy with your wounded shoulder, but we'll make it work."

Staten looked surprised he won. He didn't seem to know what else to say. "I can't do a very good job of undressing you with this arm in a sling. You may have to do most of that yourself."

"You moved a piano for me. Surely you can remove a few clothes."

Still frowning, he winked at her.

She laughed. "And if you're sleeping in my bed, we're making love. I'm putting my foot down, Staten, that's the way it is."

Finally he smiled, obviously knowing she was mocking him.

Knowing that his rough demand didn't frighten her one bit. "Is that an order, Quinn?"

"Yes. If I'm going to put up with you for the next fifty or sixty years, I need to have some say."

He watched her every move. "How you going to put up with me if you refuse to live in my house? If you won't come to me, I promise you I could never live in this little dollhouse of a place with its tiny bathroom and kitchen so small we keep bumping into each other." He smiled. "Correction, the bumping into part isn't so bad to put up with."

Quinn wanted to bring an end to the discussion that seemed to have no answer. She tugged her top off and Staten seemed to lose the power to speak.

She waited.

Finally, he whispered, "Your breasts are so beautiful. You are so beautiful."

She took his hand and led him to the bedroom. While he studied her, she undressed him. Then she stood very still as he placed his hands on her waist and slid her silk slacks and panties down in one movement.

"Don't hurt your shoulder," she whispered.

"I swear, Quinn, this causes me no pain in my shoulder. I might have to do it as a regular exercise."

They moved under the covers so that she rested on his good shoulder.

"I know most folks say I'm a cold man, Quinn."

"You've never been cold with me, just silent sometimes. You've always been kind. Maybe not so much in words, but in your touch."

"I need to say the words, if only once. You deserve as much and more. I want you in my life. I want you living at the Double K. I want to raise our child together and sleep with you every night. I want to see you in white in front of all our friends so we can promise forever."

"You want a great deal, Staten."

"It's not just a need. I'm not alive if I'm not with you. I have to say it all. I love you, Quinn."

She cuddled against him. "I know, Staten. I love you, too. I have for a long time. You may not know it, but you're my hero. I might have been the one charging the dragon tonight, but you were the one who stood beside me ready to fight."

"All the details can be talked about later, Quinn. Now is the time to show you how much you mean to me."

His big hand moved over her in a gentle embrace. "I don't want just to be in the corners of your world anymore. You've become my entire world."

All night she'd held herself in check. She wouldn't cry. She would not allow herself to break. Only now, as Staten began kissing her, she felt tears bubbling from her eyes.

"What's wrong?" he asked.

"Nothing," she answered. "Absolutely nothing."

The boy who'd always been kind to that shy little girl. The man who opened up to her as he did with no one in his world. The lover who always waited for her to make the first move. The father of her child who wanted her safe and near.

The man who'd just discovered he loved her when she'd loved him all her life. All were with her tonight.

"I love you, Quinn," he whispered against her hair.

"I know," she answered. "I know."

CHAPTER TWENTY-EIGHT

Lauren

Lauren sat on the tailgate of Lucas's old pickup and swung her legs as he draped a blanket over her shoulders. The night really wasn't cold, but she liked the thought of him taking care of her.

He was her first boyfriend. The first guy who liked her, really liked her. It was exciting, newborn and somehow very grown up, all at the same time.

They were back in the pasture where Lucas loved to watch the stars. It was his favorite place, and she knew when he was away at college it would be hers. That is if she ever got a car and could come out here.

She knew it was on the Kirkland ranch and didn't belong to them, but somehow it was their secret spot. Maybe she'd write about tonight in her diary, then when she had a few friends over, she might read about exactly what it was like in the moonlight.

"I can't believe your dad looked at me and ordered me to take you home." Lucas laughed. "Man, did he look mad at all those old folks after the concert. I think if he'd had access to a cattle truck, he would have loaded them all in, walkers and canes included."

Lauren smiled. "He wouldn't have trusted you if he knew you'd bring me here first and not straight home. I'm sure he thinks I'm safe at the house by now."

"I know. If he knew we'd be stopping out here alone, he'd probably be madder than hell." Lucas sat beside her. "This is where you're supposed to say that he'd be all right with it."

She giggled. "I can't lie. If he knew we were here, he'd shoot you. It's nothing to do with you, though. It's just that he hasn't finished lecturing me yet about boys. I think I've got at least another year of lectures before he'll trust me to go out."

"I'll wait," Lucas said. "Now and then, when I'm home, I'll call and we can talk, but, Lauren, we got to do this right. It's too special not to."

She smiled up at him. "You make me feel good when you say stuff like that. Even if you don't mean it."

"What if I did, Lauren? Would it scare you?"

"A little, maybe. I don't think long-term like you do."

He covered her hand with his. "We're going to both change in the next few years. We need to start out as friends. I'd like that."

"Me, too." She'd never had a date. She had a great deal to figure out before she could even talk about what happened after friends.

He must have felt the same way because they talked about the stars and the few months of school that were left. He told her again about what the Texas Tech campus was like and how different life would be for him there.

They talked about the night at the Gypsy House and how she still owed him a blood debt.

Half an hour passed, and she finally said she needed to go home. Even though she loved being with him, Lauren felt like she was lying to Pop. For the second time in her life, she knew she was doing something he wouldn't approve of. Maybe when she was a little older it wouldn't matter, but now she didn't want to lie to him.

Lucas must have felt the same way, because he didn't try to kiss her. He'd said he'd wait. Maybe he knew that what might be growing between them was more than a few stolen dates. Or, maybe he simply didn't want complications right now.

They were folding up the blanket when she heard the rumble of an engine.

"Someone's on the ranch," he whispered.

They climbed into the truck and listened. After a while Lucas whispered, "It sounds like they are driving the fence lines. Like they're checking for something."

"But what?"

"Maybe a break in the fence. But cowboys do that in daylight, not at night. They wouldn't be checking this fence anyway. There are no cattle here."

Lauren thought for a minute and asked, "When are cattle moved in this pasture?"

"Another week, maybe sooner. Mr. Kirkland is buying calves now." Lucas turned toward her. "That's it! Whoever is driving out here is checking to see if the cattle are on grass yet. Somehow they know a herd is coming. They just don't know when."

"Who sets the date?"

"Kirkland, but there are lots of factors to consider before they're moved. We all know the work is coming, but which pasture, how many cattle, even when the trucks come, all has to be figured out along with a dozen other details like weather and the vet's schedule. Collins has a ranch hand named Arlo who sets his dates and the number of cows moved on the Collins place, but from what I hear, Kirkland makes the call here on the Double K."

"So," Lauren whispered, "if I were a cattle rustler, I might come out every night to check."

Lucas nodded slowly. "And if I wanted to make sure none of

the cowhands were wandering around, I'd shoot at the first one I saw." Lucas thumped his head against the back glass. "I heard one of the men say he didn't plan to check this pasture at night, no matter what the foreman said. Some, if not all the men, are leery of the chore."

"Take me home, Lucas, and we'll wait for Pop. I want to tell him our theory."

An hour later they were watching a movie when her dad stepped through the front door. He looked tired, but when he saw Lucas he didn't react like she thought he might.

"You didn't have to stay, Lucas," he said, straightening to his sheriff's stance. Pop was acting like Lucas had stayed to babysit her until an adult got home.

Lucas stood. "I wanted to talk to you, sir. Lauren and I have a theory about what happened on the Kirkland ranch."

"Can't it wait till morning?"

Lauren jumped in. "When Lucas was bringing me home he told me about seeing a car driving the back pasture road late last night."

Together they told her father all the facts, except that they'd been on the land tonight. To his credit, the sheriff listened.

"Why didn't you go to Kirkland with this?"

Lucas answered. "We tried calling both his house phone at the ranch and his mobile. He didn't answer either."

"I can believe that." Pop smiled as if he knew a secret. "Thanks for telling me. I promise I'll check on it tomorrow morning. Good night, Lucas. Thanks for seeing my daughter home safely."

"You're welcome." Lucas walked to the door. "Good night, Lauren. See you at school Monday."

"See you," Lauren answered.

When the door closed, she expected her pop to start his lecture on never letting anyone into the house when he wasn't home, but Pop just picked up one of the bowls of popcorn and asked what movie was on.

"Aren't you going to lecture me?" she asked.

"Nope. You must have trusted the guy or you wouldn't have let him in. Plus, you two came up with the best theory on why Kirkland got shot that I've heard."

They went over facts of the case in a way that he'd never talked to her about his work. It was as if, now that she was sixteen, she wasn't a kid anymore. Or maybe Margaret had convinced him he was being too hard on her. Who knew, maybe Pop was just getting old and more relaxed.

As they turned out the lights, she asked, "So, Lucas is okay?"

"I wouldn't have asked him to see you home if he wasn't. Kirkland thinks a lot of the kid." Pop reached his bedroom door and turned to say good-night.

"So, it's all right if I go out on a date with him sometime?" She opened her door a few feet down the hall. "That is, if he ever asks me."

"No. He's too old for you."

"But only by a year." She forgot to add that they were only a year apart in age by three days. "He's graduating early."

"We'll talk about it later." Pop closed his door before she could build her defense.

CHAPTER TWENTY-NINE

Yancy

Yancy loaded all the old folks into their cars, then walked the few blocks to the retirement community. Ellie had already driven to the other end and promised to make sure each got to their little bungalow safely.

He didn't mind the walk. He needed to clear his head. The only danger might be one of the old folks running over him, and he hoped they were all ahead of him.

When he was in prison, his mind mostly drifted. Every day was about the same. Now that he was out, it was like waking up in a new world every morning. There were things to figure out. Reading hidden meanings in what folks said and what they didn't. Trying to jump into the conversation at the right time. Knowing when to shut up. Part of Yancy wanted to go back to his cell, just for a day or two, to rest his brain.

He straightened and walked faster. The sheriff said he was a deputy tonight. Him, Yancy Grey from nowhere, who didn't have a family, or a driver's license, or a bank account, or much of anything else. He was a deputy, if only for tonight.

Slowly his shoulders slumped as he remembered what the ex-con named Cowboy had told him. Yancy knew he was in trouble the minute he'd seen them, and it hadn't taken the pair long to figure out who he was. Cowboy said he was one of them and always would be. If he didn't go along with them, they'd name him as one of their gang if they got caught, and he'd get the same time they got. So, like it or not, Yancy was a part of their gang. If all went as planned, Cowboy promised he'd get a cut; if it didn't, they'd meet up again in prison.

The first time he'd gone, Yancy had been caught stealing. He really had no one to blame but himself. If Cowboy turned him in just to get back at him, every day of prison would seem ten times as hard. Yancy didn't want to go back. He couldn't.

That night in the shadows of Dorothy's Café, Yancy hadn't said a word. He'd simply listened. Part of what they said had to be true. Both Cowboy and Freddie knew the ropes. They had a man at the Collins ranch helping them, filling them in on details no one in town would know. A guy named Arlo would keep them informed and hide the cattle truck they'd stolen until they made the raid.

The plan was to go in right after Kirkland moved his cattle to the far pasture and round them up the first night. This wasn't going to be a small operation. They planned to pack the truck and be a few hundred miles down the road before dawn.

Cowboy said they'd get rid of what they were driving now, so no one would catch them. The truck they'd stolen to haul eighty head was already hidden on the Collins place. Cowboy knew someone in New Mexico who'd take the calves off their hands. Freddie promised they only wanted Yancy as a lookout. Someone far enough back from the crime to give them warning.

It crossed Yancy's mind that he should report the cons to the sheriff, but he didn't know any details. Not the man's full name on the Collins ranch or the night it would happen. All they'd told him was that they had a plan in the works, and when it came through, they'd be rolling in money.

Freddie had even hinted that Yancy could make more in one night than most folks around town made in a month.

But, Yancy didn't care about the money. He had enough to take Ellie out on a date, and that seemed enough. But he was too scared to say anything to Cowboy or Freddie. All he'd done was nod as if he was going along with whatever they said.

A few days had passed and, when he didn't hear from them, Yancy figured they'd either changed their plan or moved on. He didn't care as long as they didn't bother him.

Yancy turned into the Evening Shadows Retirement Community trying to figure out what a normal person would do, not that he'd ever be normal with guys like Cowboy and Freddie turning up to remind him how worthless he was.

Plan or no plan, they'd reminded him that the life he was living would never work for long. There'd always be someone who noticed something different about him, or one of the cons showing up to remind him he wasn't like most people.

When he saw Ellie waiting for him on the office steps, he forgot about being a deputy or worrying what Cowboy had planned. It wouldn't happen for a while, if ever. He had plenty of time to think about how to handle his problem. With luck, he'd have a few more days to be normal. Maybe that's all a guy like him could hope for.

"Did they all find their own little houses?" he asked as he walked up to the steps of the office. She looked so prim and proper in her dress-up clothes, but he kind of missed the cape.

"I think it was a full night for them." She patted the step beside her. "I'm just happy that they made it back home safe and sound. A few of them got so wound up, I got worried."

"Me, too. I'm getting attached to them." He sat down so near they were touching. "The day I got to town someone stole my backpack. I had no money, no clothes, nothing. The guys got together and gave me what I needed, but it was the women who had the idea to hire me to help out around the place. I figured it'd last a month, maybe more, but they're talking about building more bungalows and reopening the pool and getting the city to put in a park over where we burned the tree branches that first day. When that happens they won't just need a handyman, they'll need a manager for this place."

Ellie leaned back with her elbows on the next step. "So you're thinking you might stay? I've lived here all my life, and I think it's a great place to live."

Yancy thought of Cowboy and Freddie. Maybe the best thing to do was run. "I might. I have to see how things work out."

His brain fell off track again when he noticed that without her cape she didn't seem so round. She did have big breasts, though. He had to remind himself not to look at them again, and again, and again.

He decided to step out on a limb. "Ellie, would you mind if I kiss you?"

"No, I wouldn't mind. I've already rubbed my lipstick off."

He decided that was a definite yes. He leaned in, liking the way her breasts cushioned the contact just before his lips hit hers. There were a few things about kissing a chubby woman that made it downright delightful.

Half an hour later, when she left, Yancy figured he'd practiced kissing until he had it down pat. Funny thing about kissing, it pretty much erased every other thought in your mind. He wouldn't be surprised if there wasn't some kind of kissing overload disease that could happen if he got too much of a good thing.

He made it to his room, undressed and fell into bed thinking that if heaven was just reliving one day in your life over and over, he hoped it was this one.

Unfortunately, at dawn the next morning hell came to call.

Yancy opened his eyes to see both Cowboy and Freddie perched on the end of his bed like hungry vultures looking for roadkill.

Cowboy started talking before Yancy was fully awake. "We need you to do us a little favor."

"I can't." Yancy sat up. "I have to work today."

"This won't take long." Freddie pushed hard against Yancy's chest. "We need you to be somewhere tonight at exactly midnight. All you have to do is be there as a lookout. If you spot any trouble riding, fire one shot. We'll do the rest."

"I don't have a gun."

Freddie dropped an old dirty .45 beside Yancy. "You do now. Set up at the county road where it turns off toward the Double K."

When Freddie straightened, Yancy couldn't miss how the man patted the knife at his side.

Both cons backed away, but it was Cowboy who left the parting promise. "Be there at midnight and be armed, or we'll be back, and you and that chubby little girlfriend of yours won't look so pretty when we get through with you. You don't want to see what Freddie can do with a knife faster than you have time to yell."

Yancy didn't breathe until he heard the office door slam behind the men. He was afraid to move. Afraid to touch the gun. Afraid to picture what might happen if he didn't play along with their plan.

The nightmare he'd had for years in prison had come to haunt him. There was no way out. He had to do what they said, and when he did, he'd give up the chance to be a normal man…he'd be a criminal. Again. And, if they got caught, he'd be back in prison.

He no longer had to worry what normal people do. Yancy Grey knew he wasn't normal and never would be. That one night of kissing Ellie would be his last. Even if they didn't get caught on Kirkland's land, Yancy knew he'd have to run. Staying in town would just be asking to get caught.

All morning he worked, swearing he would not take anything from the old folks. Tonight, he'd take Cap's keys and do his midnight watch, then he'd park the car back in the same spot and catch the six o'clock bus out of town. He'd take a few clothes and all the money he'd saved, but he'd leave the leather shaving kit and the warm wool coat and the good gloves.

If he didn't do exactly that, Ellie might get hurt. He might get killed. It was time for him to wake up from his dream of living a normal life.

He worked until dark trying to get as much done on his lists, then he walked to his room behind the lobby.

Yancy was so tired and worried he almost didn't notice the tray of food on the counter. Pot roast with all the trimmings, and a slice of cherry pie.

A small note had been shoved under the plate. It read: *Enjoy your supper. We don't know what we'd do without you. Miss Bees.*

CHAPTER THIRTY

Staten

Staten moved among his men inside the main barn. The sounds of horses stomping and blowing out air surrounded him, along with the rub of leather against leather and spurs jingling as his men saddled up.

Most of the guys had been working all day, but their horses were fresh and ready to run. Even the animals seemed to pick up the excitement circling in the air like a dust devil on freshly plowed ground.

For a moment Staten felt he'd stepped back in time to the wild days of the West. And maybe he had. For miles around they only had one sheriff and one ranger. Not enough lawmen to stop what was about to happen on his land. Even though both lawmen would do the legal thing, the right thing, they didn't truly understand what the land meant to him. It was in his blood, his backbone, his heart.

Smiling, he remembered how his granny used to set the pies on the windowsill to cool. She'd always comment the wind would dust the meringue, so he'd have Double K mixed in his blood. She'd been right. Staten didn't just own the land, he *was* the ranch.

He moved between two mares and stopped near Dan Brigman. "You going to be able to handle a horse, Sheriff? Jake and a few others are following behind us in pickups. You're welcome to ride with them."

"I can make it fine on horseback." Dan grinned. "I was a Boy Scout."

Staten nodded. He'd given the sheriff a great horse that would run with all the others. As long as Dan held on, he'd be fine.

Staten stood on one of Jake's stools and yelled, "We leave at full dark and ride down into the canyon. It's not the shortest way to the back pasture, but it'll get us there unseen and hopefully, thanks to the wind tonight, unheard.

"Once we get to the arroyo, we form a single line, three or four horse lengths apart. We travel slow and silent. I don't want any of you flushing a covey of quail from a clump of yucca if you can help it."

The men nodded.

"Once you all clear the ridge, stand about six feet apart. When the last man clears, wait for the lead rider's signal. Then, pull your rifles from your scabbards and stand ready. When he makes a sign, I want every rider to lock and load. Those of you with shotguns rack them loud. There is no mistaking that sound."

Dan took over. "Remember. We're not expecting any trouble. We want this arrest to go smooth, without any gunfire. You men will keep the peace simply by standing. These fellows tonight are dangerous. If they thought they had us outnumbered they might try to gun us down.

"Once the ranger and I have them under arrest, the two pickups will come in and back us up. Light should flood the pasture about then, and it may spook a few of the cows."

Staten added, "When the men are handcuffed and safely in custody, I want those rifles put away, and every man on horseback will help take care of the herd. Everything you'll need to fix fences is in Jake's truck. I don't want a man or a calf hurt tonight."

Every cowhand nodded. They'd heard the orders and understood what was said, as well as what wasn't said. No rustler would be getting away. They'd all be in jail before dawn. The trouble the ranches had with rustlers around the area would be over tonight. By using all the men, they were making a stand.

Staten led his horse toward Jake. "You drive one pickup and let Lucas follow in mine. Make sure both are mounted with floodlights."

Jake spit into the darkness. "Lucas is saddled and ready to ride."

Staten shook his head, hating the idea of the kid being involved so closely in this. It was too dangerous, even with the precautions they were taking. Lucas could get hurt. Anyone of his men might be hurt.

Jake stared at Staten. "He knows the canyon as good as you do, boss. He's ridden through it all his life. Plus, he's got a cell phone. He can keep in touch with you." When Staten didn't move, Jake added, "He's a man who rides for the brand, just like all these men. Don't make him less. It wouldn't be the right thing to do."

Staten nodded, knowing that if he pulled Lucas, he'd be saying the kid wasn't as valuable as his other men or as good. "But, who'll drive the other truck?"

"How about that new guy the sheriff brought over tonight? The one that the prairie dog gnawed on. I've been watching him. I may be wrong, but I don't think he knows which end of the horse is which. I asked him if he rode and he said, 'How hard could it be?'"

"You're right. Tell him he's driving the truck and keep tailing you all the way. If he fell off a horse when we cross down into the canyon, we wouldn't find him for a month."

Staten raised his hand and motioned for every man to be ready.

Five minutes later, forty men were riding toward the canyon wall. There was an excitement dancing with the dark shadows of men on horseback racing. Staten could feel it. Breathed it in with the wind. What they were doing tonight would change things.

He only hoped they would change for the better.

Ten minutes later, one by one they pointed their mounts down into the canyon. Lucas took the lead, raising his arm as if about to ride his first wild pony. The kid made the descent look easy.

Staten swore he heard Lucas laugh as he followed the kid down.

All his men had gone down into the canyon before to look for strays. They knew to lean back and let the horse pick his way.

Glancing back at the sheriff, Staten hoped the Boy Scouts taught him well. Dan was wobbling but hanging on. If he took a fall his biggest worry would be the horse rolling over on him. Second worry, he'd roll off a cliff. The fall might only be twenty or thirty feet before he hit rock, but the landing would probably break a few bones.

Once they leveled out on the wide canyon floor, the men rode slowly in groups of two or three. The moon was out and offered enough light to see ahead. The horses needed rest, and Staten knew they had a few hours ride before they circled around to the far pasture.

He thought it strange how all the pastures had a name. He'd heard a few of the huge ranches just used numbers, but as long as he could remember, each of his pastures bore a name not written on any post. The north pasture, the south, timber pasture, Miller pasture, named after the man who'd sold his grandfather the land. And, of course, the far pasture.

Lucas pulled his gray alongside Staten. "It's a good plan," he said. "One that will get the least people hurt. Too bad we couldn't just arrest them at the gate."

"I heard you came up with the reason men were on my land at night. Makes sense." Staten wasn't surprised. Lucas had a way of worrying a problem until he figured it out.

"Lauren and I were just talking about it after the concert." Lucas paused, then added, "The sheriff asked me to take Lauren home. He seemed to have his hands full. We may have thought of the reason men were watching the land, but how'd you know it was going to be tonight?"

"The sheriff told me he had an informant who said there's a man on the Collins place who is working with the rustlers. Said the guy has a stolen truck stashed on the place. This is a crime that has been in the planning stage for at least a month. Have you noticed any extra trucks around the Collins place?"

"Maybe." Lucas shrugged. "There are lots of barns almost empty of hay right now. It wouldn't be that hard to drive an empty cattle truck in the back. Collins men might not question it. But wouldn't someone miss a truck that size?"

"Not if it was stolen across the state lines. It could already be in the barn before state troopers realized it was gone." Staten saw the kid putting together all the facts in his head.

"When we climb out of the canyon, only the sheriff, me, and two other men will ride toward the rustlers. They won't expect anyone coming from the canyon side of the pasture. I want you to stay with the other men and make sure they fall into line. I don't want someone rushing in before we get the bad guys rounded up or, worse, firing to spook the rustlers or the cattle. I'll call your cell and let it ring once when it's time to move the men to the ridge."

"Any advice on how I do that?"

"Start giving calm orders when you ride along the ravine. Repeat exactly what each man is to do. Tell them if they get mixed up, follow your lead."

"Yes, sir." Lucas didn't sound too sure.

"Keep your voice calm and strong. Hard as a rock. They'll follow."

They moved on in silence, and Staten thought of Quinn. She'd be upset if she knew what was going on. In fact she'd be panicked. Even when this was all over, he knew he wouldn't tell her the whole story.

For the hundredth time he tried to picture himself living at her house. Maybe if he knocked out a wall and built a couple of rooms on, or took all the gingerbread trim off, or went up and built a second floor.

Nothing worked. He might hate his dark house on his land, but at least he could live in it without bumping into walls. He could never relax there on Lavender Lane knowing he needed to be here. There wasn't even an extra drawer for him to put his stuff in or a place for his shaving kit on her sink, or enough counter space in the kitchen to keep his supplies.

Funny that he was thinking about such a little problem when he was riding into what might turn out to be the biggest battle of his life.

What did the house matter? It was Quinn and the baby that he wanted. That he *needed*.

As the night aged he worried where they'd put the baby's things in her house. A crib in a bedroom not big enough for a king-size bed. The swing, the high chair, the changing table, the toys. Quinn had never had a kid. She didn't know that they came with a van load of junk.

Only, he couldn't see a child in his house. Not Quinn's child. At one time the house hadn't seemed so bad, but now sadness seemed to hang in the corners like leftover dust.

"You all right?" Lucas broke into his thoughts.

"Yeah, why?" Staten snapped.

"You were mumbling and cussing under your breath."

Staten wasn't surprised. In the five years he'd lived alone, he'd caught himself talking to no one a hundred times. When it happened, he usually took the time to cuss himself out.

"I'm thinking of giving up cussing," he said to Lucas. "Bad habit to get into."

Staten wanted to change the subject. "You got any bad habits, kid?"

"My mom says I'm always planning for the future and sometimes don't see what's going on in the present. She says I might fall over today while I'm dreaming about tomorrow."

Staten smiled. "I guess I do the same thing, except I worry about someday and don't take the time to just walk through today." He laughed. "Hell, kid, we sound like we're damn philosophers."

"You still getting rid of cuss words, Mr. Kirkland?"

"Yep."

They grew quiet and began to watch the side of the canyon. Both didn't want to miss the ribbon of red, sandy mud that would mark the place they'd have to climb.

Staten tasted excitement peppered with a dash of fear. He'd never felt so alive in his life.

He'd never wanted to live forever as much as he did right now.

CHAPTER THIRTY-ONE

Sheriff Brigman pulled his horse to the front beside Staten when they reached the end of the ravine. The far pasture spread out before them like a midnight blanket of grass barely starting to green.

Lucas dropped back, raised his hand, and all the men behind stopped to wait for their order to ride. They'd stay behind in the shadows just below the ridge until it was time.

Staten pulled his rifle and laid it over his arm. The sheriff and the ranger did the same.

Slowly, like a thundercloud moving low over the land, Staten and the two lawmen rode their horses toward the shadow of a cattle truck backed up against the loading chutes at the corner of the pasture. Two men were running the cattle in one at a time while a third man loaded them onto the truck.

Staten heard the quick jerking movements of the cattle, their hooves clicking against the rock and metal, their low cries of complaint at being bothered. He could have been blindfolded and still known what was happening.

This was no haphazard operation. Seventy or eighty head of yearlings would be a substantial loss. These men weren't some small-time farmer feeding his family with one stolen cow. This was an organized crime.

Staten circled in the shadows until he was behind a tall man who almost looked like a real cowboy, but his movements were too impatient. He might be accustomed to riding, but he wasn't skilled at working cattle.

The sheriff and the ranger moved toward the truck, coming up on the back side, so the one loading wouldn't see them until they were a few feet away.

The other two men who'd followed Staten out of the ravine took the rustler closest to the road. He was shorter, less skilled than his partners.

The click of Brigman racking a round into the chamber sounded almost as loud as a gunshot in the silent night. Staten touched his phone so it dialed Lucas. The glow of the phone drew the cowboy's attention.

Staten wasn't surprised when the rustler in the Stetson pulled his gun.

"Aim that weapon and you're dead." Staten's voice came hard and clear as the barrel of his rifle leveled on his target.

The tall cowboy hesitated, as did the bald guy near the fence.

For a few seconds he saw the tall man's head turn, as if he might try something. Then, like a whisper, came the sounds of rifles being racked along the ridge. Forty weapons were pointed directly at the three men in the pasture.

A line of shadows, rifles raised to take aim, stood as silent guardians.

All three of the rustlers raised their hands. They might have had a chance with the men before them, but they knew they'd be sitting ducks for the men on the ridge.

One by one they climbed from their horses. The cowboy and the man at the truck didn't protest, but the bald guy jerked as if he thought he might pull free and run.

Dan Brigman fought him to the ground.

In a single flash of light from the pickup pulling up, Staten saw a knife reflect. Without hesitation, he slammed his boot against the hand that held the knife.

The rustler yelped in pain as Brigman pulled the outlaw's injured hand behind his back and cuffed him.

"Thanks," the sheriff said as he pulled the man up. "I appreciate the help."

"Any time," Staten answered, suddenly feeling like laughing. It was over. They'd done it. The plan had worked.

Staten didn't take a deep breath until all three men were crammed into the back of the cruiser. A tall rustler known as Cowboy, his friend who went by Freddie and a third man who worked for the Collins ranch who only gave a first name of Arlo.

When Cowboy saw Yancy talking to the sheriff, he yelled that Yancy was one of his gang.

The sheriff leaned down by the window and said, "Wrong. He's one of *our* gang."

The men moved like ghosts in the night repairing the fence, removing the cattle truck and making sure none of the cows were hurt. They'd be checked again in the morning. Every man was back to doing his regular work, but this night would be talked about for years.

Staten tossed his saddle and bridle into Jake's pickup. He turned his horse loose, climbed into the cab of his truck and looked back at the handyman from his granny's retirement home. "How about I give you a ride home, Yancy?"

"Okay," he yelled, just seeming to realize there was not any room in the cruiser with three prisoners in the back and a ranger riding shotgun.

As they drove back to town, they went over every detail of the night. Finally, Staten admitted, "None of this would have happened if you hadn't tipped us off."

"I had to," Yancy said. "I didn't want anyone in this community to get hurt. You know, I don't have a family, but if I did, I think it would feel like this."

"You're one of this community now, Yancy, for as long as you want to be. If the job disappears where you are, you're always welcome at headquarters. I can always use a good man."

"Would I have to ride a horse?"

"Yep, but how hard could it be?"

CHAPTER THIRTY-TWO

Staten drove back to headquarters, feeling as if he hadn't slept in weeks. His shoulder and arm ached, but he refused to put the sling back on. He could handle the pain. First, he needed to check on his men.

He found most of them in the bunkhouse having breakfast, as if they hadn't been up all night. After half a pot of coffee and half an hour of talk, he told them all to sleep in shifts and run a lean crew for what had to be done.

The foreman and Jake took over, making assignments, and the cowhands groaned as they moved away from the table.

Staten headed back to his truck. He had one more errand to do before calling it a night. Dan Brigman had been by his side all night, and the sheriff's work probably wouldn't be done for hours. Staten wanted to help any way he could.

He wasn't surprised to find Dan toiling in his office. Without wasting time with small talk, they went to work putting down every detail for the report. The three men who'd tried to rob him needed to go to jail for a long time. No telling how many times they'd attempted smaller operations.

Two hours later Dan offered to buy Staten breakfast, and they walked down to Dorothy's Café.

Once they were settled and the specials were ordered, Staten said, "You mind if I ask you something, Sheriff?"

"Go ahead."

"Well—" he'd talked to the guy most of the past twenty-four hours, but this was hard to say "—I was wondering if you'd consider being my best man. I'm thinking of getting married."

Brigman laughed. "To who?"

"Damn it, who do you think?" Now, after he'd risked his life beside Dan Brigman, Staten found out the man was a nitwit. "Hell, forget I asked."

The sheriff simply laughed. "Of course I'll be your best man, but Quinn's not going to say yes to you. Not even if you ask her real nice like you just did me."

Staten grumbled over his coffee. "You're probably right. But she sees a better me than I am, so I can always hope."

"Most women do. Except my wife. I think a wife sees the worst every chance she gets or at least mine does."

As Sissy set the platters on the table, both men gave up talking in favor of eating.

"When you going to deliver, Sissy?" Dan asked as she refilled their coffee.

"Ellie says I'm two weeks overdue. So who knows." The little waitress laughed. "Half the retirement home is eating either breakfast or lunch here every day. Mrs. Ollie said she's seen the birthing film they show in Child Development a hundred times. She thinks she can deliver in a pinch."

Dan shook his head. "When you get that first contraction, call me. I'll be here before you get your apron off."

"Thanks, Sheriff. I'll consider the offer."

Staten just kept eating as if he wasn't listening to the conversation.

Finally, when most of the six-inch stack of pancakes was

gone, Dan said, "Ask Quinn to marry you, Staten. The worst she can say is no, and I'm guessing, saying no to you won't be an easy job."

Staten stood and grabbed his hat. "I think I'll go home and clean up. You're right, maybe it's time I went courtin'."

As he walked out the door, he heard Dan yell, "Long past time, Kirkland!"

Ten minutes later as headquarters came into view, the first thing he noticed was his grandparents' old place setting back in the breaks of trees. It always shone in the dawn light. For a moment he wished they were still there. They'd built their place exactly like a ranch house should be, blending into the landscape, not perched on a rise, cutting the view up.

Every time he looked that direction, he smiled. They'd been happy in the house that had birthed generations.

As he watched, his granny stepped out on the front porch and began sweeping.

For a second Staten thought he must be dreaming. Granny was in town at the retirement community. She'd never even mentioned coming back to the old place.

But there she was. Older, thinner, but standing looking at him just like she'd been all those years while he'd grown up.

Staten turned his pickup toward the old house. If this was a mirage, he might as well find out now. It had been more than twenty-four hours since he'd slept. Seemed right he could be losing his mind.

By the time he reached the front porch she'd gone inside, but he could smell pies baking.

Impossible. No one had lived in the place in twenty years. Three months after his grandpa died, his grandmother had moved to town. She'd said the place had too many memories.

His spurs jingled as he stomped up the steps, waiting for his granny to come out. The windows on the old place were clean, and a few were even open to the sweet spring air.

The old screen door creaked as Quinn stepped out, wearing jeans and an old flannel shirt. "About time you came home," she said.

Staten thought his heart might explode. "You're moving in with me?"

"No," she answered. "I'm moving in here. Granny told me I could have the place." She smiled. "I was kind of hoping you might move in here with me."

He fought from grabbing her and holding her so tight she'd never leave, but he had to do this right. "I can't do that, Quinn, not unless you'll marry me. This is no fling or affair between us. This is forever. If you live in this house, you'll take my name."

She smiled. "I could agree to those terms."

He pulled her close, lifted her off the ground and began swinging her around and around.

Granny leaned out one of the windows. "Put her down, Staten, you'll make the baby dizzy."

He stopped but didn't turn loose of her. "You know about the baby?"

"Hell," Granny Kirkland, who'd never cussed in her life, said. "Half the town knows about the baby. Several of us have been planning the wedding and the baby shower for a month or more. Do you two really think anything happens in this town without me knowing about it?"

He kissed the top of Granny's head. "You know, I don't think I ever need to sleep again. I'm dreaming right now."

Then he turned, and right in front of his grandmother, he asked Quinn to marry him.

And as he knew she would, Quinn said yes to the man she'd always loved.

CHAPTER THIRTY-THREE

Lauren

"Hello, Lauren. Did you hear the news?"

"About the capture of the rustlers?" she whispered into her new phone. "Everyone is talking about it. Are you all right, Lucas? I heard you were in on the fight, and you weren't at school today."

He laughed. "I slept all day, and it wasn't much of a fight. We kind of walked softly and carried a big stick."

She giggled into the phone. "You sound like Reid quoting Teddy Roosevelt."

"I felt like a Rough Rider last night." He was silent. "I've decided what I'm going to major in."

"What?"

"Law."

"Me, too," she said.

Lucas laughed then whispered, "Good night, *mi cielo*."

Yancy

A few miles away, Yancy Grey stepped from his room to the office. All the aging dwarves were gone from their usual spots in the sunny area. Mr. Halls had forgotten to wash the coffee cup he always drank cocoa from, and Miss Bees had left one of her bats by the door.

He felt like the den mother picking up after a meeting. Despite being tired, they'd all been talkative tonight. Several said the sheriff told everyone at the café that Yancy had been a hero during the capture of criminals last night.

He smiled. The sheriff had kept his secret. No one would find out how he'd known that the crime was about to be committed. When he'd gone to the sheriff's office yesterday morning, he wasn't sure if he would live to see another day. Cowboy and Freddie had been his nightmare for years. But, sometimes a man has to face his fears before he can have any hope of living a normal life.

As he walked back to his room, Yancy noticed something propped against his bedroom door.

An old backpack. The one he'd carried with him from prison.

Slowly he picked up the pack that had been missing for almost three months.

It felt heavier than it had the day he arrived in Crossroads.

Yancy dumped out all he'd owned a few months ago on the bed.

Then for a long while Yancy just stared at the contents. Brand-new underwear and socks. The bloody shirt he'd worn when he'd been arrested more than five years ago had been washed and folded neatly. His initials had been embossed onto the leather shaving kit. A brand-new wool coat and gloves, the tags still on them. The three hundred dollars he'd lied about having was in a wallet.

Who, he wondered. Someone had stolen his pack and then returned it with all he'd dreamed of having in it.

A tear ran down his cheek. He'd achieved his goal. He was rich.

Walking out into the night he smiled out at the midnight sky and knew there was only one thing left to do in his life.

Set himself some new goals.

★ ★ ★ ★ ★